Unintentionally Yours
By Marina Black

I0533502

ISBN: 978-0996648622

Dedicated to Jo, Jess, & Ceci. I don't know what I'd do without you. You are my kru.

To my supportive friends and family. I love you all.
-M.B.

Chapter One

Reno O'Keefe sat up, stretched, and buried his face in the palms of his hands.

A headache thundered in the back of his brain, equal parts hangover and pressure from the storm currently raging outside. Last night was lost in a haze of tequila and bad decisions. Reno remembered cracking open a bottle with two of the barbacks at The Watering Hole. After his fifth shot, he vaguely recalled demanding a private dance from a gorgeous dark-haired woman and getting slapped upside the head. Everything after that was a blur…

Sliding his legs over the edge of the bed, Reno glanced at the blinking numbers on his alarm clock and swore. The power must've been knocked out sometime last night. It was fairly regular occurrence, thanks to the out of date electrical wiring in the building. Reno had been living in the same bachelor pad for twelve years now. The studio apartment was cluttered, smelled like old socks, and there wasn't anything in the fridge except beer and old Chinese takeout. As far as Reno was concerned, it was paradise.

Scrubbing a hand over his stubbled jaw, he sighed. Reno needed a shave badly, not only of the two-day beard he was sporting but also his head. He'd gone cue ball in college and had stuck with it ever since. If he let it go another day, wavy brown hair would start growing in odd patches around his temples and he'd resemble a mad scientist. Reno tried growing it back once and decided after a week it wasn't worth the trouble.

Given the dreariness of the day, Reno had no idea if he had time for his usual grooming activities. He fumbled for his cellphone and the cursing becoming more violent as he realized not only was it late in the evening, but he also had fourteen missed calls and half a dozen voicemails.

Celia was *seriously* pissed.

She and Reno had been hanging out for the last couple weeks. He'd taken her to dinner once, but it was mostly bumping uglies in the back office after a long shift. Maybe if he actually cared about her, he'd have taken a moment to call back, but Reno had exactly twenty minutes to shower and get to the club. It wasn't even a competition. He didn't have time to waste on angry girlfriends—ex-girlfriends, as it probably was now anyway. There were far more important things to be taken care of.

As Reno jumped into the shower, his mind wandered. He wasn't exactly heartbroken by the thought of breaking things off with Celia. Sure, she was gorgeous but there wasn't a future for them. At the end of the day, she was just another checkmark on a laundry list of chicks he'd banged over the years. Celia was too clingy anyway. Vincent "Reno" O'Keefe didn't *do* clingy…

Well, he *did* them but he didn't care for the dramatic fallout after the fact.

It was an act of God that he managed to get into work with five minutes to spare. Jogging into the kitchen,

Reno grabbed an apron and tossed it on over the dark jeans, black button down, and worn black tie that served as his uniform. He'd been the bartender, bouncer, executive chef—oh, and owner, of this club for the last five years. It wasn't the classiest place in town. Hell, it wasn't even the classiest strip club in town, but it kept food on his table and his rent paid. What more could he possibly ask for?

The Watering Hole stood proudly in the heart of Carson City, just off 395. It was nestled between a warehouse store and a gas station; across the street was St. Teresa's Catholic Church. When Reno bought the place, he got rid of the dingy, rotting wooden exterior that made the club an eyesore and put in vinyl siding the color of soft cream. The nasty old carpet had been torn out and replaced with shiny laminate floors. Previously whitewashed walls had been painted a dark blue that complemented the ruffled fabric that adorned the stage area. He'd even redone the employee areas to entice his dancers to stick around. The only thing Reno hadn't changed was the name. The Watering Hole was a quirky, hilarious double entendre that he adored from the moment he first heard it.

The acquisition of the club came at a time in his life when he was searching for a change. Reno had partied his way through undergrad at Emerson College and found the job market an unfriendly place when he finally graduated. With very few marketable skills, he applied for any job he could find until he got an interview at a telemarketing company. Initially, he worked in Boston near where he'd grown up, but they eventually closed down operations due to cost of living in the metro area.

The bigwigs offered Reno a deal: take a measly severance package and face the job market again or move to Carson City, Nevada and join their team out there. It didn't seem like much of a choice at all. Reno packed up his life and moved three thousand miles away. After a year, he took a position in management. Twelve years later, he was dejected, depressed, and desperate for a change.

As luck would have it, Reno was perusing the real estate page when he noticed a club in the foreclosure section. To this day, he couldn't pinpoint what made him curious about the dingy old place. The only good explanation he could come up with is that it had to be fate. The minute Reno walked through the front door, he knew it had to be his. Purchasing The Watering Hole outright depleted almost all of his savings but even after five years, he didn't regret the decision at all.

The cherry-colored doors to the kitchen swung open, dragging Reno out of his hazy, hungover reverie.

"Hey! Smith wants a basket of chicken fingers. And make it snappy! He's got that wild look in his eyes tonight," she barked.

Reno's back was turned but he would've known that voice anywhere. Mona Gallo was born in the heart of the bayou and had the accent to match. She was the kind of woman who didn't take any disrespect from anybody and made it her duty to keep everyone in line. Mona had kicked the crap out of more than one patron who got a little handsy over the years. She was tough, but fair…although lately, she seemed ornerier than usual. Reno decided to let it ride. Beneath all the bluster and cussing, she had a heart of gold. If Mona wanted him to know what was going on, he trusted her to tell him.

A smile ghosted over Reno's lips when he thought back to the first time he saw her. Mona had been in the middle of stripping to Joe Cocker's 'You Can Leave Your Hat On' and she had the whole place enraptured. Honestly, it was her performance that made him feel confident this club would succeed. Reno offered the girls an opportunity to stay on when he took over management. Mona agreed to his terms but made it very clear that this was her turf. Obviously, Reno hadn't agreed. They clashed horribly at first. He'd even fired her twice…but she showed up like clockwork the next day and he'd given her a raise both times. Reno needed her and they both knew it.

It had taken several years for Mona and Reno to find their rhythm with one another. There were still times they disagreed but for the most part, they'd learned to deal with each other. Hell, he'd even say they were friends…even though he didn't know much about her. Reno knew her middle name was Renee, she preferred lemonade to liquor, and she knocked around with some big-time businessman Reno didn't care for. Mona was elusive in the best kind of way. Maybe that was why she was the only woman who had remained constant in his life for all these years.

Mona popped her head back into the kitchen, her pouty red lips curled downward in a frown. "I'm sorry, did I say take your time in here?" she scoffed at him. "I *meant* to say get me those damn chicken fingers before that little weasel starts knocking money off my tip!" She folded her arms across her chest and glared.

Reno tossed a couple frozen pieces of chicken in the fryer along with a handful of fries. "Anything for you, pumpkin," he called back. He washed the grease off his hands and looked her up and down. There was something different about Mona tonight, although he couldn't quite pinpoint what it was. She hadn't gotten her hair cut; it hung long and dark, with waves that cascaded to her shoulder blades. Her jade eyes sparkled in the dim light. The outfit she was wearing wasn't new either; she still filled it out so perfectly. "You look especially gorgeous tonight. Got a hot date?"

"Don't you sass me, Reno O'Keefe." Mona shifted uncomfortably under his scrutiny. Black leather pants molded to her body and the lace tank top both hid and revealed her curves in ways that made men go crazy. At least for now, anyway. Her whole body felt raw and she wasn't sure if it was hormones or because Reno was undressing her with his eyes. She folded her arms across her chest and set her jaw.

A quiet Mona was absolutely terrifying. On any given day, she'd rip him up one side and down the other. Reno knew instantly that something was off and it shook him to the core. "Hey, what's wrong?"

"I'm a foul-mouthed, short tempered bitch," Mona deflected. It was her signature move. When the going got tough, she got even more sarcastic than usual.

Reno knew that better than anyone. He tossed the freshly cooked chicken and fries into a red plastic basket. "You want to talk about it?"

Mona shrugged him off, grabbing the order and walking it out to her impatient client. Reno followed. He cracked open a beer and set it on the table beside Smith's food. He stared while she tossed ketchup and napkins on the table, and dogged her every step. Mona ignored his incessant hovering like a pro. It wasn't the first time she'd had to deal with his overbearing concern and it wouldn't be the last. She needed to get away from him for a while and the best way to do that was to head downstairs. The dressing area was for dancers only and he wasn't allowed there during business hours.

Destiny was tearing it up on the pole tonight. She'd recently gotten accepted into a dental hygienist program at the local junior college and was over the moon with excitement. That exuberance carried over to her dancing and she was sure to make a killing with the Thirsty Thursday crowd. Liberty had just finished her set and was counting her tips while perched on the edge of the makeup counter. She glanced up as Mona flopped onto the couch. "Girl, you look awful..."

Mona groaned and covered her face with her arm. "Yeah, well I feel even worse. If I thought Reno could run this place without me, I'd have stayed home." Fifteen years she'd been working at this club and she hadn't called out once. She wasn't going to let a little morning sickness slow her down. Rolling onto her side to find a more comfortable spot, Mona sighed. "Celia quit this morning."

Liberty shook her head. "Nice kid, but she just didn't get it. It's bad enough she was screwing the boss. Then thinking it was serious. Ha! They were together less than a month and she was already talking about wedding venues." Tossing the stack of bills onto the makeup counter, she rested a hand on her hip. "That chick was warped."

"You don't get into this business for love. You get into it for the tips and the free drinks," Mona replied curtly.

"That's for damn sure." Opening up her bag, Liberty slid the money inside and pulled it tightly closed. "So where does that leave us? We're already short...I'd offer to pick up but my mom can only watch the kids on Tuesdays, Thursdays, and Saturdays now."

"Nah, it's okay. We already planned on holding open casting tomorrow. We'll see what turns up."

Liberty hurried for the door. "Great, I'll see you Saturday! Feel better!"

Once again, Mona was alone with her thoughts.

Liberty was younger than Mona by a couple years and had been married and divorced twice. She had two daughters with her second husband and things had been rough during the early months of their separation. Mona didn't need another reason why getting too close to anyone or anything only led to heartache and pain...but after five years of dating a handsome, wealthy man, she let herself get lax. And she'd forever have to suffer the consequences.

Kyle Andreas was born with a silver spoon in his mouth and added to the coffers by heading up a very successful Las Vegas real estate business. Mona met him at a New Year's Eve party. He offered to buy her champagne, she told him to fuck off, and they'd been dating ever since. Kyle didn't want to rush into a serious relationship but Mona didn't mind taking things slow. They had a good thing going, so why mess with success? Mona wasn't the traditional type anyway...Ring? Picket fence? No, thank you. They were committed to each other in their own way and that was all that mattered. Or so she thought...

Mona's frown deepened. She was angrier at herself than she was at Kyle, honestly. The signs had been there all along: he never wanted her to meet his friends or family, he travelled a lot which meant the time they did get to spend together was often short, and she never stayed the night at his place. Five years of being his dirty little secret and all she had to show for it was a broken heart and belly full of baby.

The pregnancy had come as quite a shock. Mona hadn't thought anything of it when the doctor prescribed antibiotics for a sinus infection two months ago. Suddenly she was late, moody, and sore. According to her new OBGYN, the medicine likely interfered with her birth control pill. Since Kyle hated using condoms, it was the perfect setup for an unplanned pregnancy.

Mona considered freaking out...but the timing wasn't exactly catastrophic. She had a job, a savings account, and an apartment. She was thirty-three; this could be her only chance to have a baby at all. A supportive father for her child would've been great, but when Kyle stood there and told her he wasn't interested, Mona walked away with no regrets.

Destiny burst into the dressing area and Mona sobered. She couldn't sit around all day and worry about things she had no control over. There was work to be done. "Hey Des, you interested in picking up time? There'll be a bonus if you can pick up all Celia's shifts for the next two weeks. Reno and I'll pay the registration fee for your first semester of school?" With Destiny's 'yes' still resounding in her ears, Mona headed back to the main floor. Usually she wasn't exerted by a single flight of stairs but she'd been nauseous for most of the weekend and had no appetite. When she got to the top, Mona's vision swam and she felt her balance start to waver.

Reno saw it happen in slow motion. Mona looked like she'd seen a ghost; all the blood drained from her face. Panic speared through him and he leapt over the bar, wrapping his arms around her waist to steady her and keep her from tumbling backwards. For a moment, it seemed like she was going to fight him but he crushed her against his chest and she instantly succumbed. "Easy, pumpkin," he murmured into her ear. Reno pulled her over to a chair, kneeling beside her. "Get her some water," he commanded one of the waitresses, whose name he couldn't remember. Mona was the one who knew all these things. It was just one of the many reasons he needed her to be okay. Brushing her dark hair away from her face, he cupped her cheek. "Are you alright?"

Mona accepted a cup from Tiffany with a softly spoken word of gratitude. A cold sweat had broken out over her shoulders and upper lip. Reno's hands were warm against her skin and she found herself leaning against him for support. She took a moment to get her bearings, her eyes fluttering closed as she breathed in the scent of Reno's musky cologne mingled with the crispness of laundry soap. It wasn't until his fingertips accidentally brushed over her belly that she felt the need to move away. Nobody could tell she was pregnant yet, but she wasn't going to take any chances. "I shouldn't have come in tonight, I think I'm coming down with something. I'm going to head home, boss." She swallowed hard. "I got Destiny to cover Celia's time and we have auditions tomorrow morning…"

"Celia quit?" Reno asked. "She say why?" He honestly wished he was devastated, that would've been a welcome change from the emptiness of not caring about anyone or anything. The moment he met her hot gaze, he winced. Oh shit, Mona was *pissed*.

"You're kidding, right?" Mona moved to stand but immediately regretted it. She was still incredibly dizzy and stayed firmly planted in her chair. "You really need to stop screwing the girls, Reno. We've lost some of our best dancers because you can't keep it in your pants!" She'd said all of this to him before, but it was time to bring out the big guns. "You're about to turn forty!"

Reno scoffed, "That's not true!"

"I know when your damn birthday is!" Mona countered. "If I didn't think I would barf all over your ten dollar tennis shoes, I'd kick your ass right now! You want to hook up and play around and you don't give a crap about anyone's feelings but your own. I'm not going to turn a blind eye anymore. Get your shit together, Reno! I won't clean up any more of your messes." It wasn't that Mona wanted to be harsh. Deep down, Reno was a great guy. The only thing standing between him and happiness was his own damn self.

Reno's chestnut brown eyes were firmly fixed on his aforementioned ten dollar tennis shoes. If anything Mona said had been incorrect in any way, he would've had a leg to stand on. Unfortunately, she knew him inside and out. He couldn't hide a damn thing from her. He really didn't want to admit she was right…so he whipped out his cell phone to call her a cab. Distraction was the best medicine. While they waited, Reno refreshed Mona's water and gave her a couple packets of crackers to help settle her stomach. She was still sickly pale when the taxi arrived.

Mona stood on her own but Reno wrapped his arm around her waist for support. "Make sure she gets in safe or I'll have your ass," he warned the driver. "I'll pick you up at eight tomorrow. Get some rest, pumpkin." He went immediately back to work but Mona's words turned over and over in his head. Even after he locked up the club and headed back to his apartment, he couldn't stop the wheels from turning. He *was* going to be forty in a couple weeks and what did he have to show for it?

Reno was born into a massive Irish-Catholic family and grew up in the suburbs of Boston. His mother, Martha, was a waitress and his father had been a cop. They were married at eighteen and his mother gave birth to Mark just nine months after the honeymoon. Luke arrived eleven months later, then Stephen two years after that, and Rob the following year. Vincent—Reno, as he preferred to be called now—was the baby of the family, born just months after his father had been diagnosed with colon cancer. They used every available resource for treatment but his dad passed away while he was just a toddler. The only memory Reno had of his dad was seeing him laid out in a casket at St. Joseph's.

Times were tough after Vernon O'Keefe passed away. Reno's mother knuckled down and worked three jobs to make sure they had food on their table and clothes on their backs. He was five when Martha met Richard. He showed up at the restaurant one day, swept her off her feet, and they lived happily ever after...

It was quite a shock when, at the age of 42, his mother found herself pregnant again. Lizzy was Reno's baby sister and even though there was a seventeen year age difference, they'd always been thick as thieves. There was nothing they didn't share with each other and nobody who could ever come between them. It was actually her call that snapped Reno out of his funk tonight...

A smile ghosted over his lips as he brought the phone to his ear. "Hey, Squirt, how's it going?" The shrieking on the other end turned his stomach to lead. He couldn't understand a single word she was saying and there was a sense of urgency to her voice that terrified him. "Lizzy!" he gasped, the icy fingers of panic spreading over him, "Breathe! What's wrong? Is it mom?"

Lizzy let out another screech. "I'm getting *married*!" she cooed. "Raymond proposed to me tonight! He got down on one knee and everything. Oh you should see the ring, it's *so* perfect! It was his grandmother's…" she sniffled suddenly. "I know it's late and I'm sorry. I just *had* to tell you right away."

Reno was suddenly glad he was sitting down. How was it that even his baby sister was getting married before him? "Christ…" He scrubbed a hand over his five o'clock shadow. "Isn't this kind of fast? How long have you been dating this guy?"

If Lizzy took offense, it didn't show in her voice, "A year. But we've known each other for four. We were friends before we started dating and I always thought he was so cute!" Lizzy sighed dreamily. "He's such a good guy. I think you two are really going to hit it off." Reno could hear her chewing her bottom lip over the phone; she always did that when she was nervous. "The other reason I wanted to talk to you is because the wedding is next month. I know it seems fast but our dream venue opened up unexpectedly and I knew it was a sign!"

"Elizabeth Ann-Marie O'Keefe, are you knocked up?" Reno shouted into the phone. He was certain steam was about to come pouring out of his ears.

"Vincent, if I was knocked up we wouldn't bother booking Hayden Castle. We'd have a double wedding/funeral at St. Joseph's followed shortly thereafter by my taking Holy Orders." Lizzy giggled. "You know I made a promise to wait until marriage. I finally found a guy willing to respect that. It's how I knew he was the one! I keep pinching myself because I'm afraid I'll wake up and find all of this was a dream." Lizzy's exuberance was unwavering. "I started making a list of people to invite and I want to include your girlfriend. I'm dying to meet her!"

Reno furrowed his eyebrows. He was truly at a loss as to who she was talking about since he hadn't had a *girlfriend* since he broke up with his high school sweetheart. "Who are you talking about?"

"*Mona*, stupid!" Lizzy demanded.

"Huh?" How the hell did Lizzy know about Mona and why did she think they were dating?

"There's no use trying to lie. You are *constantly* talking about her, Vince. Ever since you bought the club, it's been 'Mona and I hired a new girl, Mona and I got into a fight, Mona and I are thinking about adding onto the champagne room'," Lizzy gabbed. "Mona, Mona, Mona!" There was a smile in her voice. "You spend almost every night together. And when I called you yesterday, she picked up your cell phone and informed me she was carting your drunk ass home. We only talked for a few minutes but she sounded lovely." Lizzy huffed into the phone. "I'm not taking no for an answer!

I'm the bride and I demand to meet the woman you've been hiding from us for so long!"

Reno was so stunned he couldn't think of a thing to say. Did he really talk about Mona that much? Bringing her up was only natural, he supposed. They *did* spend an awful lot of time together. It also made perfect sense now as to how he got home from the bar in one piece. Mona must've driven his car home and then taken the bus back to her place in the middle of the night. No wonder she was weak and exhausted. A wave of guilt washed over him. "I can't make any promises but I'll ask her, okay?"

Lizzy was making that god awful high-pitched noise again and Reno's head was still pounding from last night's overindulgence. "Congratulations, Lizzy, I am so happy for you. You need to get your beauty rest and so do I. I'll call you tomorrow, alright kiddo? Goodnight."

Flopping onto the bed, Reno stared up at the ceiling. Today had been a whirlwind. When he went to sleep last night he was a happy, drunk bachelor living out a fantasy…today he was a lonely, hungover, almost-forty-year-old whose only meaningful relationship was with the scariest stripper he'd ever met.

The more he thought about it, the more he *wanted* Mona to attend Lizzy's wedding. He was going to be at this big fancy event with his brothers. They were all happily married and had a gaggle of kids between them. It had been years since the last family wedding and it was a guarantee that every aunt, uncle, cousin, neighbor, and family friend was going to show up in force. He really didn't want to think about going to a wedding alone…it would be a bloodbath.

Mona was right. It was time for a change and overhauling his personal life was the top priority. Reno reached for his cellphone, chewing his bottom lip as he contemplated what to say. He thought about asking her to the wedding right then but decided against it.

Across town, Mona finally slogged out of the bathroom. Thankfully, she hadn't actually vomited but it was touch and go there for a while. After an hour of deep breathing exercises, she finally felt well enough to move. Mona dragged herself off the floor and plopped down on the bed. She'd almost fallen asleep when the buzzing of her cell phone startled her. For half a heartbeat, she thought it might be Kyle changing his mind about her and the baby. It wasn't. Her eyebrows furrowed as she stared down at the screen.

Reno (02:11am): Hope you're feeling better, pumpkin. Call me if you need anything. Sleep tight.

Mona contemplated sending back a text but eventually decided against it. She pulled the covers up to her chin and closed her eyes. Tomorrow was another day. Hopefully, it would be a better one for both of them.

Chapter Two

Friday morning dawned with a vengeance. Yesterday's stormy skies gave way to bright sunshine, but it did nothing to boost Mona's mood. Reno texted her at seven offering to pick up breakfast on the way to auditions. Normally she would've asked him to get the biggest, blackest, strongest coffee he could find but she heard a rumor caffeine could be harmful to the baby. None of the articles she'd read online were definitive, so she decided to err on the side of caution and go for a chai latte.

Reno had to check his phone six times to make sure he'd texted the right person. Two years ago, he promised to stop smoking if Mona gave up coffee…during that time, he had never been so fearful for his life. He was so concerned, as a matter of fact, he forgot to crave cigarettes at all. After being smoke-free for a week, they made the mutual decision to resume her caffeine intake and promised never to speak of the incident again.

As he pulled into the driveway of her condo, Reno bumped the horn to alert her he'd arrived. Mona stepped out a minute later, wrapped up in a sweater and a pair of dark jeans that hugged her hips. Once she was buckled in, she gratefully accepted the tea. There was a softness to her in these early morning hours that disappeared by the time the first patrons walked into the club in the afternoon. He wouldn't admit it to anyone but he cherished these moments with her. Cautiously backing out of the driveway, Reno took off down the familiar road to the club. Neither of them was awake enough to be chatty just yet but they settled into a companionable silence as he weaved his way through traffic.

Once they made it to the club, Reno jogged ahead and held the door open as Mona stepped inside. They set up shop while munching on breakfast sandwiches from her favorite place. He was glad to see her appetite had returned in full force. She ate all of her sausage, egg, and cheese on a croissant and both their hash browns. Reno didn't mind, he was quite full after packing away a football sized breakfast burrito. While he cleaned up, Mona admitted the eager interviewees into the club. She compiled a stack of resumes and headshots and they hunkered down for what could only be a frustrating day.

Auditions were never fun. Every amateur who'd ever taken a pole dancing class and newly minted eighteen year old who wanted to piss off mommy and daddy showed up in force. The herd thinned out a little bit after Mona went over mandatory background checks and drug testing. With the basics settled, they took dancers one at a time. By mid afternoon, Mona had listened to 'Lady Marmalade' no less than twenty times and a tension headache settled itself behind her eye. When the last dancer headed out, Reno and Mona breathed a sigh of relief. He went to crack open a beer but Mona was glaring at him so hard he decided against it. He got them both water and greeted the crew as they began to trickle in for their shifts.

When the club opened for dinner, Mona and Reno headed to the office upstairs to discuss who they were going to hire. "What about Cadence?" Mona slid the picture closer to Reno for inspection. "She has potential. I'd like to teach her a couple new moves but I think she'll do real well with the bachelor party crowd. She's real all-American you know?" Reno leaned back in his seat and she frowned at him. "You got a problem with her because she's chubby?"

"I didn't say that!" Reno balked.

"You were thinking it." Mona folded her arms across her chest. "She's got great tits and a bubbly personality. If she doesn't pull in good tips, she won't stick around anyway. What's the harm?" She pressed. Reno shrugged at her and she knew she'd won. "I think we ought to hire another one too. Destiny's going to be starting school soon. We need to think ahead. Plus it'll give our regular staff some options if they need time off. I know Liberty wanted to take the kids to Disney this year. She's been saving up."

Reno nodded eagerly. "Well, I liked Valentina." He glanced up at Mona, expecting her to disagree. Shockingly, she was nodding in agreement. He grinned from ear to ear. "So we hire Cadence and Valentina." He drummed his fingers on the mahogany of his desk. It was made special for the pimp that used to own this place and Reno adored it. "I say we keep Ginger's profile just in case. She wasn't *terrible*."

"All she did was move her damn hips from side to side. I've seen grannies thrust better than that." Mona stood up. "If you want to call her for a date, do it, but don't try and reel her in under the pretense of a job she ain't going to get."

Reno was constantly astounded at how well Mona knew him. She was absolutely right. He wasn't interested in hiring Ginger…but he was interested in seeing her naked. Tossing the girl's profile along with the other rejects, he leaned back in his chair. Mona was already starting to put the paperwork together and she didn't look pissed. Now was the perfect time to ask her about the wedding. "So, Lizzy called me last night." Reno cleared his throat and waited for Mona to look up from her paperwork before he spoke again. "She's engaged."

"Isn't she a little young for that?" Mona raised an eyebrow at him. She glanced at the framed picture on his desk, staring at the petite blonde. The photo had been taken at Lizzy's high school graduation…it seemed like just yesterday. Reno seemed a little uneasy and she moved closer to soothe him. "This has got to be a big deal for you. I know how close you are to your sister."

"Yeah, especially since they're getting married a month from now," Reno muttered. Her eyebrow rose higher. "And before you ask, she isn't expecting." He exhaled sharply. "Their dream venue opened up and they jumped at it. Or maybe they're just eager to screw around. Lizzy made a promise to wait until marriage…" He looked up at Mona and swore he saw something akin to pain flash in her eyes. It was gone almost as soon as it came and Reno wasn't even sure it had been there at all. He couldn't trust his instincts when it came to Mona's emotions. She was an enigma. "I know it might be a little awkward but I really need a date. What do you say?"

Mona waited for the punch line. "I don't know anybody to set you up with, Reno. Besides, you don't want to take a stranger to meet your parents."

Reno shuffled uncomfortably. "I don't want to take a stranger…I want to take *you*."

Mona stared at him. "You want me to go to your sister's wedding with you?" She floundered, trying to find the right words. "Why?"

"A wise woman recently told me to get my shit together. I'm not going to find someone suitable to bring home to my family with just a few weeks to the wedding." Reno inched closer to her, his gaze was pleading. "I can't show up to this wedding alone. I swear, I will pay for everything. Plane ticket, hotel, the works. I'll even give you paid time off. I *need* you Mona, please say yes!"

It was an interesting offer. Mona's instinct was to dismiss the idea immediately but now that she thought about it, getting away for a little while had its appeal. In a few months, traveling would be ill advised and by this time next year, almost impossible. This could be her last chance to take a real vacation for a long, long time. Add in the fact that this trip would be on Reno's dime and it got even better. Mona licked her lips. "Who's going to run the club while we're gone?"

"Tito and Otis can handle it and I'll ask Liberty to look out for them." Reno grinned. "You are going to *love*

Boston. I promise you, it'll be a good time." Mona would've argued harder if she intended to say no to him. He was pleasantly surprised he hadn't had to beg...

Mona wasn't about to let him get off that easy. "I'm going to need a day off next week to go shopping. I don't have anything to wear to a wedding. Let's make it Thursday, I was going to be late anyway because I have a doctor's appointment." She made the decision not to tell him it was with her OBGYN.

"Deal!" Reno beamed. Lizzy was going to be so happy and he was too. Knowing he'd have Mona at his side made him feel like this wedding was actually going to be a good time. "I'm going to head down to the kitchen. You need anything?" He lingered beside her a moment.

"Nah, I'm fine." Or she would be. Mona nudged him playfully and sent him on his way.

Reno threw himself into prepping Tito and Otis to take over while he was in Boston. They had to know the kinks of the fryer, where the emergency kit was, the list of contractors to call if something went wrong, and where the spare set of keys was. Meanwhile, Mona explained the schedule to Liberty and went over some conflict resolution tips that had served her well over the years.

That evening, same as yesterday, Mona started to crash around ten. Her stomach roiled, her skin broke out in a cold sweat, and she felt absolutely miserable. Reno blamed it on the breakfast sandwiches, claiming his stomach had been a little off too, but Mona knew the truth. This was going to be her life for the next few weeks. The OBGYN told her morning sickness was common and as long as she was taking in enough food and staying hydrated, it would pass.

Shockingly, Reno wasn't a dick about her commandeering his office and curling up on his chair. He didn't say a word when she fell asleep, drooling all over his day planner. Instead, he wrapped a sweatshirt around her shoulders and left a bottle of water at the edge of the desk. The nap only lasted twenty minutes but she felt better afterward. She at least managed to finish the introductory packets for Cadence and Valentina. She'd also done this week's payroll and started adding the new girls to the schedule where they'd have the support of more experienced staff. Once that was finished, she set about cleaning Reno's private bathroom for her own personal use.

The club shut down at two. Tito shooed out the last customers, making sure they had rides if they were too impaired to drive. Otis cleaned up the kitchen. Reno padded upstairs, pausing to watch Mona as she stared out the office window. He'd never seen her look so lost and it did something to him. Despite the sweatshirt he loaned her, she was still shivering. Without thinking, he reached out and placed his hand on her forehead. "Well, you don't seem feverish…and I don't see any track marks."

Mona's entire body clenched and she wrenched away from him. "I'm *not* on drugs!" It hurt deep in her soul he could even think she'd be using. Then again, she never told him where she'd come from or that both her parents had been backwater hicks, shooting up in the bayou between stints at County. The wounds still bled after all these years. Mona's jaw was set and there was murder in her eyes.

Reno raised his hands in mock surrender. "Christ, I was just kidding!" She was wicked pissed but he rested his chin against her shoulder and she started to unwind. "I didn't really think you were using. I'm just shit at making jokes, it's part of my charm." This time, her posture relaxed and he shot her a tender smile. "I'm sorry you're still not feeling well. Let me take you home?"

Mona wanted very badly to let him…but she also didn't want to rely on him any more than necessary. Reno was trying to get his life in order and she was going to be raising this baby on her own. Part of being a single parent was learning how to manage things alone. Then again, she ached for the companionship of someone she cared about. Maybe it was the hormones or perhaps she'd just had enough rejection in the last couple days, but she needed someone to lean on. It might as well be Reno.

Peering down at his arm as it encircled her waist, Mona swallowed hard. She wanted to tell him about the baby, but she was terrified of his reaction. Reno didn't deal well with change and she couldn't take any more heartbreak this week. Since he couldn't tell she was pregnant yet, she wasn't going to rock the boat. "You sure it's not too much trouble?"

Reno looked properly affronted. "Let's go." Why did she

always insist on making everything such a big deal? It was a ride home. He'd much prefer bringing her home himself and making sure she got in safely than worry all night. He stayed close to her side as they headed downstairs. Tito and Otis could manage closing up tonight; it was a great test run for when he and Mona were in Boston.

As they made it out to the parking lot, Reno half expected her to push him away. Mona didn't need anything from anybody and had no issue telling them so. To see her so vulnerable evoked an instinct that he didn't even know he had. When they got to his car, he pried open the rusted door of his beat up jalopy. It used to be beautiful. Fourteen years ago he'd bought the lemon colored car from an elderly couple moving into assisted living. The inside was still immaculate, but the outside had begun to show signs of its age. It didn't usually bother him but seeing Mona in the front seat of the rust bucket made him feel uneasy. "I have to get a new car…"

Mona furrowed her eyebrows as she buckled herself in. "Why? You love this car." It was the very first purchase he made after getting a job out of college and he was so proud. When he relocated to Nevada, he drove it from Boston to Carson City with his life in the back seat. Mona didn't know why she felt so emotional about a vehicle that wasn't even hers, but all the insecurity she'd been feeling came welling to the surface. "Just because she's not the prettiest girl at the dance doesn't mean you should just throw her away! It's not right!"

"What the hell is going on with you?" Reno demanded.

"I've never seen you so riled up. I'm starting to wonder if you've been body snatched!" He reached over, gripping her hand. "Talk to me."

Mona felt her chest tighten with sadness. She couldn't tell him about the baby, so she decided to go with the other half of the truth. "Kyle and I split, okay?"

Reno wished he could be sympathetic but it just wasn't happening. "Good!" he declared. "I don't know what the hell you even saw in that loser in the first place. You deserve so much better." After two tries, the engine turned over and Reno threw the car into reverse. Mona didn't say much on the ride home or when he pulled up in front of her condo but she certainly did when he followed her into the house.

"What are you doing?" Mona turned to face him. Reno was already kicking off his shoes. He brushed past her and she groaned in frustration. "Whatever this is, can it wait until tomorrow? I'm exhausted."

"Nope! You dodged a bullet, pumpkin. We're celebrating!" Reno announced. Mona wasn't a drinker. He'd never seen her have more than a glass of champagne on New Year's. Tonight, though, he intended to get her wasted so she could forget all the pain she was feeling. It always worked for him…at least for a little while. "What've you got to drink?"

When Reno knelt to look in the cabinet, Mona swiped her prenatal vitamins off the counter and shoved them into her purse for safekeeping. If he were more observant, he might've noticed. Mona wasn't worried at all. "I'm not feeling well. Adding a hangover onto what's bugging me is the worst idea I've ever heard. Just forget it."

Reno paused, his shoulders sagging slightly. "You are always there for me when things go sour. Lizzy told me you drove my drunk ass home the other night. Is that true?" Mona didn't have to say anything; he knew the truth. "I owe you, and I don't like it hanging over my head."

"I never said there was any debt," Mona soothed. "So, I drove you home a couple times. I didn't want you to hurt yourself or somebody else. It wasn't a big deal!"

"It's a big deal to me," Reno replied, licking his lips. "Whatever you said made a huge impression on my sister…what did you two talk about anyway?"

Mona considered lying. She truly wished she didn't have to keep any secrets from Reno; she liked things better when all the cards were on the table. She couldn't tell him about the baby yet but at least she could be honest about this. "I was getting you to the car and you were doing a god-awful impression of Elvis. It was four in the morning and when your phone started ringing, I thought it might be an emergency." Pulling open the fridge, she grabbed two bottles of water and handed Reno one. "Lizzy was very upset. She thought her boyfriend was cheating on her since he'd been so squirrelly lately and she was worried that saving herself for marriage was the wrong move."

Reno's heart was hammering in his chest. "What'd you

tell her?"

"That she needs to trust her instincts. If that boyfriend is going to tuck tail and run when the going gets tough, he isn't worth her tears." Mona's heart ached. Why hadn't she had this advice and wisdom while getting mixed up with Kyle? "We talked it out. I think Ray's a good kid." She took a long sip of water. "Sounds like he was nervous about proposing. It all makes sense now." Huffing slightly, Mona padded into the living room with Reno hot on her heels. "I still think she's too young to get married…"

A chuckle passed his lips as he snuggled beside her on the couch. "My mom got married when she was eighteen years old. Pretty much everyone in my family married young and wedded the love of their life." Reno shook his head. "I'm the only holdout."

"There's nothing wrong with that." Mona nudged him. "You don't want to do it just because everybody else is doing it. People who get married for all the wrong reasons end up miserable and divorced." Her mind wandered to Kyle and what she would've said if he'd asked her to marry him instead of walking away. Would they have made it work? Or would they have flamed out and wrecked their kid in the process? It hardly mattered now. Kyle was gone and Mona had other things to worry about. "Look, I was a little rough on you yesterday—"

"No, you were right," Reno interrupted. "That's why I'm swearing off women for a while." He turned to face her, grinning. "Except for you, pumpkin. The club couldn't run without you and neither can I." He leaned his head against her shoulder. "We'll go to the wedding, spend some time with the family, see a few sights, and once my cleanse is over, I'm turning over a new leaf." Reno glanced at her out of the corner of his eye. "You really don't have to apologize."

The way they were positioned on the couch, it made it difficult not to snuggle into him. Mona stopped trying. "Lesson one: When it comes to women, don't interrupt." she warned. "I was hard on you, yeah, but I'm not sorry about it. I just want you to be happy." Mona patted his thigh. "I also want you to get the hell out of my house so I can go to sleep."

Reno sighed exaggeratedly. "You're a party pooper." Even though Mona told him to take a hike, she clearly wasn't in a hurry to get up. If anything, he got the feeling she needed him to stay. Reno peered down at her, a smile ghosting over his lips. "You mind if I watch the weather before I head home? We lost power last night during the storm and I bet the cable is still knocked out."

Mona nodded, her eyes drooping as he grabbed the remote and flicked the television on. Reno's warm body and the dulcet tones of the weather station were too powerful to resist. She tucked her legs beneath her and within a matter of minutes, she was out cold.

The local weather played on the eights and by the time he got to the weekend forecast, Reno had become a human pillow. He peered at the woman snuggled against him and tenderness welled in his chest. Mona

Gallo was the most beautiful woman he'd ever seen. Without tension and annoyance marring her features, she was flawless. Her lips were rosy pink, even without lipstick. There was a soft glow to her skin, even though it was dimly lit in the living room. Reno brushed a strand of silky dark hair from her cheek and stopped cold. He'd always been attracted to her but he'd never been so compelled to act on it before. It was Mona, for God's sake! Of all the women out of his league, she was at the very top of the list.

Reno kept thinking back to his first night as The Watering Hole's new owner. Since he'd been a manager at the telemarketing firm for so long, he was sure he knew what he was doing. He didn't.

Issues arose with a rowdy customer and in the midst of sorting it out, Reno vaguely remembered calling Mona a bimbo. To her credit, she waited until they were in the back room to put him in his place. She nailed him in the gut so hard he dry heaved for the rest of the night. Looking back now, he deserved it. He'd been condescending, rude, and sexist; to this day he was still mortified at how he'd treated her.

Thankfully, they were solid now. Reno focused on the overall maintenance of the club; he did repairs, ran the kitchen, and made sure the big bills were paid. Mona did payroll, was the face of the club, and kept their permits were in order. She'd also been unanimously elected as the club's den mother; she made sure the girls were healthy and happy, and she wasn't afraid to get rough if she had to. Reno trusted Mona implicitly.

A soft sigh passed Mona's lips and she burrowed deeper into Reno's side. His heart fluttered when she smiled in her sleep. The rational part of his brain must've already gone to bed a long time ago. Instead of getting up and leaving, he wrapped his arm around her waist and hunkered down beside her.

Sometime the next morning, Mona was startled out of the first good night's sleep she'd had in weeks by what she believed to be a wild animal. Sitting up quickly, her heart thundered in her chest as she wildly glanced around. It wasn't a bear who'd gotten into her condo…it was Reno's thunderous snoring. For a split second, she considered throwing him out. Then again, she hadn't been bothered by his presence until the windows started rattling. Mona poked him in the gut, causing him to shift on the couch. Just like that, he was breathing quietly again and she rubbed her weary eyes.

She considered getting up and going into her bedroom but Reno's hand snaked out and tugged her back against him. She wondered if he knew what he was doing, but he was clearly still asleep. It was too early in the day to weigh the pros and cons of her decision. Mona was sleeping comfortably and there was no reason to fight it. She rested her head on his chest and went back to bed. She'd be up before him anyway, so she had nothing to worry about.

Mona's phone rang sometime around eight and she dragged herself up off the couch. For some ungodly reason, she was disappointed Reno wasn't there. He must've snuck out sometime after she went back to sleep. What shocked her was that she slept through it.

Mona had always been a very light sleeper; it was how she'd kept herself alive as a kid. She must've been more exhausted than she thought.

A soft thud from the other room drew Mona's attention. Her eyes widened in shock when Reno stepped out of the bathroom with a towel around his waist. "I hope you don't mind I helped myself." He chuckled. "I had quite a drool spot on my chest when I woke up this morning."

Heat suffused Mona's face and she wiped away a bit of spittle at the corner of her mouth. "I do not drool!"

"My shirt begs to differ, pumpkin," Reno teased. "I borrowed one from a pile in the laundry room." The morning banter wasn't as awkward as he thought it was going to be. "What do you say I take you out for some breakfast? It'll be my way of saying sorry."

Mona was feeling very hungry this morning, which was kind of a miracle since she'd been so nauseous the last couple days. "Sorry about what? Lying about me drooling in my sleep?"

"No," Reno smirked. "For imposing on you last night. I shouldn't have stayed. I wasn't thinking straight." He dragged a hand over his shaved head. "I wanted to make sure you were okay…"

"Forget it." Mona shrugged it off. "Breakfast sounds awesome. I'll get dressed." She paused in the doorway of her room, glancing back at where Reno had settled himself down. He'd flicked on the news, taking in the morning headlines while stroking his jawline. In the last five years, he'd been over to her house only a handful of times and never for an extended period of time. Oddly, it felt like he'd always been here. Mona felt like he belonged.

Tossing on a pair of jeans and a t-shirt, she piled her dark hair in a bun on top of her head. Reno stood, following her out to the car, his warm palm ghosting over the small of her back. Mona decided not to read into it...getting too close to him, or anyone, especially right now could only end in disaster. She had to keep up her guard or risk getting hurt all over again.

Chapter Three

The invitations to Lizzy's wedding arrived on Tuesday. It was only then that Reno realized there was more on the calendar than just her special day. Lizzy had a whole week of events laid out on a separate itinerary. It all began with the bachelorette party and Ray's stag night on Saturday. Reno considered skipping it, but he wanted to find out what kind of man Ray was before he married his baby sister. Then there was a Jack and Jill brunch on Sunday. Tuesday was a family barbecue at Ray's parents' home. Wednesday was the final fitting for dresses and tuxes. The rehearsal dinner was on Friday and finally, the wedding/reception on Saturday. Reno wanted to be there for all of it, which meant he had to convince Mona she deserved an extended vacation.

As soon as he got into work, he headed upstairs to the office. A smile slid over his features as he caught Mona stifling a yawn. "Evening, pumpkin," Reno called. She turned to face him without fanfare, inclining her head in a quiet hello. "You got a second?"

"As long as you don't mind sharing my attention," Mona replied. She still had two hours on Friday that she needed to fill and, so far, nobody could take them. Liberty couldn't get a babysitter, Cadence had another gig scheduled, Valentina had requested the night off, and Destiny needed some kind of break or she'd dance herself a into coma. "I'm trying to fill between midnight and two on Friday and I'm not having any luck…"

Reno plopped down beside her. "You haven't been up

there for a while but I know you've got the moves. Why not fill it yourself?"

On the one hand, doing it herself would alleviate some of the stress of trying to find someone; on the other, Mona was concerned. The morning sickness came and went these days. A call to the doctor offered some insight into the fact that she wasn't eating enough. Mona started a regimen of small, frequent meals that seemed to be helping. She was at the cusp of the second trimester, which meant she wasn't exactly showing yet but there was a slight softening to her belly that hadn't been there before. Her breasts had filled out too. Mona didn't fit in her own bras, let alone her old costumes. It also made her extremely uncomfortable to think about being leered at by drunks during such a personal time. "I don't think so."

Reno furrowed his eyebrows. "What's the big deal? You're a stripper. It's what you do." It only took him half a second to realize he'd just shot himself in the foot. Mona's lips pursed into a thin line. "I didn't mean to say you aren't good at other things!" She was still glaring at him and he sighed. "I didn't come up here to piss you off…"

"Really? Because you're doing such a great job at it," Mona replied curtly. "Forget it." Standing abruptly, her entire body tensed when Reno grabbed her by the waist. It was just a gentle touch, his warmth bleeding through the thin cotton dress she was wearing. Mona had no fear of him harming her or the baby, but her hand instinctively covered his as it rested over her belly. Her throat clogged with unwelcome emotion. "What do you want, Reno?"

If he didn't know better, Reno would've sworn there were tears shimmering in her eyes. It couldn't be. Mona never flinched. "I want to talk to you about the wedding." He sighed and dropped his hand. "I feel like I should wait until you're in a better mood, though..."

Mona huffed in annoyance. "Spit it out, O'Keefe!"

"I got the invitation to Lizzy's wedding this morning and there's a lot of pre-wedding stuff I didn't know about. I really want to go." Reno licked his lips. "I would love to say I've been a great son and kept in touch, but the truth is I haven't been back to Boston in over a decade. This would be a really great chance for me to spend time with my brothers and sister, my mom and Richard, and see some of my old friends." He hesitated. "I want you to come too, Mona. We could take two weeks, see Boston, see my family...I promise I will pay you for all of it."

"I'm not an escort!" Mona's skin crawled just thinking about it. "If you want to go for a few extra days, I'm fine with it. I just don't want you getting the wrong impression about what this is. We're friends. It's not that serious."

It *was* serious to him. Mona was putting a pin in her life to go across country with him. She was signing up for his massive Irish Catholic family and all of its quirks. None of that fazed her...in fact, the only thing that bothered her was the fact he offered to pay her. Reno rubbed his palms together. "I don't deserve you. You

---

know that, right?"

Mona inhaled the masculine scent of Reno's soap and deodorant, mixed with the pomade he used to keep his bald head shining. She was suddenly warm, body and soul. The weakness in her was more frightening than anything else. "I've been telling you that for years," she ribbed him. "So, what are all these events? I was going to just get a dress for the ceremony but I guess I need some other stuff, huh? Casual or formal?"

Tugging the invitation out of his pocket, he handed over the typed page Lizzy had included. "This is the list. If you ask me, you don't need anything special. You always look amazing." He grinned at the slight blush tingeing her cheeks. He thought about commenting but then thought better of it. "I'm going to book the hotel and the plane tickets tonight. Everything is happening so fast." A little too fast, if anyone asked him. Reno chatted with Lizzy for an hour last night and he was exhausted just *talking* about planning the wedding. "You have any special requests about the trip? Window seat? Vegetarian meal?"

Mona shrugged. "I'm not hard to please, sweetheart." She patted his shoulder. "I've really got to get down to the floor." It was busy tonight and with the two new girls still settling in, she barely had a second to breathe. "Don't forget I'm off on Thursday. While I'm shopping, I'm going to pick out something from Lizzy's registry. Unless you already did?"

"What registry?" Reno cocked his head, confused.

"For her wedding?" Mona wanted to laugh at the stupid look on Reno's face. "She and Ray must have picked out presents they want. Right?" Moving toward him, she grasped the invitation. "See at the bottom? Registered at Crate and Barrel and Target. I'm going to be at the mall anyway. I'll have the gift shipped to Boston."

It had been so long since he'd been to a wedding; he'd almost forgotten there was etiquette to be followed. "That'd be great. You know, I actually need to get a new suit and tie. Why don't we go together? I could use a woman's opinion so I don't end up looking like I'm going to a rodeo instead of a wedding. I could pick you up?"

Mona shifted nervously. "I actually have some stuff in the morning." She had her doctor's appointment and first ultrasound. This was the appointment she'd been waiting for. After the initial confirmation, which had been at the urgent care clinic in the local Wal-Mart, she'd obtained a referral for an OBGYN. Dr. Harris accepted her insurance and, on their first meeting, had a calm demeanor and gentle touch that put Mona immediately at ease. The good doctor had been one of the people to validate her decision not to tell her friends about the pregnancy until the second trimester. "I have a doctor's appointment, remember?"

Reno hadn't remembered and was immediately concerned. "I'm coming with you!" he blurted.

Mona was startled by his outburst. There was a darkness in Reno's features she'd never seen before. "It's a routine visit…" She couldn't discount that it'd be easier to have the OBGYN tell him she was pregnant rather than finding the courage to do it herself. Then again, she didn't relish the thought of Reno coming to the OB and complicating things even further. After telling Kyle and his outright rejection, Mona needed a couple weeks before dealing with anyone else's reaction. Reno looked like he was about to jump out of his skin. "I've never seen you like this. What's wrong?"

Reno paced the length of the office, his hands behind his back. "I…" He cleared his throat with more force than was necessary. He couldn't stop thinking about his mother recounting stories of Vernon growing weaker, falling, and sleeping more, especially near the end. "My dad died of cancer, okay? If you're sick, you need to tell me. I will be there for you, no matter what."

Mona grasped his shoulders and stared into the fathomless depths of his warm brown eyes. "Look at me, I'm *fine*." Her thumb stroked his cheek gently; the stubble was slightly rough against her fingertips. "I'm a little tired and run down. It's nothing life threatening." Reno threw his arms around her and rested his forehead against her shoulder. He could feel her heart beating steadily against his chest, as they embraced. There was such relief in knowing she was okay. Reno took a moment to revel in their closeness. Mona smelled like sunshine and there was a soft coconut scent to her hair. When she pulled back, he found himself staring at her pouty lips. It would be so easy for him to lean in and kiss her senseless. Mona was staring at him, those green eyes boring into his soul…

A soft cough from the doorway drew Mona and Reno's attention away from one another. Liberty folded her arms, "I'm sorry to interrupt. Cadence is freaking out. I tried to calm her down but she wants to talk to you..."

"Yeah, I'm coming." Mona tugged away from Reno, her cheeks flushed with embarrassment. "I've got to take care of that." She chattered, feeling slightly nervous. "We're all set. On Thursday I can pick you up after my appointment. Your place is on my way to the mall."

"Yeah that's—"

"Good." Mona cut him off. She turned and fled down the stairs.

Reno was left standing there, frustrated. Mona always kept him off-balance but it seemed worse lately. He was seeing her in a different light. His fortieth birthday loomed on the horizon; maybe this was the start of a midlife crisis. Five years working with Mona and he'd been attracted to her, sure—any straight man with a pulse and a penis would be. Still, he'd never considered anything more than fantasizing about her. Lately, it took all the strength in his body not to touch her and some days he wasn't even succeeding at that.

Grumbling to himself, Reno opened up his computer to check out airfare deals. Lizzy said they'd contracted with a hotel in the heart of the city. The rooms were expensive but she'd worked out a huge discount. Besides, he wanted Mona to enjoy her time in Boston and getting a nice room would help with that. The flight was a solid eight hours and he made sure they got nice seats, not quite in first class but he sprang for the extra leg room. He'd also rented a car so they could get around the city without having to rely on family for transport. The whole trip made a dent in his life savings, but he'd do anything for Lizzy…and Mona.

Reno printed out two copies of the itinerary and confirmations, one for him and one for Mona. He fired off a quick text to Lizzy, which ended up becoming a twenty minute phone call of more excited shrieking. She would've gone on for longer but Reno had work to do. He gently explained he loved her and would see her soon, before getting back to the to-do list Mona handed him this morning.

Even as Reno completed his chores, his mind continued to wander. By this time next week he'd be on plane heading home with Mona at his side. He could hardly wait. Everything was finally falling into place.

Chapter Four

Thursday came a lot quicker than Mona expected. She'd spent so much of Wednesday trying to get Cadence settled into a routine that the night flew by. The girl had talent, but also a lot of insecurity. Once Cadence got over the initial worry, she was going to be an amazing addition to the Watering Hole lineup...until then, Mona worried she was going to pull her hair out in frustration.

None of that mattered right now, though. She was sitting in Dr. Harris's waiting room, reading an educational pamphlet about breastfeeding. It seemed like the best option for her baby, and would certainly be cheaper. Every penny counted, especially if Reno decided he didn't want her around once she gave birth...the thought turned her stomach over.

"Mona Gallo?"

She faked a smile as the nurse ushered her into the examination room. Mona had already given blood and a urine sample, so she was weighed, measured, her blood pressure checked, and she was given a yellow gown to change into. It was another twenty minutes before the doctor actually came in and Mona had chewed her fingernails to the quick.

"It's good to see you again." Dr. Harris smiled gently, settling herself on a stool across from the examination table. "How are you feeling? Has the nausea subsided?"

"Yeah, I have been eating every couple hours like you said and it's been working great. I only get a little twinge now and again, usually when I smell perfume or potato chips." Mona shrugged. "I picked up a copy of '*What to Expect When You're Expecting*' and everything I'm experiencing seems normal." There was a hint of a question in her statement.

Dr. Harris nodded enthusiastically. "Before we start the physical exam, is there anything specifically worrying you?"

"I want to make sure it'd be okay to fly. I'm planning on going to Boston for a wedding. Everything I read said it's usually fine but to check with my doctor so..." Mona chewed her bottom lip. "Do you think it's alright?"

Flipping through the chart, she glanced back through Mona's vital signs. "I'd like to examine you before I make a final decision but it's generally not an issue this early on. Lay back for me and I'll take a peek." After thoroughly assessing Mona, Dr. Harris settled back in her seat to make a few notes. "Everything looks great. You can fly, have sexual intercourse, and have a great time at the wedding. As far as I'm concerned, you have no restrictions. " She grinned wider. "Although from personal experience, I want to encourage you to pace yourself. Drink plenty of water and make time to rest. You're growing another person and that can take a lot out of you."

Mona jotted down notes throughout the appointment, pausing when Dr. Harris said she could have sex. Being intimate with anyone was honestly the last thing on her mind. Besides, it wasn't like she had anyone who wanted her anyway. When Dr. Harris informed her it was time for the ultrasound, Mona's heart leapt into her throat. "I've been waiting for this all week." She admitted, "I'm a little freaked out…"

"That's a very normal reaction," the doctor replied gently. Dr. Harris placed the wand over Mona's belly, moving it around until the baby came into view. "Here's your baby." She pointed to the silhouette. "Judging from these images, I'm going to say gestational age is approximately thirteen weeks." Dr. Harris made a few quick annotations and then shifted the wand. "Everything looks great." She pressed the print button to send the images she'd captured to the printer and handed Mona a tissue. "Welcome to the second trimester, mama."

Sitting up on her elbows, Mona furrowed her eyebrows. "Thirteen weeks? But I was on birth control," she argued. "And I didn't get the antibiotics until later."

Dr. Harris crossed her legs as she scribbled measurements onto the chart for future reference. "Birth control can be affected by a lot of things. There's no telling if it really was the antibiotic or if it was a hormonal fluctuation or simply a twist of fate." Closing up the file, she set it aside for now. "I really admire you for taking this so well." She folded her hands. "During our first consultation, you told me your significant other is no longer involved?"

Averting her eyes, Mona picked at an errant string on the gown. "Kyle's not a part of either of our lives anymore."

"Pregnancy and childrearing are challenging, even on the best of days. Do you have anyone you can count on? Family? Friends?" Dr. Harris rested a comforting hand on Mona's shoulder.

Mona's mind immediately slipped to Reno. As hard it was to believe, the overgrown frat boy had actually been something of her rock over these last few weeks. He'd driven her home when she wasn't feeling well, they'd slept in each other's arms the other day, and then ate waffles. It wasn't exactly one of those big, romantic love stories that people wrote novels about, but she felt she could rely on him. Then again, she was terrified he was going to freak out and fire her when he learned about her new addition. Everything was confusing right now and she couldn't immediately answer Dr. Harris.

Instead, she swallowed. "It's just me. I'm doing it on my own."

There was a moment of silence and Dr. Harris stood, walking over to her desk. She pulled out a booklet. "I'm not saying you need it, but there are resources available for single parents." The doctor placed the literature into an envelope with the ultrasound pictures and Mona's appointment card for a follow up in six weeks. "You call me if you have any questions, alright?"

It wasn't that Mona wasn't appreciative of Dr. Harris' generosity but it also pissed her off the doctor didn't seem to think she could do this alone. She accepted the envelope and headed to the car with her jaw set and mind racing. There were millions of single parents out there. She knew several of them personally. No, it wasn't easy, but at least the kid would have one parent who loved it unconditionally. Mona hadn't even had one stable parent growing up, and she'd turned out just fine.

Slamming the car door, she grabbed her cellphone to check her messages. Reno had texted several times asking for updates and she stabbed the dial button. He picked up on the first ring and Mona laid into him. "Keep your pants on, O'Keefe. I'm coming to get you now."

"You sound mad. Are you—"

Mona hung up.

She ripped out of the parking lot and down the road to Reno's apartment. He was already standing outside when she arrived. Creases of concern lined his face as he opened his mouth, but Mona cut him off. "Don't start with me," she warned, "I'm fine, okay? I'm not dying in some tragic, horrible, terrible way."

Reno scoffed at her. "Hello, pumpkin, I'm glad to see you too," he drawled sarcastically. Leaning over, he intended to give her an icy peck on the cheek, except Mona turned her head and he kissed her full on the mouth. Fire erupted in his veins as he pulled back. "Shit! Mona, I'm sorry..."

Why had she been angry again?

Reno's lips touched hers and Mona instantly forgot.

She cleared her throat, trying to ignore the heat scorching her cheeks—and other less visible places. Turning to face the windshield again, she could feel Reno's warm brown eyes boring holes into her. "Buckle up," Mona demanded. The best thing she could do right now was not make a big deal about this.

"Sure." Reno would've agreed with anything she said right now. How could he have been so stupid? She pulled out of his apartment complex and onto the freeway. Not a single word was spoken the entire trip to the mall. In fact, there were several times he wondered if she was even breathing.

Mona found a space in the back and was out of the car a millisecond after she threw it in park. Reno was hot on her heels as they headed into the department store. Bealls wasn't the nicest or the most comprehensive, but it was the best they were going to get without going to having to drive into Las Vegas. She turned to face him, her jade eyes flashing dangerously. "Take a walk, O'Keefe."

"Can we talk about what happened?" Reno pouted. "Will you at least allow me to apologize profusely?" he called after her. Mona stomped into the lingerie section and he groaned, straightening his spine as he stalked in after her. After nearly giving a little old lady a heart attack, Reno followed Mona to a rack of lacy bras. Ignoring the desire that began to stir in his belly, he cleared his throat. "I was just going to give you a fake kiss…I thought it'd be funny."

"Oh yeah, I'm really laughing," Mona countered. She

wasn't mad at him. She was mad at herself for getting swept up in feelings she shouldn't be having. She was pregnant for God's sake! Thirteen weeks, to be precise. It wouldn't be long before he figured it out on his own. The more she thought about it, the more terrified she became of his reaction. What she needed now was her space. "I'd like a little privacy here, Reno."

He shifted uncomfortably, scrubbing a hand over his jaw. Reno couldn't help but notice Mona was practically falling out of the bra she was wearing right now. She'd picked up a couple pounds in a few desirable areas and every part of him was appreciative of it. The more he realized how attractive she was, the more he remembered why he needed to get away from her. This was Mona he was thinking about. He didn't have a shot in hell. "I'll meet you in the men's section."

Mona exhaled sharply. "Thank you." She could see worry on his face and she folded her arms for a moment. "Pick out a suit that actually fits you. None of that *'I'm still a 34'* crap. You're not. Try something in a 38." Reno looked annoyed and she grasped his arm. "Pants too. Not just jeans. One each in black, blue, and khaki. Two belts. And a handful of ties."

"I have ties," Reno groused.

"You have a Scooby Doo bowtie and a tie with naked ladies on it." Mona folded her arms. "Oh, and that black one that's faded and has grease stains on it." She shook her head. "This is a wedding. Lots of opportunities to look your best." Patting his chest, she flashed him half a smile. "Wait for me before you try

---

51

anything on."

"Fine." Reno huffed. Mona was bullheaded, but at least she forgave quickly. He really fouled this afternoon up. What he wanted to do when she arrived was get some answers about her health and ensure she would be alright. Mona was far too feisty and stubborn to up and die on him but she had been extra ornery lately, and he wanted to know why. Now, he was alone in the department store, wishing he never fought with her at all.

Mona thumbed through several items before a saleswoman came over. "I'm actually looking for some maternity bras?" Her throat was dry just asking. The associate walked her over to a smaller section that had exactly what she was looking for. She also found several nightgowns that would be great for nursing, and they were on sale. Mona purchased everything and had them placed in bags so Reno wouldn't see what she was getting…especially not the spicy little number she'd bought for his sister to wear on her wedding night.

By the time Mona reached the menswear section, she was starting to feel peckish. Opening up her purse, she grabbed a granola bar and took a few bites. Reno had several of the sales associates at his beck and call. It didn't surprise her at all that they were pretty young girls, batting their eyelashes and giggling at him. Mona's frown deepened. Jealousy she had no business feeling welled to the surface and spilled over. "I can take it from here." Her accent was thicker than usual, but that always happened when she got angry. Tossing her bags down on a chair near the dressing rooms, Mona set her jaw. "Let's see what you've got."

Reno scratched his neck guiltily when she came barreling upstairs. The girls he'd been chatting up scattered to the far corners of the store. He didn't exactly know why he felt ashamed, though. Mona wasn't his wife or his girlfriend. Hell, after their little tiff this afternoon, he wasn't even sure they were friends anymore. He carried his items into the dressing area. "They were just helping me pick things out. And by the way, I'm a 36—in case you were wondering!" He pulled the cream colored pants up but even sucking it all the way in, he couldn't get them closed. He narrowly avoided cursing…why did she always have to be right?

"Uh-huh," Mona replied incredulously. "Well, come out then. I want to see." There was a long silence and she stood up. "Take them off. I'll go grab everything in a 38, okay?" Without judgment, she collected everything he'd already picked out and slipped it in to him.

Much to Reno's dismay, the new size fit perfectly and when he stepped out of the dressing room, he really looked great. The way the suit hugged his muscular arms and cupped his butt. A rakish smile spread over his features. "You sure it's not too sexy?"

Mona laughed. She picked a piece of lint from his arm and smoothed her hands over his shoulders. "I think it's a risk we have to take." She peered at the two of them in the mirror, her stomach tightening in response. It was strange how natural they looked together. Mona had to shake the thought away. "Let's see the ties you picked out." She went through the pile, setting aside a light blue, a dark blue with diamonds on it, a black tie, and she grabbed a green and a coral colored bowtie off the rack.

"Pink?" Reno stared at her incredulously. "Are you out of your mind?"

"It takes a real man to wear pink." Mona held it up to his neck and smiled. "It's perfect for the wedding. Lizzy will love it." Reno's warm hand slid up, taking it from her and sighing. Mona knew then and there she'd won. "You won't regret it, Reno." She smiled. "Now come on, I want to see those other pairs of pants."

Reno grumbled to himself as he went back into the dressing room. "Does this mean I get to watch you modeling dresses?"

Mona smirked. "Fair's fair, I guess. Besides, I need opinions. I want to make a good impression…" She glanced down at her lap, feeling raw all of a sudden. "It's not too late to back out, you know."

Pushing open the door to the dressing room, Reno folded his arms over his bare chest. He was wearing the new pair of jeans he'd picked out and they fit him like a glove. "What the hell are you talking about, pumpkin?"

"I…don't have a good track record with families." Mona picked at her ragged cuticle. "The last thing we need is for the people you love to be talking about the hussy you brought to your sister's wedding for years to come."

"You're not a hussy! Don't ever say things like that about yourself." Reno closed the distance between them. "You must have *some* experience with family gatherings, right?"

Mona shrugged. "I went to AA meetings with my ma before I was old enough to be left home alone. That's as close as I got to extended family."

Reno was quiet for a moment. Mona went out of her way not to tell him anything about herself or her past, so he didn't want to press. He reached out. "Just think of my family as a random group of drunks. That's actually more accurate than you think..." He grinned at her. "Plus, I'll be there with you every step of the way, pumpkin. You don't ever need to feel awkward." Stroking the back of her hand gently, he smiled. "My sister already adores you."

"I guess you're right..." Mona exhaled, some of her fear alleviated. "Get all the pants, the two white dress shirts, the blue button-down, and the ties we picked out. There were belts by the checkout. I'm going to go ahead and look for a couple dresses. Then we can head over to Target and pick something off the registry. I also need new luggage. I don't have a suitcase big enough for almost two weeks in Boston." Not to mention she was pretty light on prenatal vitamins and was hoping she could sneak some past Reno so she didn't have to drive back there later.

A smile was permanently plastered on Reno's face as he headed to pay. Mona was pretty amazing. He'd already guessed she'd grown up rough and she was

—

jaded because of it. That's why she tried to push everyone away. Mona was trying to help him get his life together and to settle down a little bit; maybe he could help her open up and realize she deserved way better than that weasel Kyle.

After lapping the place twice, Reno frowned. "Mona?" He called, moving toward the dressing room. The door opened up and she stood there in a dress that had to have been made for her. It was black but it had green swirls that accentuated her eyes. As lovely as it was on her, he ached to pull it over her head and kiss her senseless. "You look amazing…"

Mona twirled in front of the mirror. "Are you sure it doesn't make me look fat?" Maybe it was the power of suggestion but her belly seemed bigger now than it had this morning. Actually, that had been happening for a couple days now. When she woke up, her stomach was fairly flat but by the end of the day, she clearly had a bump. Mona chalked it up to the eating, but maybe it was a normal part of pregnancy…either way, she felt self-conscious.

"Are you kidding?" Reno shook his head. "You're getting that one. Let's see what else you've got." Women never ceased to baffle him. The next two dresses she tried on were just as perfect. A black cocktail dress that hugged her curves, a maxi dress that flowed down to her ankles, and a shimmering party dress with an empire waist completed her collection. "I'm going to have the hottest date at the whole damn party."

It wasn't true, but it felt nice to hear nonetheless. Mona picked up a couple pairs of control top pantyhose before she made her purchase. Reno insisted on carrying everything for her and they got back in the car a lot calmer than they left it. Target was ten minutes down the road and Mona sent Reno to customer service to get a copy of the registry. She quickly bought her vitamins at the pharmacy and shoved the bag and receipt into her purse before Reno was any wiser.

Mona found the perfect suitcase and Reno rolled it across the store as they shopped for Lizzy. After some discussion they decided to pick up the stemware and a cake plate from the middle of the list. And by 'they decided', Reno meant Mona had directed him to the correct gift and he purchased it. He was grateful for it too. It would've taken him hours to decide on how much he should spend and which items were most important. As they headed back to the car, he could see Mona was tired. "Hey, what do you say we head back to my place? I'll order us a couple pizzas and we can watch one of those chick flicks, if you twist my arm." He grinned.

"What the hell are you talking about? *Pretty Woman* is your favorite movie," Mona snorted. Reno couldn't deny it. "Pizza and a movie sounds good but don't you have to close up the club?"

Reno shook his head. "Nope, I handed the keys over to Tito. I'm trying to give the boys more responsibility while I'm around, so they can fall back on me if they need it. We're going cross-country for almost two weeks. I need to make sure they can handle things while we're away."

"That's actually a really good idea…"

"You don't have to act so surprised." Reno leaned back in his seat as they got back on the highway and headed for his place. "And just so you know, I *am* sorry about earlier. I was a jerk." He glanced over at her.

Mona sighed. "Yeah, well, I came in kinda hot. I'm sorry too." It was clear Reno wasn't expecting her apology and she rolled her eyes. "You don't have to look so surprised, I admit when I'm wrong." He shot her a withering look and she pursed her lips. "It just doesn't happen all that often!"

She pulled up in front of his place, slid out of the driver's seat, and followed him into the apartment. It was cluttered but Mona felt oddly at home in his space. "I want sausage, mushrooms, and onion on my pizza. Ooh, get the stuffed crust! I'm going to make sure your new clothes get hung up properly."

"You got it, pumpkin. I'm getting hot wings too," Reno called. He could see Mona from where he was standing, shifting things around in his closet to make room for his new clothes. After she finished, she tidied up the bed and picked up several used glasses from his nightstand. "Hey, I didn't bring you over here to clean up. Sit down and relax."

"I don't mind," Mona replied. She found herself elbow-deep in dishes before Reno could say another word. *What to Expect When You're Expecting* had a whole section on nesting but Mona never thought she would be 'nesting' at Reno's place. By the time the pizza arrived, she'd run the vacuum and forced him to dust. There was a sheen of sweat on her upper lip, her hair was slightly mussed, and she really felt like she'd earned her meal.

Reno wasn't sure what the hell got into Mona, but he got into the cleaning mode and half an hour later, the place was spotless. "Man, I should've invited you over here weeks ago." He grinned.

Mona grabbed a piece of pizza and took a large bite. This was exactly what she had been craving, even if she hadn't realized it until this moment. "So, what are we watching?" She peered over at him, chuckling at the expression on his face. "*Pretty Woman* it is."

"I do not deserve you." Reno already had the DVD queued up and he pressed play, resting his arm over her shoulder as the familiar music filled the room. Mona made a pretty good dent in the pizza and the wings. It was good to see her eating more than just the crackers and peanut butter she'd been noshing on at random intervals during the day.

Reno split his attention between the screen and the woman cuddled beside him. It wasn't late but she was starting to fade. For the second time in as many weeks, Mona fell asleep at his side. This time, he wasn't going to let her sleep on his crummy couch. It took a little maneuvering but he hoisted her up, carrying her the few steps to his bed. She didn't even move when he pulled the blanket over her shoulders.

Padding back into the living room, Reno finished watching *Pretty Woman* while he put the leftovers away. After a quick shower he changed into a clean pair of boxers and slid into bed beside Mona. The moment he closed his eyes, she curled against him and a smile ghosted over his lips. There was no telling how she'd react come morning when she realized she was sleeping in his bed.

Well, at least he'd die a happy man.

Chapter Five

Mona awoke on Friday wrapped in Reno's tender embrace. She was so stunned, she couldn't find a single word to say. He didn't seem eager to delve into where their relationship was going. Instead, he made breakfast and they kept their mouths full so they wouldn't have to talk about the elephant in the room.

With a couple mumbled words, Mona headed home to shower and change before work. Reno was already at the club by the time she arrived. They orbited around each other, keeping their conversations strictly professional.

That's the way things continued until the following Thursday evening. Tomorrow they were flying to Boston and Mona was not in a good mood. Reno could instantly tell this wasn't her usual gruff demeanor. There was something about the way she moved that made him legitimately concerned. At the end of the night, he cornered her. "You got a minute?"

Mona looked up from the register and nodded curtly. She dropped off a receipt to one of the regulars before heading upstairs to the office. She paused in from of the mirror, tugging her apron up a little higher. It had only been a week but she was definitely starting to look pregnant. Thankfully, Reno seemed blissfully unaware, although there was a part of her that wished he weren't. She wanted to tell him. *Needed* to tell him…the only problem was she couldn't get out of her own way. "What do you need?"

Reno glanced up. "I wanted to talk about tomorrow. I thought I'd pick you up at five. Our flight is at seven, so it should give us plenty of time to get in and find our terminal." He cleared his throat. "There's a time difference, so we should get into Boston before noon. We can't check into the hotel until three. So, my mom invited us by the house for lunch. After we pick up the rental car, I was thinking we could head to Brighton. Are you okay with that?"

"Yeah, are you?" Mona cocked her head in confusion. Reno seemed a little unsure. "You having second thoughts about bringing me?"

"What? No!" Reno stood up, walking around the desk. "I just didn't want to overwhelm you with my family the minute you get in. If you want to get settled or if you just want to sit in the parking lot at the hotel for three hours, we'll do it." He smiled gently. "Whatever you need, I'll make sure you have it. I can't tell you how much I appreciate this." Resting his hand on her shoulder, his thumb stroked over her collarbone.

Mona shrugged him off. "I can hold my own. You said so yourself." His touch burned through the core of her and she eagerly changed the subject. "By the way, the flow sheet of family members you gave me was actually really helpful. I still can't tell your Aunt Millie from your Aunt Sophie, but I guess that's how it goes with twins." She forced a smile, despite the butterflies in her belly. "I was just wondering…" She licked her lips, choosing her words carefully, "What did you tell your family about me?

"Nothing. I just said I was bringing a date," Reno replied nonchalantly. "I've haven't brought a woman home since high school, so you're kind of a big deal." He watched Mona's expression change and he chuckled. "They're going to love you, pumpkin. I'm not worried."

That made one of them.

Mona was worried about so many things: making a good impression, helping Reno acclimate to being part of a family again, enjoying her vacation, oh, and hiding her pregnancy. What could possibly go wrong? "Right…well, I'm going to take off. I've got to finish packing." He nodded in agreement and she took off without a backward glance.

As soon as she got home, Mona switched the last load of laundry into the dryer. She checked and rechecked her list of items she wanted to bring. It wasn't like they were going to another country where she couldn't purchase a forgotten pair of socks, but she wanted to be as organized as possible. Everything in the suitcase had been washed and tried on before it made the cut. Anything that wasn't comfortable or accentuated her baby bump in any way was put aside. Thankfully, the new outfits she bought were still workable.

Sometime after one in the morning, the laundry finished and Mona closed up her suitcase. When she got up, in a couple hours, she just needed to throw in the last of her toiletries. Mona crawled into bed, expecting to fret the night away but she fell asleep quickly and didn't stir until her alarm went off at four.

It took all Mona's strength to crawl out of bed. She shimmied into a pair of jeans and threw on a green tank top, zipping a black hoodie over it. Reno warned her it was cooler in Boston and she certainly wanted to layer up for the plane ride. Slipping her extra phone charger and makeup case into her luggage, Mona was all ready to go by the time Reno got to the house.

The roads were deserted leading up to the airport and Reno had no issue finding a parking spot in the long-term lot. He dragged their suitcases behind him as they headed into the terminal and waited in a fairly short line to check in. The security checkpoint loomed ahead of them. "You go first. I have to untie my shoes," Reno offered.

"Sure," Mona replied, her voice still gruff with sleep. Placing her carry-on into the grey plastic bucket, she tossed her shoes in and took a step through the metal detector. It beeped and she watched the TSA woman eyeball her closely.

"Take off your sweatshirt and go through again," she ordered.

Mona's mouth went dry. Unzipping the garment, she found herself feeling nervous again. Her belly wasn't huge yet but she was definitely starting to show. The woman with the wand noticed immediately and flashed her a gentle smile. Mona snuck a glance at Reno but he was focused solely on getting his things onto the conveyer belt. Mona breathed a sigh of relief and tugged her hoodie tighter around herself.

After they made it through the line, Reno plopped down on a bench to retie his shoes. "What do you say we scout out some breakfast and then find our gate?" He stayed close as they went in search of something that was open. Peet's was brewing up fresh, piping hot coffee and baking something that smelled heavenly. "Whatever you want is on me," he offered.

Mona picked out a tea that smelled like mint and salivated over a cranberry walnut scone. With both in hand, she stepped back to let Reno hand the cashier his credit card. Their gate wasn't too far from the café and they easily found a seat. Mona and Reno watched the sun rise through the massive plate glass window. She rested against Reno's shoulder, sipping her tea and eating her scone. There was no need for idle chatter as they waited and a comfortable silence stretched between them.

Forty-five minutes before takeoff, the plane began to board. Much to Mona's dismay, she had to use the restroom twice before they took off. The baby seemed quite content to squash her bladder and she couldn't seem to get comfortable. Reno glanced at her as she finally settled into the seat beside him. "I don't blame you," he leaned into her, "I don't like to fly either."

Mona just nodded, allowing Reno to come up with his own explanations for her frequent bathroom trips. She wasn't really afraid of flying. However, she *was* terrified of him finding out her secret. The trip was only ten days; she could hide her pregnancy that much longer. Then, on the way home, she'd drop the bomb and they could deal with the fallout. He'd be less wound up and

Mona would be in a better place to deal with his reaction—at least she hoped she would be.

The moment the plane began to shuttle toward the runway, Reno morphed into a completely different man. He was terrified. He gripped the arm of the seat between them and his jaw clenched so tightly she was afraid he was going to hurt himself. "Hey," Mona murmured. Her fingers brushed against his wrist by accident. Suddenly, he grabbed a hold of her and didn't let go. Instinctively, she laced her fingers with his and stroked the back of his hand with her thumb. "Everything is fine. Just focus on me, okay." Gentle reassurance didn't seem to be working; she'd just have to distract him. "Why don't you tell me more about your family?"

Logically Reno understood he had a greater chance of getting struck by lightning than dying in a plane crash. Unfortunately, his anxiety was not listening to reason. Mona was his only saving grace. He closed his eyes, inhaling the sweet scent of her shampoo and focusing on the warmth of her palm seeping into his skin. "I can't think of anything right now except how we could drop out of the sky, and about my dad…"

"You mean Richard?" Mona pressed him for an answer.

"No, " Reno choked out. "Richard is amazing. I love him and I couldn't be happier he married my mom but…he isn't my biological father." He paused a moment, building up the courage to pry open his eyes. "Vernon O'Keefe is…*was* my dad." Swallowing hard, he stared into her expressive jade eyes. "My brothers all have

———
66

these great memories of him before he got sick. There were picnics and parades and going out to breakfast after church on Sunday. I've seen the pictures. We all look so happy." He practically choked on his grief. "You know what I remember? The funeral...that's all."

Mona leaned closer, resting her opposite hand on his knee. "He died when you were little. It doesn't surprise me you don't have many memories," She soothed.

"You know what I'm thinking about? If I died right now, I'm not even sure I'd make it to heaven. I run a strip club, for God's sake." He licked his lips. "But if by some miracle I did get in? I don't think I'd recognize my own father." Reno's voice shook and he averted his gaze. "Shit, that was morbid. I'm sorry, I—"

"Reno, stop," Mona demanded. Grasping his face between her hands, she wouldn't let him pull away. "First of all, one little plane ride to Boston isn't going to be what takes us out. We're tougher than that." Her fingertips brushed over the warm skin of his temple. "Second of all, you don't have to hide what you're feeling from me. I'm not some bimbo you picked up at the airport. I know you better than you think." Exhaling sharply, she leaned in, resting her forehead against his. "If there is some celestial palace where good boys and girls go, you'd definitely get in. And they must have a way to streamline finding your loved ones once you get there. Otherwise heaven would be a little bit like trying to find the right line at the DMV...*impossible.*"

In spite of everything, Reno laughed. Wrapping his arms around her back, he drew her close to him. "What the hell would I do without you, pumpkin?" Honestly, he'd been asking himself that question a lot lately. Mona prided herself on being closed off but something had changed. She was letting him in and he was amazed by how much he enjoyed the woman beneath the bravado.

The tension began to ease when the seatbelt signs came off and they were cruising at thirty-seven thousand feet. Reno felt a rush of guilt. Poor Mona looked uncomfortable twisted to face him; he shifted slightly so she could sit a little more naturally. Part of him wanted to ask how he'd gotten so lucky as to coerce her into going on this trip with him. The other was scared shitless of her answer. Thankfully, the flight attendant came by and he focused on sipping his soda and opening up the packet of pretzels that accompanied it.

Mona wasn't feeling nauseous but she ordered ginger ale anyway. It was better than waiting to see if her stomach went sour. The inflight movies didn't interest Mona and she buried herself in a novel Liberty had recommended. It was naughtier than she expected but not altogether unpleasant. Mona hadn't even thought about sex since she learned she was pregnant…now she couldn't stop thinking about how she'd probably never get any ever again. Slamming the book closed, she jammed it into her bag.

Reno tugged the headphones away from his ear. "You alright?"

"Yeah, just feeling a little cooped up. I'm going to take a

walk." Mona took the opportunity to use the bathroom, stopping to freshen up her mascara and fix her hair. Once they landed in Boston they wouldn't have a lot of time. The thought of greeting Reno's loved ones looking like a ragamuffin made her blood run cold. Suddenly, she was rethinking wearing the pair of stretchy jeans and this particular hoodie. Maybe she should've picked a dress or at least some nicer slacks. Hurrying back to her seat, she pulled Reno's headphones off. "Do you think I should change before we get to your mom's?"

Reno looked her up and down. "Why?" Mona was honestly the most beautiful woman he'd ever seen. "My ma was a waitress her whole life and Richard's a plumber. We're not exactly the Kennedys, pumpkin." He slung his arm around her shoulder. "You're gorgeous."

Mona was prepared to lambaste him for lying to her face, but when she looked into his eyes she actually believed him. Simmering down, she plugged in her headphones and watched the rest of the movie. She wasn't sure what it was about but there were a lot of explosions, bleeped out cursing, and car chases. Reno seemed to like it but Mona was glad when it was over.

They touched down in Boston right on schedule, which was a miracle given how massive Logan airport was. Mona worried they were going to get lost in the crowd and she reached out, grasping Reno's hand as they navigated their way to baggage claim. He flashed her a soft smile as they waited for the carousel to spit out their belongings.

Reno tried to take Mona's bag but she gently rebuked

him. He still watched her like a hawk as they waited for the shuttle to take them to the rental place. By the time they got everything into the SUV and the GPS fired up, it was half past noon.

Boston had changed a lot since Reno had last been in town. They'd finally finished the Big Dig, which he never thought was possible. All the businesses had changed over and the exit numbers were different as well. Once they actually got on the highway, he found himself navigating quite easily. Mona was tight-lipped and a little stiff, but he didn't comment on it. If their roles were reversed and he was about to meet a giant group of strangers, he'd feel exactly the same way.

It took a solid forty minutes to get into Brighton. Reno wound his way through the old neighborhood, counting the things that had changed and finding many more that had not. Nostalgia flooded him in waves as he turned down the street he'd grown up on. "Damn…"

Mona sat up straighter. "What's wrong?"

"I'm having déjà vu. Right over there was where I crashed my bike when I was eight years old. That's how I got this scar." He traced the faded mark at the side of his mouth. "I busted my lip open and had to get two whole stitches. I was the coolest kid in third grade." Reno chuckled to himself. "The empty lot at the top of the street was where the old Jenkins place used to be. We were all convinced it was haunted. On Halloween we would always camp out and see if we could catch a glimpse of the ghost. It was a death trap. I'm surprised it took them so long to tear it down." He shook his head.

"My high school sweetheart lived in the blue colonial across the street. God, I thought I'd marry that girl…but Gwen was way too good for me. She was going to change the world." Silence hung between them for a moment. "It's strange being back." Reno eased the car into the driveway, staring at the house he'd grown up in. "Welcome home…"

Mona wasn't sure what she was expecting, but a charming yellow cape with a massive wraparound porch wasn't what she pictured. The front yard was small but a white picket fence quarantined a playscape in the backyard that had clearly built by hand. Although it was weathered, it looked sturdy. Mona was confident the children would be safe to play on it…not that *her* baby would ever be here. Wiping that thought from her mind, she eased out of the car. Reno was waiting for her, a wide smile on his face. His hand hovered over her lower back and she leaned into him, keeping close as he led the way up the porch. They were seconds away from ringing the bell when the door flew open and a dark haired woman threw herself into Reno's arms.

"They're here! They're finally here! Richard, get the camera!"

"Ma," Reno groaned. "Come on. We don't need to take a million pictures!"

"Yes, we do!" Martha countered, her tone leaving no room for argument. "Now, can it and smile!"

The flash of an antiquated digital camera was slightly disorienting to Mona. Reno must've sensed she was a bit off center because he pulled her against him and his palm rested over her belly. Her mouth went dry...he didn't even know she was pregnant but he still instinctively protected the baby. The realization affected her more than she wanted to admit.

More people poured into the foyer and Mona couldn't tell who was talking anymore. Strangers were hugging her, kissing her cheeks, and talking all at once. As they moved toward the living room, Mona came face to face with a massive crucifix. Jesus Christ was right. She had never seen anything so gruesome hung on a wall...and she'd had grown up in New Orleans.

Reno leaned in, his warm breath fanning her neck. "They'll settle down in a minute," He whispered. "Hang in there, pumpkin." She was holding her own, which was more than he expected of anyone. Mona was a trouper.

Mona nodded, smiling softly. Whatever was cooking smelled amazing; they hadn't eaten since that tiny pack of pretzels on the plane and the scone she'd had for breakfast didn't exactly tide her over. Martha seemed to know immediately that someone in the house was hungry and clapped her hands together. "You two must be starving! The lasagna is cooling now. Can I offer anybody a drink? Wine? Beer? Soda?" Folding her hands, she smiled sweetly. "Mona, dear, what can I get you?"

Reno had already warned Mona that refusing an offer of food or drink was extremely offensive to his mother. "I'd love some water, if it's not too much trouble."

Martha nodded enthusiastically and Mona grinned. "Thank you, Mrs. O'Keefe."

"None of that!" Martha exclaimed. "Call me mom!"

"O…kay." It took Mona a moment to force the words out. "Thanks, uh, *mom*." She cast a sidelong glance at Reno, who didn't seem at all concerned. Everyone else was calling Martha 'mom'…then again, everyone else belonged to this family, except for her.

Luke was the second oldest O'Keefe. His wife, Lisa, ran a nonprofit in New Hampshire and they'd chosen to make their home there. He'd been working as a preschool teacher when they first met but made the decision to stay home when their daughter Lana was born with Down syndrome. Of all his brothers, Reno was the closest to Luke and they talked often about his goddaughter. Reno could hardly believe the chubby baby he'd fallen in love with at first sight was now almost ten. He was really regretting not coming home sooner.

Martha returned with a cup of water a minute later. "Here you go, dearest." She paused in front of Mona, her eyes shiny and bright. "I'm so glad you could come for the wedding. I can't wait to get to know you better." In a flash, the tears were gone and the authoritarian was back. "Lunch will be served in five minutes!"

"Can I help you with anything?" Mona offered.

"Nonsense!" Martha scoffed. "You've had a long flight. Relax, mingle, and help yourself to anything you'd like."

She bustled back to the kitchen, giving orders as she went.

Mona turned her attention to the brother standing in front of Reno. His hair was jet black and wavy…which meant he was either Mark or Luke. Stephen had somehow been born with flaming auburn locks, and it was a longstanding family joke that he belonged to the milkman—even though Vernon's side of the family were primarily redheads.

The brothers were chatting idly when Luke huffed in annoyance. "So, are you going to introduce me to your mystery woman or am I going to have to be rude and do it myself?" He didn't miss a beat. Luke extended his hand and grasped Mona's firmly. "I'm Luke and this is my wife, Lisa."

"Mona Gallo," she replied warmly. Her thick Southern accent stood out starkly in a room full of Bostonians. "It's so nice to put a name to a face. Reno has told me so much about you."

The ice cube in Lisa's white wine clinked against the glass as she leaned in, hugging Mona warmly. "We're just thrilled you could make it. We've been waiting a decade for the black sheep of the family to bring a girl home." She nudged Reno playfully. "So, I want all the details. How'd you two meet?"

Mona took a sip of her water before setting it on a coaster. "Well, we—"

"Met at the club," Reno interrupted. Clearing his throat

several times, he faked a grin. "Mona was dancing. It's really a boring story. Right, pumpkin?"

"Oh? Are you a professional dancer?" Lisa probed.

"You could say that." Mona chuckled, ignoring Reno's glare. "To be honest, Reno's right. It's not an interesting story at all. We fought like cats and dogs when we first met and now look at us! I honestly can't imagine my life without him…"

Damn, Mona was an amazing actress. Reno almost believed her. To really sell it, he pulled her against him again, pressing a kiss to her temple. "I'm a lucky man."

Luke and Lisa exchanged a look.

Martha carried the last tray of food into the dining room before whistling over the murmur of voices. "Alright, everybody! Dig in!" Lisa went first, grabbing Lana a plate and helping Mark's wife Elina carry over portions for her twins, and three of Rob's four children. His wife, Karen, was taking their youngest for a doctor's appointment that had been scheduled long before Lizzy announced she was getting married. Rob, unused to being the sole caregiver for his children, seemed very overwhelmed.

Mona was a little disappointed she wouldn't get to meet Lizzy until Friday. The bride and groom-to-be were scrambling with last minute wedding details and wouldn't be around for lunch. Though everyone was very welcoming, Mona got the sense all the whispering going on was about her…she squared her shoulders,

---

smiled a little wider, and made an effort to fit in.

Reno couldn't tear his eyes away from Mona. He slipped away during lunch, taking a moment to greet the family he hadn't seen in so long. Mona was enjoying a hearty portion of lasagna and salad, which made his mother incredibly happy. She chatted animatedly with Richard. Hell, she even seemed to get along with Elina who had a tendency to be a bit standoffish with strangers.

Lana finished her meal quickly and bounded over to where Mona was sitting. The girl grinned ear to ear, her dimples showing as threw herself into Mona's lap. She smoothed Lana's blonde hair, braiding it per the girl's request as they talked quietly about school and all the girl's other favorite activities. It was obviously love at first sight. Lana curled at Mona's side, her head resting against Mona's shoulder as the twins crawled in and out of her lap.

"She's lovely, Vincent." Martha wrapped her arms around her son, hugging him tightly.

When he turned to face her, Reno's heart ached when he realized his mother's eyes were filled with tears. "What's the matter, ma? Are you sick? Is it dad?" Richard had a very mild heart attack in his fifties and Reno always feared the worst.

Martha dabbed at her eyes. "It's nothing like that. I'm just so proud of my kids. I love you so much, sweetheart." She brushed a strand of salt and pepper hair behind her ear; as usual her long locks were secured in a knot at the base of her neck. The years had been kind to Martha O'Keefe. She had more wrinkles since the last time he'd seen her but she looked radiant. It wasn't that he felt she had been hard on him for not settling down and marrying, but it was always at the back of his mind that he was the odd man out. At the last family wedding, Rob married Karen and it made Reno stop and think about what he wanted. Unfortunately, what he decided upon was a string of short-term flings and one night stands.

Of the last ten women he dated, Reno couldn't imagine a single one of them in this house—let alone snuggling under a pile of his nieces and nephews. Ian, Rob's youngest at only two years old, had found his way to the center of the couch and was currently napping with his tiny head tucked beneath Mona's arm. Her fingers gingerly brushed the child's hair, smoothing the cowlick at the back of his head. Reno looked over at his mother and found her smiling knowingly at him. He squeezed her in a hug once more. "You've done so much today. Go sit down and put your feet up! I'll clean the kitchen."

Martha padded over to grab something to eat. Mona leaned toward her, "You need to show me how you did that. I can't even get him to wash a dish at home." By 'home' she'd meant Carson City, but she watched the surprise register on Martha's face and immediately realized her mistake.

"I didn't realize you two were living together!" Martha cooed. "In my day, you had to be married to live with a man…" She straightened her shoulders. "I understand, of course. Things are different these days! I have no

—
77

delusions you and Reno are abstinent."

If Mona hadn't been grounded by a big pile of children, she might've run for the door in shame. "Oh no, I wasn't—"

"You don't need to be embarrassed, honey. I didn't just fall off the turnip truck, you know." Martha smiled sweetly, cupping Mona's cheek. "I'm thrilled you support one another. As for helping around the house, remind Vincent that a happy wife means a happy life. I can see how much my son loves you. He'll do right by you."

It took all of Mona's strength not to choke on her own tongue. Martha was clearly mistaken. Reno love Mona? There was a greater chance of him running her over with his car. The thought was laughable really. The little crush Reno had harbored for her when he first bought the club would be instantly obliterated when he found out her little secret. Instead of arguing, Mona grinned through her discomfort. "You never know!"

Except she *did* know. It wasn't going to happen.

Lisa bustled around the living room, gathering Lana's things. "We'd love to mingle a bit longer but Lana's fading." Luke woke Lana slowly. The girl stretched and then whimpered, clinging tighter to Mona for a moment before her father coaxed her up the stairs. "Mona, it was a pleasure. I'm sure I'll see you this weekend for Lizzy's bachelorette?"

"Oh, I'm sure she doesn't want me intruding…"

"Are you kidding?" Martha cut in. "She hasn't stopped talking about it since Vincent let us know you were coming to the wedding! My son was supposed to tell you that you were invited…" She folded her arms. "I'm going to set that boy to rights!" Martha announced before marching into the kitchen.

Mona covered a laugh when Reno pushed his way out of the kitchen. "Ma, I know!" he sighed. "I'll make it right." Sidling over to her, he extended his hand. "Well, I have some serious apologizing to do and I think it'd be better if I did it at the hotel." He watched her flush and he realized how suggestive that must've sounded. "I didn't mean…" Reno cleared his throat. He was flustered as she was now. "I'm going to be quiet before I make an even bigger ass of myself." He grabbed his keys and gave his mother one last kiss. "We'll see you guys soon."

Without protest, Mona hugged several more family members and followed Reno out to the car. As she slid into the passenger seat, she leaned back. "I'm exhausted."

"I can barely keep my eyes open," Reno replied honestly. "My family is great but they will suck every ounce of energy out of you." Carefully, he eased his way out of the driveway while Mona set the GPS to the hotel. They both needed time to rest and decompress after a long trip and a day with the family.

Chapter Six

The Hartland Hotel was the focal point of Regan Street. Its brick facade and canopied windows were quintessentially Boston. Reno found a parking space fairly easily and they stepped into the hustle and bustle of commuters heading home from work. Mona found herself swept up in the sights and sounds whirling all around her. It wasn't that she was unfamiliar with city living; she'd grown up just outside of New Orleans and Carson City was not exactly the Styx. Still, this area had its own personal flair and she liked it instantly.

As they stepped inside, a crystal chandelier illuminated the atrium and reflected off the pristinely kept white walls. The sun was just starting to set and the whole place seemed hopelessly romantic. Reno headed to the check in desk, handing over the itinerary to a gangly twenty-something. Mona moved to Reno's side, glancing at the display of pamphlets. There were museums galore, bus tours, the Freedom Trail, the aquarium…she was excited to explore.

"Your suite is located on the fifth floor," the kid explained. "Our onsite restaurant and lounge is one of the best in the area. You two should check it out. If there's anything we can do to make your stay more pleasant, just let us know." He grinned broadly and handed over a welcome packet. "Have a nice stay, Mr. and Mrs. O'Keefe."

Mona didn't bother to inform the attendant that she wasn't Mrs. O'Keefe. She simply nodded her thanks and followed Reno to the elevator. She managed to lug her suitcase all the way to the room without incident. Her breath hitched in her throat when he opened up the door and she glanced at the lavish accommodations. The room had a full kitchen with a refrigerator and microwave tucked in the right corner. Straight ahead was a living room area with the television and a small table for dining or writing. The king sized bed was massive…but there was only one in the room.

Reno cleared his throat, "I wanted the room with all the stuff and they only have king beds." He carried his bag over to the side of the couch and leaned it there. "I should've mentioned it earlier. Don't worry, I'll sleep on the couch."

"Don't be ridiculous." Mona shrugged him off. "We've slept in the same bed before. This one's much nicer than your lumpy old mattress too," she chuckled. If Reno was offended, it didn't show. He smirked at her and started to unpack. Mona did the same, immediately hanging her garment bag in the closet. She put her toiletries in the bathroom, pausing to revel in the grandeur of the place. "This must've cost you a fortune…"

"You don't need to worry about it. I wanted you to have the best." Reno kicked off his shoes and plopped down on the couch. "Especially after the show you put on this afternoon."

"What show?" Mona queried, settling herself beside him. "What're you talking about?"

Reno raised an eyebrow at her. "This afternoon with my

family? You were charming."

"Are you saying I ain't charming *all* the time?" Mona asked threateningly. She snorted when his expression changed from neutral to concerned. "I get what you're saying. At work I have to stay tough. You show weakness in our business and you end up in trouble." Well, more trouble than she was already in anyway. "Our clients know they can't mess with me or my girls. If they thought they could, they *would*. I know from experience…"

Reno rested his head against his palm. "It was like that at your last job?" It was a simple question but he could see the hurt flash in her vibrant green eyes.

Mona shuddered. "There's a club deep in the heart of the bayou called The Gypsy. It was real rough. I knew more people who were used up than who got out…it wasn't pretty." Staring down at her hands, she swallowed hard. "I needed the money." Tightening her grip on the arm of the couch, she chewed her bottom lip. "I worked there for three years, saved up every penny. Cheapest bus tickets I could find were to Carson City. So I picked up my life and moved." Mona picked idly at a string at the edge of her shirt. "Worked out well that there are a number of strip joints in the area because I'm not good at anything else."

"You're smart as hell, Mona. You could be the CEO of a company if you decided that's what you wanted," Reno pressed. "You better not *ever* leave me, though. I will put up a fight."

Mona chuckled. "How many CEOs do you know who never graduated high school?" She shook her head.

Reno's eyebrows shot up. "You never finished high school?"

"Nope." Mona's tone belied no embarrassment but her cheeks were flushed. "I don't have a nice family like yours, Reno. I grew up crawling around on bar room floors, picking slivers of glass out of my knees and learning not to get underfoot during a fight. I don't remember much of my father either, except he rarely talked to anyone and went to County when I was six." Her chest ached with emotion. "Damn it…"

"What's wrong?" Reno pressed, his hand sliding over her shoulder.

Mona swallowed past the emotion that burned in her throat. "You don't want to know this shit."

Reno *did* want to know. "I think it's only fair, right? You get to know my family, I learn about yours." He'd always known she'd grown up rough, it was etched into her soul. He just wanted to know more. In an effort to loosen her up, Reno massaged Mona's shoulders. "How'd you get through it?"

"Sometimes I wonder the same thing." Mona froze for a moment. "My mother wasn't bad when she was sober. Thing is, she was never sober long. She died with a needle in her arm when I was fifteen." She found herself leaning against Reno for support. "After that, the trailer got repoed and I had to take that job or I'd have ended up in the system. The Gypsy was scary but the stories I'd heard about foster families were worse…" A tear escaped and before Mona realized what was happening, tears were burning down her cheeks and he was murmuring sweet words into her ear while rubbing her back.

Reno hugged her tighter, his fingers brushing away the dark hair that clung to her dampened cheeks. "Maybe it's not what you wanted to hear but everything that happened made you who you are today. It brought you into my life and I'm so glad for that. I couldn't run the club without you, Mona. Hell, I couldn't run my life without you."

Mona snuggled deeper into his shoulder, dabbing her eyes with a tissue he produced from a box sitting on the end table. She chuckled slightly at his assertion that he couldn't manage without her. "I guess that's true."

Reno smiled again. "What do you say we get in our pajamas, order a bunch of room service, and spend the rest of the night relaxing?"

Mona nodded eagerly. The last thing she wanted to do was go out right now. It was bad enough Reno saw her like this and she was closer to him than anyone else. Complimentary water bottles had been provided with the room and she cracked one open, sipping until she trusted her voice again. "I'm definitely looking forward to getting some rest…and I'm *starving*." She thought about apologizing for her reactions and for divulging so much, but Reno made her feel as if she didn't have to. He grabbed the room service menu and handed it over to her to peruse.

"You want something stronger than water? Champagne? Beer? Wine?" Reno flicked through the bar list.

"Nah, I think it'd be better to keep my wits about me on this trip." Mona was not much of a drinker. Even on special occasions she stayed sober to make sure Reno got home safely. She worried, at first, he might find her sobriety suspicious but he shrugged it off and she relaxed again. "Oh man, the bacon Swiss burger looks awesome. And I want the curly fries and a lemonade."

Reno grinned and picked up the phone to dial. "I'll make that two." He watched Mona pick out her pajamas. It occurred to him that she had been different lately. There was something softer in her words and actions; she was still tough but he could see cracks in the façade. The Mona he knew would've never told him about her family or the pain in her life. Whatever the reason for the change, he liked it.

"I'm going to take a quick shower before the food comes," Mona called. Reno told her it was going to be half an hour, she had plenty of time. She desperately needed to wash away the stress of the day and the saltiness of tears that had dried on her face. Some of her reaction was hormonal but a much larger part of it was festering pain she'd been keeping inside for so long. Her mother passed away when she was still so young and innocent; Mona thought she was so grown up and she'd been so wrong. Her baby wasn't going to know the pain of coming from a broken home and having to fight for survival every day of his or her life. That was a promise.

Turning the water to warm, she settled the bath mat on the floor. There were luxurious shampoo and conditioner bottles sitting on the sink and she placed them on the side of the tub. After Mona undressed, she paused to stare at herself in the mirror. Her fingers traced over the soft curve of her belly and she chewed her bottom lip. Keeping this pregnancy from Reno felt wrong, especially after everything they'd shared over the last few days. After she finished with her shower, Mona was resolved to tell him the truth.

She lathered her hair and washed with the floral soap provided by the hotel. The warm spray sluicing down her body felt delightful. By the time she stepped out, she felt prepared to handle what was to come. Slipping on the silky red pajama bottoms and tank top, she zipped her hoodie back up and swallowed her fear. "Hey Reno?" Mona called as she stepped out of the bathroom. "There's something I've got to talk to you about—" Her mouth fell open at the sight of Reno wrapped in the arms of a woman who had to have been a model at some point in her life.

"Oh!" The blonde clasped both hands over her mouth. "You must be Mona!"

Before Mona could stop her, the stranger hurried over and wrapped her in an uncomfortably tight hug. Standing there stiffly, she didn't participate in the embrace. This woman definitely wasn't included in the flow sheet of family members Reno had given her…it was too much to hope for that she was some long lost cousin, right?

"Mona, this is Gwen Hartland. We grew up across the street from one another. She owns the hotel...which I should've realized it sooner. I had no idea you were in this business. Last I heard you were going to law school..." Reno shifted on his feet. There was something in Mona's posture that made him wary. Her jaw was set the way it did when she was about to deck a rowdy customer. He approached Mona with extreme caution, putting himself between the two women. "I was just telling Gwennie we were over at the house earlier today."

"I wish I could've made it but I was stuck in meetings all day. I just can't get enough of mom's lasagna!" Gwen grinned broadly. "Well, I just wanted to let you know your meal is comped and if there's anything you need, I'm going to give you my personal cell phone." She scribbled her number onto a pad of paper and slipped it to Reno. Leaning in, she kissed him sweetly on the cheek. "Vincent, I'm so happy to see you. And Mona, it was a pleasure meeting you as well!" With that, she swept out of the room.

Reno stared at the number in his hand. When he turned, Mona had an odd expression on her face. It almost looked like she was jealous, but that couldn't be it...maybe he was reading too much into it. Reno picked up the plates and settled them on the coffee table in front of the TV along with their lemonades. Mona picked up the controller, flicking through channels silently in search of something to watch. It suddenly occurred to him she'd been talking about something when she first came out of the bathroom. "Was there something you needed to tell me, pumpkin?"

Mona hated how vulnerable she felt right now. She was so close to Reno just minutes ago. Seeing him in Gwen's arms reminded her why she couldn't allow it to happen again. "Nah," she lied. Mona grabbed a curly fry from the plate and chewed thoughtfully. It tasted fine but she wasn't feeling hungry anymore; nausea was starting to churn in the pit of her belly again and she didn't want to add fuel to the fire.

"Are you sure? You came out of the bathroom and said there's something you needed to tell me about..."

"I, uh, just wanted to warn you I used all of the shampoo. I guess it doesn't matter anyway." Mona knew the fib was ridiculous. Reno shaved his head; he didn't need shampoo. It didn't faze him though. He just smirked and she turned her focus back to the TV.

After going through the channels several times, Reno sighed. "Nothing's on." He leaned back on the couch with his burger in his lap. "The weather is supposed to be pretty nice tomorrow and we don't have any wedding stuff, it'll be a great day for sightseeing. I was thinking maybe we'd walk the Freedom Trail and hit Faneuil Hall for lunch. Then Gwen was thinking maybe she and I could grab a drink and catch up?" Mona nodded but he could tell she was pissed. "Are you going to tell me what's wrong? The whole point of bringing you on this trip was so I didn't have to deal with this silent treatment bullshit."

White-hot anger seared in Mona's veins. She laughed but it wasn't a happy sound. "You brought me on this trip because you don't know a single breathing female you haven't screwed over." She leapt from the couch and stormed over to the fridge. She'd eat later. Right now, her stomach couldn't handle it. "And while we're on the subject of who the hell you think you are: what kinda club does your family think you run, *Vincent*?"

Reno blanched. "They think it's a nightclub. I just never corrected them. We have dancing and drinks…" Reno stuttered. He furrowed his eyebrows. "That's not what we were talking about!" Moving beside her, he leaned against the counter. "Look, Gwen was my high school sweetheart. She was smart and pretty and popular. I don't know what the hell she even saw in me but there must have been something, right?" Reno swallowed hard. "When she dumped me, I was crushed. Sometimes I wonder if the reason I've never found someone else is because I've been hung up on her." Reno plopped down on the arm of the couch. "And she's *single*, Mona! This could be my shot."

A wave of nausea passed over Mona. She glanced down to try and compose herself but found herself staring at her belly again. Of course she knew Reno didn't care about her like that. It was the hormones again. She finished wrapping up her dinner and padded over to the couch. "Your family thinks we're involved."

"I know," Reno replied quietly. "There's no reason they need to think any different. Gwen knows how my family is. She's been a part of it for as long as I can remember. She can keep it quiet so it won't upset any of the wedding activities." He swore he saw Mona shudder. "It's just a drink. It's not like I'm going to fuck her!"

"What do I care if you do or not?" Mona snapped back. "I'm not your keeper." She needed to get away from him. He was too close to her and she was feeling off center. "I'm tired. I'm going to bed."

Reno frowned deeper. "It's seven o'clock!"

Mona ignored him. She grabbed her bottle of water from the table and walked around to the other side. The bed was comfortable but she was having trouble finding a good spot. Reno aggressively flicked through the channels. She could hear him chewing his fries and mumbling about women.

Pulling the blanket up to her shoulders, she flipped through her e-book copy of *What to Expect When You're Expecting* for a while. It reassured her what she was feeling was normal. The only problem was: nothing Mona was going through was normal. She had been abandoned by the father of her baby and was shacking up with her boss in a hotel room thousands of miles from her home. At least Reno hadn't figured out she was pregnant, which was a blessing and a curse.

After an hour of silence, Reno gave up pretending to watch television. He couldn't concentrate. After shooting Tito a quick email to check in, he slipped into bed beside Mona. She was reading something intently and ignoring him. Clicking off the light on his side of the bed, he rolled toward her. One lesson he remembered his mother telling him when he was a boy: Never go to bed angry.

"I'm sorry for pissing you off…"

"I'm not pissed off." Mona faced him head on. "I get it…she's the one that got away. You need to see where it goes." Saying it out loud didn't make it hurt any less.

Reno nodded sadly. "I would've married her, Mona. I had a ring in my pocket on graduation night…" He glanced over at her. "I don't even blame her. I was a punk in high school. I was reckless. I loved partying and flirting. Thirty years later, I'm a different man."

"Really?" Mona peered at him. "Two weeks ago you were so blasted I had to bring you home from work. Your girlfriend dumped you because you blew her off. On her birthday, no less."

"Shit, it was her *birthday* too?"

Mona just shook her head in annoyance. "You're older, sure, but you ain't any wiser." She rolled away from him with a huff. "If she's what you want, then go for it. I'm sure as hell not standing in your way." With that, she flicked the light off. "Good night, Reno."

A heavy sigh rumbled through his chest. Mona was right. As much as he didn't want to hear it, he wasn't the kind of guy Gwen deserved. She was a successful business owner. Somehow, she was even prettier than he remembered. He didn't even deserve her…but he'd regret it the rest of his life if he didn't at least try.

It had been a long day of traveling but it was still too early for bed in Reno's opinion. Mona was out cold, her breathing soft and even. The last rays of sunshine lit the room and he stopped to stare at her…she looked like an angel. Even with no makeup and puffy eyes, she was gorgeous. Damp waves of dark hair fanned out over the pillow and he ran his finger over a strand.

Mona turned over in her sleep, her shirt dangerously low on her heavy breasts. It took every ounce of strength in his body not to reach over and touch them too. Reno shut his eyes tightly, but there was no rest for the wicked tonight. A few minutes later she was snuggled at his side, her curvaceous body pressed up against his. Ignoring the throbbing ache in his loins was pure torture. He didn't sleep a wink that night…Libido: 1. Reno: 0.

Chapter Seven

When Reno awoke the next morning, Mona was already up. Going to sleep at seven meant around three in the morning, she was wide awake and raring to go. She'd walked to the Starbucks down the street and picked him up a coffee. Although she didn't say anything, Reno knew it was the closest thing to an apology he was going to get. Taking a swig of the strong brew, he muttered a sleepy 'thank you' before getting in the shower.

Mona sipped her chai latte and watched the local news. There was a continental breakfast downstairs but she honestly couldn't even think about eating. Her stomach was upset and her screwed up sleep cycle didn't help either. In the light of day, Mona realized she'd been out of line getting so mad at Reno last night. They weren't together and if he wanted to give it a try with his high school sweetheart, she was in no position to stop him. The coffee was a peace offering and she was very grateful he didn't rub it in her face.

Reno stepped out of the bathroom with a towel slung low on his hips. He stood in front of the closet for a moment before selecting one of his new pairs of jeans and a black polo from the drawer. Reno slid a pair of Snoopy boxers over his hips before he turned to face her. "Did you already eat breakfast, pumpkin?"

It was very hard not to watch as Reno got dressed. Mona forced herself to stare at the television until his pants were zipped. "I'm really not hungry," Mona replied tersely. She did her best to ignore the gnawing ache of desire that warmed her belly.

"I'm not either. Faneuil Hall is always crowded anyway. We can hit it early and avoid the rush." Grabbing his wallet and keys, he tipped his head toward the door. "You ready to go?"

Mona nodded enthusiastically. She'd never been further East than Alabama and was really looking forward to exploring. Reno wasn't kidding when he said Boston was unlike any place she'd ever seen. It had all the charm of historical landmarks with the hustle and bustle of city life she appreciated. Reno parked the car at the visitor center and picked them up a couple of maps.

They set off at a leisurely pace. Mona paused to snap pictures every once in a while. One day when the baby was older, she'd show him the pictures with pride. This trip was her last hurrah before motherhood and she was making memories she would always treasure. "I can't believe you grew up here." She paused to gaze at the Bunker Hill Monument, taking in the beauty of the landscape around them. "This place looks like it was ripped out of a fairytale."

Reno grinned. "I didn't appreciate it much as a kid but I get it now." Watching Mona newly discovering places he'd visited dozens of times was amazing. He was enjoying her reactions more than seeing the sights. Her enthusiasm was palpable.

Mona and Reno looped around by the park, sauntered across the bridge, and paused in front of the Old North Church. Mona looked a bit overheated so Reno bought them a couple of waters and they sat on the steps for a moment. Even though it was late September, the afternoons were still warm and there was a heaviness to the air that made it difficult to take a good deep breath.

Even after they set off again, Mona was still looking peaked and Reno slid his arm around her waist to steady her. It surprised him when she brushed him off, walking a few steps ahead but he decided not to comment on it. They took a detour off the beaten path when Mona heard about a farmer's market in the area. They hit the Haymarket and found themselves up to their eyeballs in fresh produce, meat, eggs, fish, and spices. She bought more than enough to stock their fridge for the week and was looking forward to eating something other than takeout. With bags full of goodies, they hurried toward Reno's favorite destination of all.

Faneuil Hall stood before them, warm and inviting. The air was fragranced with an odd combination of chocolate, aged cheese, honey, and saltwater. The way Reno described this place, Mona thought it was going to be a very large food court. It was so much more. She shopped around, pausing at little booths to try a sample here and there. Mona got herself some Nutella gelato and a pink lemonade, which she ate while making the rounds. Just that little bit of sustenance made her feel like a whole new woman.

Reno ate his way through the plaza. Falafel, pizza, bite sized hamburgers, and apple pie. They just didn't cook like this in Carson City and he was taking full advantage. He was full up and starting to think about resting again when Mona suddenly stopped. She darted into a shop with hand-sewn items and embroidery, her fingers lingering over a quilt that hung in the window. Moving to her side, his lips quirked into a smile. "Don't tell me Liberty's expecting again…"

Mona's heart ached as her fingers brushed over the sturdy but soft quilted fabric. It was a buttery yellow color with white accents, tiny flowers embroidered by hand. Even the edges had been scalloped in delicate hand stitched lace. She had to have it. When she turned the price tag, Mona's felt sick to her stomach. "Two hundred dollars!" And the item was already on sale. It was just too expensive. Mona had money saved, sure, but this was simply too much. Rationally she knew it was stupid to feel so emotional over a blanket…then again, Mona wasn't feeling particularly rational at the moment. It felt as if her heart had been wrenched from her chest. She envisioned wrapping her tiny baby up in this blanket and rocking him into a gentle, peaceful sleep.

All hell broke loose.

"Hey," Reno murmured gently, sliding his palm up her arm. "What's the matter, pumpkin?" He would've had to be blind to miss the shimmering of tears in her eyes…then she began to sob. Reno panicked. "If you want the blanket, I'll get you the blanket. *Please* don't cry." There she was, standing in the middle of the embroidery shop with tears pouring down her face. "Ma'am!" he yelled to the woman sitting behind a cash register. "We want this blanket wrapped up."

"No!" Mona croaked. "It's too expensive."

"I don't care!" Reaching into his pocket, he pulled out his credit card and practically threw it at the saleswoman. The shopkeeper flashed him a knowing look…though he wasn't sure exactly what she knew. It didn't matter. With the box in hand, Reno smiled at Mona. "Alright, we've got the blanket. See? It's going to be okay."

Mona cried harder. Great gulping sobs wracked her chest and her shoulders were shaking. It was one of the most embarrassing experiences of her life, but she couldn't stop herself. Frustration and rage, pain and fear all came flooding to the surface and she was powerless to stop the onslaught.

Reno shepherded her through the crowd, hailing a cab that would take them back to the car. He didn't care about the cost; he just needed to get Mona somewhere safe and secure. Once they got to the parking lot, Reno switched the bags into the rental car and then eased Mona into the front seat. He threw money at the cab driver and told him to take a hike. Sitting in the seat beside her, Reno felt like crying too. "Pumpkin, I just need to know if you're hurt. Do you need to go to the hospital?"

Shaking her head fiercely, Mona reached out and grasped his hand. "Home," she choked out and Reno sprang into action. He threw the car into reverse and took off toward the hotel. Instead of searching for street parking, he screeched up to the valet and handed over the keys. With a twenty in the pocket of the attendant, he instructed their bags be carried up to the room. Reno had his hands full with Mona.

The room had been freshly cleaned and a bouquet of yellow roses had been placed on the table with Gwen's regards. Mona narrowly resisted the urge to throw them across the room as she collapsed on the couch. Reno was right beside her, his hands seeking her body again. When she withdrew from him this time, it was not just a rebuttal but a violent reaction. "Don't touch me!"

Reno pulled back as if he'd been burned. His chestnut eyes widened in shock. Sympathy turned to anger and then boiled over. Why the hell had he ever thought things would be different just because they left Carson City? As soon as he got even a little bit too close, she shut down and pushed him away. It was infuriating. "I don't get you, Mona. One minute you're telling me we can sleep in the same bed and the next you're going to bite my head off for touching you! This hot and cold routine is insane!"

Mona was raw. At fifteen years old she'd learned to hide her feelings and her fear. If she kept everything locked behind walls, never feeling or wanting anything, she couldn't be hurt. Lower your expectations and everything seems like a dream come true. Reno was right that she couldn't decide if she should trust him or not. She had been clinging to the edge for so long, she forgot what it meant to actually have support. Then she began doubt Reno's loyalty to her. Mona growled low in her throat, jade eyes flashing dangerously. "Oh, so you think I'm crazy? I'll *show* you crazy!"

This time, Mona gave in to the urge. She picked up the vase and hurled it against the wall. Unfortunately, the stupid thing didn't break…it fell over, drooling water and loose flower petals onto the kitchen floor. It didn't even make that much of a mess, Mona lamented, it just irritated her. She grabbed a paper towel and threw it over the spill, then picked up the vase and hurled it into the sink.

The vessel sat there, mocking her, as it remained unbroken and resting on its side. Whatever the hell this vase was made of, Mona wanted a baby seat of the same material…

What were once lovely yellow roses were now bruised petals and broken stems. Hurling the carnage in to the trash, Mona vigorously washed her hands. Reno was just staring at her as she stomped around like a madwoman on a rampage. She mopped up the floor and then turned her attention to the counter. There were still bits of flower around and she erased any trace of their existence.

A knock on the door startled both of them. Reno moved to open it but Mona blew past him. The startled bellhop was holding their purchases from this afternoon and she accepted them silently. She noticed Reno taking another twenty out of his pocket to give to the terrified bellboy, but she didn't say anything about it. It wasn't until Mona turned away from the fridge that she found Reno in her face again. Suddenly, he grabbed her. Her body melted against his warmth but her mind raged on. "What the hell are you doing?"

"You won't stop moving so I'm holding you still until you tell me what the hell is wrong with you?" Reno barked. "Are you having some kind of psychotic break?" He was stronger than her by far. Reno looked her dead in the eyes, his hands tightening around her shoulders. Mona gritted her teeth and something truly terrifying flashed in her eyes. It wasn't anger, it was fear.

Reno's heart stopped. "Jesus Christ! I'm not going to hurt you, Mona." Seeing her so frightened ripped a hole in his chest. He loosened his grip and his hands slid across her back. She wasn't crying anymore, at least, but he felt her emotion as acutely as if it were his own. "I don't want to fight with you, pumpkin. I want to *help* you." Mona slumped against him and he cradled her in his arms. After a long moment, he sighed and rested his chin atop her head.

"Maybe I am having some kind of psychotic break…" Mona murmured against his shoulder. She felt out of control lately and her growing attraction to Reno wasn't doing anything to help that. It would never work between them. Even if he wasn't still in love with Gwen, there was no way he was going to want a woman pregnant with another man's child. Besides, they worked together quite well. There was no point in rocking the boat simply because she had hormones coursing through her that made her go berserk. "I'm sorry."

Comforting Mona was Reno's sole focus. As he held her close, he started to realize how warm she was and how sweetly she fit against him. She exhaled softly, burrowing deeper against him and rational thought started to fade. Mona was gorgeous. She put up a front to protect herself but he was starting to see how sweet the woman underneath was. He couldn't deny he was attracted to her, especially in moments like this. Reno reached up, brushing the curtain of dark hair from her face. "Whatever's going on, we'll deal with it together. Okay?"

When Mona looked into his chestnut brown eyes, she almost believed him. She'd forgotten what it felt like to be held like this. Kyle had never been the touchy-feely type. He was always in the mood for sex but once he finished, he rolled away from her and was gone shortly thereafter. Mona didn't think cuddling was ever something she wanted or needed. Then Reno put his arms around her and Mona realized how wrong she'd been.

"Whenever you're ready to talk, I'm here," Reno soothed. His hands slipped down, resting on her hips. He pressed a kiss to the top of Mona's head; it was something he'd seen Richard do to his mother a million times. It was meant as a comforting gesture and it should've been platonic…except Mona moved and his lips grazed hers.

Reno could have stopped there. He probably should have.

He didn't.

Tilting her chin up with his fingertips, Reno kissed Mona softly. A sigh of pleasure rumbled in the back of her throat and he absorbed it. She tasted like heaven and he was instantly aflame. Hands gripped her waist as he took a step toward the bed. Reno wanted so much more…

Mona was ripped out of the moment when she realized what she was doing. In between Reno's hot hands, her child slept. Another time, another place, she might've given in. God knew she wanted to. It was too big a risk. She was already in way over her head and adding sex to the mix would make it impossible for her to keep him out.

It took Reno a while to realize Mona was pushing him away. The disappointment that flooded him was quickly replaced with relief. What the hell was he doing? Mona was his coworker and friend. She was also going through something and sex would complicate things. The words stuck in his throat. Even though he knew it was wrong, he couldn't bring himself to apologize. He wasn't sorry he'd kissed her…he was just sorry it was bad timing. Rubbing a hand across his shaved head, he flashed her a sheepish grin. "So…"

"Forget this ever happened?"

Reno sagged with relief. "Deal."

Mona's cheeks still stung with embarrassment. Feelings she didn't know what to do with were coursing through her. She had to get away before she made a mistake she couldn't take back. "I'm all gross from walking around. I'm going to wash up." Mona tucked a strand of dark hair behind her ear. "I was thinking I might make something light for dinner. You interested in

Caprese salad with some of that bread we got at the market?" It wouldn't be too hard since they had all the ingredients.

"Yeah, sounds good." Reno wasn't really hungry since he'd pigged out at Faneuil Hall; he just wanted to please Mona. She washed her face, changed into a comfy pair of sweats, and swept her hair into a messy bun at the top of her head. While she tooled around the kitchen, Reno opened up his computer to check in on the club. It wasn't that he didn't trust Tito and Otis, but The Watering Hole was still his baby. According to the email report, everything went off without a hitch. Valentina had a bad case of strep and called out but Cadence was more than willing to pick up the extra time on the floor. Under Mona's tutelage, she was really coming into her own as a dancer.

It took a little bit of searching but Mona found a stash of pans. She washed them thoroughly before setting the saucepan on the stove. Making a balsamic reduction wasn't difficult, but would add a ton of flavor to the simple salad. While the vinegar warmed on the stove, she sliced up the yellow and red tomatoes, arranging them on paper plates. Next, she washed and chopped copious amounts of basil to sprinkle on top of thick slabs of creamy mozzarella. A little salt, pepper, and olive oil along with the warm balsamic reduction was truly perfection. Tearing two hunks from the soft loaf of bread, Mona carried the meal over to where Reno was sitting. She settled his plate on the coffee table and sat down across from him. "How are things at the club?" she asked, digging into her meal with gusto.

Reno set his computer aside and picked up the plate. "Everything's fine." When he took a bite, he moaned. "Holy crap, Mona, this is amazing! You could give my mother a run for her money..." He paused, pointing his fork at her. "If you tell her I said that, I will deny it to the death."

Chuckling softly, Mona shook her head. "It's just a salad, Reno. It's not that exciting."

"It's better than I'm used to. I can fry up chicken fingers pretty well but I can't make anything like this." Leaning back on the couch, he savored every last bite. "How come I didn't know you were a gourmet chef?" Reno grinned at her.

"Maybe because I'm not?" Mona shook her head. "I can make a few things really well. Spaghetti sauce, apple crisp, and I make a mean chicken enchilada. Simple recipes with simple ingredients. I'm not exactly Julia Child."

Reno mopped up the juice from the salad with the bread. "Well, I'm impressed anyway. You never cease to surprise me, Mona Gallo."

It was hard to keep the silly grin from her face. Once she'd finished her salad and bread, Mona felt better. Maybe her blood sugar had been low. She remembered what the book said about eating small, frequent meals. Maybe it wasn't just for the health of the baby, perhaps her sanity depended on it as well.

Mona stood up to clean the kitchen but Reno beat her

to the punch. "You cooked. I'll clean up," he offered.

"I barely *cooked*," Mona chuckled. "But if you want to do the dishes, go for it. I'm not going to stop you." She was contemplating watching television when her phone rang. Her eyebrows furrowed when a number she didn't recognize flashed on the screen. "Hello?"

"Mona?"

"…Who is this?"

"It's Lizzy!"

Mona stared at the phone for a minute. She wasn't sure how Reno's sister got her number. "It's good to hear from you…Reno's in the other room. I'll get him."

Lizzy giggled girlishly. "Mona, if I wanted to talk to my brother, I would've called him! I want to talk to *you*!" There was a short pause. "Mom told me you didn't think you were invited to the bachelorette party. I am so sorry you felt that way. My stupid brother should've told you from the beginning that I want you to be a part of the festivities. I'm so excited to meet you in person."

"I'm looking forward to meeting you too." Mona found herself smiling again. "Anything I need to know about this party?"

"Wear something sexy because we're going to hit the town," Lizzy explained. "If you need to borrow something, let me know. I have a bunch of cute dresses that I bet would fit you perfectly."

Mona doubted that, considering she hardly fit into her own clothes lately. A twenty-two year old probably wouldn't have a single item that would flatter her baby bump. "I've got it locked down, sweetheart. I can't wait to see you tomorrow. Um…where is it?"

"Everyone's meeting at the house and then the boys will go their way and we'll go ours. Oh, you're going to love my bridesmaids too." Lizzy squealed again. "It's going to be so much fun!"

Mona had to pull the phone away from her ear for a moment or risk going deaf. "I'll see you, Lizzy. Make sure you get to bed early, it'll be a late one tomorrow." It was such a mom thing to say but she couldn't help herself. After she hung up the phone, Mona found herself face to face with Reno. "Your sister," she chuckled. "She wanted to make sure I knew I was invited to the bachelorette."

Reno wiped his hands on a towel. "I'm never going to live that one down, huh?" He smiled. "I'm glad you're going."

Oh, Mona had no doubt it was going to be fun. Lizzy was a dynamo and she was sure they'd be fast friends. Putzing around the room a bit more, she perched on the edge of the bed. "You feel like tucking in with a movie?"

"Um, I told Gwen I would have that drink with her tonight." Reno cleared his throat. "I mean, I can cancel—"

"Don't." Mona stood abruptly. "Go for a drink. Have fun. This is your chance…don't waste it." She forced a smile. "But first? You need to change."

Reno glanced down at himself. "Why?" A pair of jeans and a polo seemed fine for a drink.

"You want to impress her, right?" Mona walked over to the closet and opened it up. She pulled out a pair of khakis and a crisp blue button-down. "Take a shower and put this on."

"Yes, mother," Reno teased. "Should I shave too?"

"No way," Mona admonished. "The stubble thing you've got going on is sexy." She blushed after she said it. "Keep it. Trust me."

Reno did trust Mona implicitly. He nodded, heading into the bathroom to freshen up for his pseudo date. He decided not to comment on Mona's assertion that his five o'clock shadow turned her on. It was already awkward enough that they were staying in the same room, sleeping in the same bed, and pretending to be dating. Kissing her this afternoon only made it worse. Reno needed to keep things carefree and uncomplicated or die trying.

After a quick shower and a spritz of cologne, Reno changed into the outfit Mona picked out and paused to admire himself. She was so right. The clothes fit him perfectly and Gwen would appreciate the effort. Stepping out of the bathroom, he did a quick spin. "So?"

Mona glanced up from her reading. "You look fantastic." Her heart was aching. "Have a good time."

Reno grabbed his wallet and the room key from the dresser. "If you need anything, we're just going to the bar downstairs." He hesitated again. "Are you sure you're alright?"

"Go!" Mona commanded.

Raising his hands in mock surrender, Reno headed downstairs. Gwen got off work at seven and he wanted to be waiting for her when she arrived. He found a quiet table near the bar. Even though he had been looking forward to this since yesterday, Reno's thoughts kept straying to Mona. Was she okay? Was she bored? Had she gotten enough to eat today? Gelato, two bottles of water, and the salad didn't seem like a lot…

Reno was so wrapped up in thinking about Mona, he didn't even notice when Gwen walked in. *Crap*, Reno thought to himself. He was in way over his head.

Chapter Eight

Gwen was breathtaking. She'd changed out of the crisp, navy blue suit that served as her hotel uniform into a lemony yellow dress with a sweetheart neckline that showed just a hint of cleavage. Her golden blonde hair fell in curly waves over her shoulders but was braided on top to keep it out of her electric blue eyes. She walked with poise and grace, her ruby red lips curved up in a shy little grin. It was that very smile which drove Reno mad in high school. Every head in the room turned to gaze upon the angelic visage who'd just graced them with her presence…but Reno was still staring at the drink menu, worrying that Mona was upstairs crying her heart out.

"Vince?"

His head snapped up and he pushed away from the table so quickly he almost knocked the chair back. "Crap!" He righted himself, heart pounding in his chest. "Sorry." Damn it…he intended to present himself as a suave, sexy businessman, not a bumbling idiot. Faking a smile, Reno walked around the table and pulled out a chair for her.

Gwen smiled sweetly. She crossed her legs at the ankle, setting her clutch at the edge of the table. A long, awkward silence hung between them and she glanced at the bartender to signal they were ready to get a drink. "I'll have a glass of white wine, please."

"Whatever's on tap is fine for me." Reno was glad for the momentary distraction. He was all kinds of messed up right now between thinking about Mona and being dumbfounded by Gwen's ethereal beauty. "So…" He gazed at her, lost in her eyes.

"There's no reason to be nervous," Gwen offered. "I know it's been a while since we've seen each other and we may not have ended things on the best of terms…but we're older now. I want to start fresh and get to know you now." The bartender brought over their drinks and she held out her glass. "Here's to new beginnings."

Reno clinked his mug against hers before taking a sip. "It's really amazing you own this hotel. It's lovely and your staff is great. I can't say enough good things about it."

Gwen blushed. "Well, it's a labor of love. I always wanted to be a lawyer and use the law to exact change in the world. It was my goal and my passion…until I got into school and realized the kind of people lawyers are." She shook her head. "I remember sitting in my Intro to Law class on the very first day and realizing what a mistake I'd made. Sophomore year I changed my major to business with a minor in hospitality and I took a job at a hotel part time. I started in housekeeping and worked my way up to a front desk position. That's where I met Jason."

"Jason?" Reno shifted uncomfortably.

"My ex-husband," Gwen clarified. "He was this cultured, rich, handsome hedge fund manager who used to stay at the hotel whenever he was in town on business. On our second date he took me on a private jet to his villa in France." She took another sip of her wine. "I was swept away. It should have been a wake up call that he was thirty-five and had already been divorced three times. I thought I'd be different..." She shrugged. "Thankfully, I knew a bunch of lawyers when he served me with divorce papers. I proved he was cheating on me during our marriage and took him to the cleaners. That's how I got the money to buy this hotel, actually." A sly smile ghosted over her lips. "You should've seen this place when I first came in. It was a disaster. Making the Hartland into the beauty it is today has kept me so busy, I haven't had time for much else. It's also hard to trust again after you've been betrayed by someone who promised to love you forever..." Gwen shifted, tightening her posture. "Enough about me! What about you? What've you been up to?" She leaned in, resting her elbows on the edge of the table. "I heard you go by 'Reno' now? There's got to be a story there."

Reno wished he'd gone for something stronger than beer. A vodka tonic would've sufficed, though he preferred straight tequila. "I'm sorry to hear about everything with your ex. You deserve better, Gwennie." He licked his lips, trying to come up with a way to explain everything going on in his life without making her want to run in the opposite direction. "I guess it's easier to start at the beginning. I took the long way around graduating from college. When I did get out, there wasn't much I could do with a major in criminal justice and a minor in history." Reno chuckled to himself. "I started working at Telecom as a marketing rep. It was a dead-end job but it paid the bills. I had been there several years when they moved operations out to Carson City." He tapped his fingers on the table. "My boss out there was this senile old coot who couldn't remember anyone's name. I was covering the Reno area so that's what he called me. It just stuck, I guess."

Gwen signaled the bartender for another round of drinks and they arrived promptly. "I think it's cute." She grinned. "So how'd you go from telemarketing to owning a nightclub?"

Reno gratefully accepted a fresh beer, taking a long swallow to wet his throat. "After a while, I was fed up with my desk job. When my boss retired, I took his position as manager but I still wasn't fulfilled. One day, I was reading the paper in my office and I noticed this ad for a club in foreclosure." He smirked. "I'm not really sure what possessed me to go out there but I walked in the door, Mona was dancing, and I knew right then the club had to be mine. I made an offer to the bank and a few weeks later, it was mine. Business has been good and I honestly couldn't be happier."

"So how long have you and Mona been together?" Gwen shifted the conversation effortlessly.

"We're just friends, Gwen," Reno explained fervently. "I know how it looks. The two of us here, sharing a room but I swear, there's nothing between us." It wasn't exactly a lie but, for some reason, he felt guilty anyway. Scrubbing a hand over his stubbled jaw, he sighed heavily. "We're not involved like that."

Gwen didn't look convinced. She leaned back in her chair, lips curved into a frown. "We're old enough to be honest with each other, Vince. It's okay to admit you have a physical relationship with her even if there's not an emotional attachment. Believe me, I'm not the naïve eighteen year old you knew once upon a time. I've had my fair share of lovers."

"We're *not* lovers," Reno pressed. "Mona just broke up with her boyfriend. They'd been together for as long as I've known her. I really didn't want to go to Lizzy's wedding stag and she wanted to get away for a while. It just worked out. Mona and I are friends, Gwen, that's it."

It was clear from her expression she didn't believe him at all.

* * *

Five floors up, Mona was going stir crazy. She needed to get out of this room. Exploring the hotel would take up some time and slake her thirst for knowledge. She wanted to see the on-site restaurant too, since she hadn't been there yet. Mona did her best to delude herself that her curiosity had nothing to do with Reno. It was mere coincidence that she found herself seated at a booth in direct sight of where he was enjoying a drink with Gwen…

Mona knelt on the far side of the where she was mostly obscured by a plant. Reno was focused fully on Gwen anyway; he wouldn't notice her across the room *not* spying on them.

The bartender padded over, his smile too wide and his

voice too loud. "Good evening, miss, are you dining alone?"

"Shh!" Mona admonished. "Yeah, I'm by myself." She glanced up at him. "I'll take a glass of lemonade to start." She'd really enjoyed it last night. "Hey, have you overheard anything interesting between those two?" Reaching into her pocket, she took out a twenty and slid it across the table toward him.

Looking both ways, the man picked up the money and shoved it into his apron pocket. "That's my boss, I could get in big trouble…" He leaned in closer, pretending to show her something on the menu. "When she heard that bald guy was staying at the hotel, she *flipped* out. She went on a juice fast, got her hair all done up, and picked up a bunch of new clothes. Rumor is they used to be together in high school and she wants him back." He chewed his bottom lip. "When she found out he was staying here with another woman, it wasn't pretty."

Mona nodded, signaling for him to keep going. "What else?"

"Well, I heard him saying he's here with that woman platonically. She's not buying it." The bartender snickered. "I'm not sure I would either. Mike at the check-in desk said the girl he brought with him is a knockout."

Hiding her smile, Mona peeked at Reno and Gwen once more. "That's great. Thanks." She handed over the menu. "I'll take a lemonade and anything interesting that comes up over there." Mona was well aware what she was doing was wrong. Reno deserved his privacy and she shouldn't be eavesdropping. Instead of listening to that instinct, she pretended she was simply in the mood for some overpriced hotel lemonade and continued to casually stalk the couple through the leaves of a synthetic plant.

* * *

Reno had been over and over his and Mona's relationship at least a dozen times. Gwen's refusal to believe him was really staring to irritate him. She was making that same face she'd worn the night she dumped him; that was the final straw. "What do you want me to say? If I was involved with Mona, I'd tell you. She's great. I care about her and want the best for her…but you were the one who got away. I want to give this a shot."

Gwen's eyes widened in shock. "Do you really mean that?"

"Of course I do. I was going to propose to you after graduation. I had a ring and everything." Reno averted his eyes. "It was pointed out to me recently that I haven't had a serious relationship since we broke up and I think it's because, deep down, I've always loved you and I never felt like I could do better."

Mona was going to throw up. It was getting late and most of the dinner crowd was gone; she could hear Reno and Gwen easily now. There he was, declaring his undying love to this woman and she looked thoroughly unimpressed. Reno was pouring his heart out to her and her lips were pursed, her brow creased, and she was staring at her manicure. Mona wanted to break her in half.

"This is a lot to take in," Gwen said finally. "I care about you. I always have. I just…don't want to get hurt again."

"I'm not trying to hurt you." Reno's frustration spilled into his tone. "I'm not asking you to do anything. You always said I never shared my feelings. That's the reason we broke up. I'm trying, Gwen…" He shook his head. "You don't have to make any decisions. I just wanted you to know." He stood up, opening his wallet to pay for drinks.

Gwen reached out, her hand sliding over his wrist. "I own the hotel. You don't need to do that. It's on me…"

Reno didn't stop. He threw several bills on the table. Gwen's hand tightened around his wrist but he didn't want to see the pity in her eyes or hear it in her voice. He paused for a moment to gather his strength. When he turned, she attacked his mouth. Gwen leaned her full weight against him without warning and if he hadn't been quick about wrapping his arms around her, she would've hit the floor.

Mona had to get out of here…she couldn't watch. She pushed the door that led to the outside and snuck through the front door. Glancing around to make sure she wouldn't be caught, she hightailed it to the elevator. Through the windows of the restaurant, she could see Reno and Gwen entangled in each other's arms until the doors finally closed. It was sickening.

"Wow." Gwen breathed, fanning herself as she pulled away from Reno. "I've never been kissed like that."

"Well, I'm happy to oblige." Reno forced a smile. His face was smeared with her lipstick and his lips tasted like chardonnay. He expected excitement and passion but honestly, he was left feeling uneasy. "They're probably eager to close up for the night. I'll see you tomorrow?"

Gwen picked up her clutch and applied a fresh coat of lipstick. "I wouldn't miss it for the world." Straightening his collar, she pressed her body against his. "The rest of the weekend is pretty busy but maybe we could get together Tuesday? I've got the day off. We could get out and do something just the two of us."

"I'll let you know what the day looks like," Reno replied coolly. Gwen batted her baby blues at him before sauntering out. He watched her go with a blank expression on his face. The girl he'd grown up fantasizing about was gorgeous and successful, well educated, and classy. She had been the object of his affection since he was in grade school. He wanted her. At least, he thought he did...

As hard as he tried, Reno couldn't stop thinking about Mona the entire evening. When he kissed Gwen, it was monotonous. When Mona's lips touched his, he caught fire...if she hadn't had enough sense to stop him tonight, he'd have pushed her onto the bed and made love to her until they were both weak from exhaustion. Reno was broken out of his thoughts by the bartender who stood there, holding a broom.

"Sir? We're closing down the kitchen for the night but the lounge is open until two if you want another drink. Is there anything else we can get for you?"

"No, thanks…" Reno wanted another drink. Hell, he wanted to drink until this day was a blur. If Mona wasn't upstairs, he might've thought about it but he made stupid decisions while intoxicated. She was right…it was time to grow up.

Mona made it back to the room as quickly as possible. She was still breathless when she heard Reno swipe his keycard and fumble with the door. Grabbing one of the travel magazines from a drawer, she opened it up to the middle and pretended to read. When he stepped in the door, she casually set it down. Reno was smeared with lipstick and looked slightly dazed. She cleared her throat in an attempt to keep emotion and her judgment at bay. "How'd it go?"

Reno shrugged. He opened up the buttons on his shirt, peeling it away and leaving his muscled chest bare as he paced the room. "Gwen's different than I remember. She's gorgeous and I can't deny I'm attracted to her. I just can't figure her out." He peered over at her. "I think she wants to get back together." Although she never actually said it…

"That's great." Mona faked enthusiasm. She stood up, pretending to yawn; her exhaustion was very real, even if the yawn wasn't. "It's everything you wanted." She tugged off her hoodie and laid it over the chair. Next, she peeled off her socks and tossed them into a bag to be washed once they got back home. After splashing some water to cool her face and twisting her hair into a bun, she was more than ready to hit the hay. Reno wasn't being forthcoming about his date and she didn't want to let on that she'd seen everything.

"Everything you wanted...?" Reno thought. Was it, though? Just like that, he was in high school again being strung along with no idea where the relationship was going. Reno sighed. He watched Mona crawl into bed and snuggle beneath the oversized comforter. She looked so soft and warm; he couldn't wait to get in beside her. He changed into his pajamas and hopped in without looking back. Propping himself up on one elbow, he stared at the silhouette of her back. "Gwen wants to go out again on Tuesday."

Pulling her arms tighter around herself, Mona peered over her shoulder at him. "Sounds like fun."

"I'm not so sure." Reno inched closer to her. "I promised you I'd show you around and I'm a man of my word."

Mona shrugged exaggeratedly. "We never agreed you'd spend every waking moment with me. If you want to go out with her, go out and have fun. I can entertain myself, Reno. Far be it for me to stand in the way of true love." She burrowed deeper into the fluffy hotel pillow. "Good night."

"Right..." Reno frowned. "Good night." Mona clicked off the light, bathing the room in darkness. He rolled onto his back, staring up at the ceiling. Reno wasn't sure true love even existed anymore. He was sure he had a moment with Mona earlier tonight. He could've allowed it to build into something deep and meaningful…but he ruined it by bringing Gwen into the mix. Now he had a shot with Gwen and all he could think about was Mona.

Covering his face with both hands, Reno groaned. He was so screwed—in every sense but the biblical one. He cast one last glance at Mona before he turned and rolled the other way. Gwen or Mona, Mona or Gwen…he had no idea what he wanted, or if he deserved either one of them. For now, Reno had a lot to think about and the best remedy was to sleep on it.

Things would be clearer in the morning. They had to be.

Chapter Nine

Mona awoke to the smell of something burning. She tumbled out of bed half-awake. Her hair was sticking up in every direction and one hand cradled the sacred space where her unborn child grew. The only thing she knew was that she had to protect the baby under any circumstances. "Reno!" she cried, choking against the smell as she staggered forward. "Reno, there's a fire!"

Reno caught her in his arms to halt her movement. She was flailing all over the place and he was afraid she was really going to hurt herself. "Mona, it's okay!" he sighed. "I was making breakfast and I burned the eggs…and the toast." Reno looked appropriately sheepish. "Did you know the windows in here don't open?"

"The one in the bathroom does…" Mona slipped out of Reno's grasp. She jogged into the bathroom and threw open the window as wide as it would go. As she dragged a lungful of fresh air in, she paused to stare at her reflection and groaned. Man, she looked terrible. There were deep purple stains beneath her eyes and her lips were dry and cracked. She closed the door, changing into a fresh pair of clothes and fixing up her hair before she stepped out. "Why don't we go out for breakfast?"

"I think that's a really good idea."

It just figured when Reno tried to do something nice for Mona, it backfired terribly. He was the main cook at the Watering Hole. Sure, all of their cuisine was made in a machine that automatically alerted him to take it out of the fryer. Still, he'd cooked eggs before. It wasn't that hard...or maybe it was. Reno was used to his own stove, which was old and didn't heat evenly. In retrospect, turning the heat to high was his first mistake. Then, using the other pan to make toast—and subsequently not watching that pan at all because he was trying to keep his eggs from exploding all over the place—was even worse. Thankfully, Mona didn't say anything. Reno just hoped the smell was gone soon.

The pair headed downstairs and the hostess showed them to their seats. By the time coffee and tea had arrived at the table, Mona had overcome the initial shock and began to laugh. She covered her mouth with her napkin, her entire body was shaking and moisture gathered in the corners of her vibrant green eyes. "The look on your face!"

"Me?" Reno was laughing just as hard as she was. "You were staggering around with your eyes half open. I'm surprised you didn't fall over!" Tears gathered in his eyes, his ribs hurting from laughing so hard. "I appreciate you trying to save me from the fire, though."

Resting a hand on her belly, Mona felt as if all the stress had left her body. She let out a heavy breath and took a sip of hot tea. "Why don't you leave the cooking to me from now on, okay?" Reno nodded in agreement and she couldn't help but grin.

Breakfast was lovely. Mona had crepes with strawberries and cream that were to die for. Reno opted for eggs, hash browns, and bacon. He didn't even mind when she stole a piece because there was far too much food for one person to eat in front of him. Conversation flowed easily. They made the mutual decision to have a leisurely day in. The clouds outside were dark and ominous; it was definitely going to rain. Besides, they needed to conserve their strength for partying tonight. When they got back to the room, housekeeping had come and the smoky smell was gone. Everything was working out perfectly.

Mona hopped back into bed with her e-reader and Reno climbed in beside her with his computer. Every once in a while she'd glance over and catch him staring at her. After the sixth time, she set her book aside. "What?"

"What?" Reno echoed. He closed his computer and rolled onto his side to face her.

"You're staring." It made Mona very nervous. Her baby bump was still small but she was very aware of it. Had he realized she was pregnant? No, she told herself. He was far too calm to have worked out that bombshell on his own. "Do I have something on my face?"

"No," Reno chuckled. "I've just..." He was quiet for a moment, gathering his thoughts. "I like this. You and me, just hanging out. There's no pressure or awkwardness. I get that you have to be tough at work. Yes, even with me—"

Mona raised an eyebrow at him cheekily. "*Especially* with you."

Reno had come to cherish these quiet moments so much. "Yeah yeah." He nudged her playfully. "I mean it, Mona. You're the best. Kyle is a fucking idiot."

Just like that, the illusion was shattered. "I don't want to talk about Kyle," Mona replied stiffly and sat up a little bit straighter.

Reno reached out to calm her, his hand sliding over her wrist. "I didn't mean to piss you off. I just can't believe any guy would ever give you up…" He could tell Mona was getting upset by the crease in her brow and immediately changed the subject. "It's going to be an interesting night for us. You know there are going to be strippers in some capacity tonight. Do you think it'll cathartic to be on the other side?"

Mona thought about that for a moment. "I guess it probably will be. Let's hope they don't suck or I'll have to teach them a thing or two," she teased. "Speaking of, any word on how Cadence is doing?"

"No shop talk," Reno pled. He didn't want to talk about the Watering Hole or Cadence or anything to do with Carson City. He wanted to get to know Mona the way he'd wanted to for five whole years. "My sister is dying to meet you, you know."

"Yeah, she's been tweeting about it all morning." Mona snorted, shaking her head. "I don't know what you told her about me but she's going to be really disappointed when she finds out I don't spin straw into gold or shit rainbows." That earned her an appreciative laugh. She loved when Reno was like this. Usually he was all flirt and no focus. This man right here was the Reno O'Keefe she'd come to know and lo…care for deeply.

Rain began to pelt against the hotel windows, drawing Reno's attention for a moment. "I think that's my fault." He glanced back at her. "You've been such a huge part of my life since I bought the club. I didn't realize I talked about you so much…"

"What exactly did you say?" Mona probed.

"Honestly, I don't even remember but my sister worships the ground you walk on," Reno replied with a shrug. "As a kid, I was always the closest to my brother Luke. He's the family peacekeeper and the levelheaded one. I would've said he was my best friend…until Lizzy was born." A wistful smile played over his features as he thought back to the day his mother brought the tiny, fussy baby home from the hospital. "I was seventeen years old and already an uncle several times over." Reno chuckled. "As you can imagine, I was not very excited that my mother had a kid when she was *so old* either." He shook his head. "Then, I held Lizzy for the first time. I remember thinking she was the most perfect kid in the whole universe. I wasn't going to let anything happen to her. I plan on keeping that promise."

Listening to Reno talk about his little sister made Mona so happy and so sad at the same time. She'd always wanted a sibling, but the way her family was, it was probably better she never had one. "Seeing how a real family is supposed to be is strange. I didn't know there were people out there who grew up like you did for real. I thought it was something they made up in movies and

TV shows…" Mona found herself sighing. "I'm jealous."

"You don't have to be. We have our fair share of dysfunction too. Big families are not all they're cracked up to be." Reno stroked the back of her hand with his thumb. "My oldest brother Mark can't stand Richard. They've been butting heads since the day my mom married him. I think it's because he remembers our biological dad more than Luke, Stephen, Rob, or I…but it can get heated, especially if he's been drinking." Reno paused, glancing down at his hand resting over hers. "I always liked Richard. I called him 'dad' growing up…"

Mona tilted her head to the side. "You don't anymore?"

Reno let out a breath he hadn't known he'd been holding. "'I've barely talked to him in ten years, Mona. I mean, he calls me on my birthday and on Christmas and Thanksgiving. He's always said he loves me and I believe him I just…" He swallowed hard. "I guess a part of me has always wondered. I'm not his biological kid. It has to be different, right? You can't love someone else's kid as much as you love your own…"

Mona's mouth instantly went dry. She'd been wondering the same thing for weeks now and hearing him speak her worst fear aloud was gut wrenching. "I'm not sure…" Her voice came out as a ragged whisper. Mona wasn't sure if she'd ever find someone who'd be willing to be in her life and raise another man's child, but she hoped it could happen. A part of her had wondered if Reno could be that man. It seemed she had her answer. "I guess we'll never know." Mona finally managed to speak, shrugging both shoulders in a way that seemed unnatural and uncomfortable. That's how she was feeling right now. Hurt welled in her chest and she was desperate to get away before Reno could see the hurt in her eyes. "I think we should start getting ready for the party tonight."

It was still early enough in the afternoon that Reno didn't feel they needed to rush, but it was clear Mona was uncomfortable with this conversation. He nodded and smiled. "Why don't you go first? Far be it for me to get in the way of a lady's routine."

"I'm hardly a lady," Mona replied with a sarcastic smirk. "But my hair takes a lot longer to dry." She reached over, running a hand over his bald head before rolling off the bed. Lizzy said to dress sexy, which meant she had to get on the full getup including the push-up bra, makeup, and a brand new pair of Spanx.

Watching Mona rifle through drawers was fascinating, especially when she pulled out some kind of pantyhose that looked a little bit like a medieval torture device. Next, she fished out a pair of lacy underwear that forced him to put his computer over his lap. He knew Mona owned things like that but now he was thinking about her *wearing* them. Reno lost his virginity when he was sixteen and since then, he'd never been without a partner for long. Actually, these last couple weeks were the longest dry spell he'd ever been through. He'd been on this no-women cleanse, but until now it didn't really feel like he was detoxing.

The sputtering whoosh of the shower turning on

reminded Reno that Mona was getting naked with only a single door between them. Suddenly he was fourteen again, rock hard and had no idea what to do. Sure, he could take care of the urge himself…but Mona had all the towels locked up in the bathroom with her. He could also proposition her when she got out of the shower, but that was the opposite of not complicating things in their relationship.

Instead, Reno turned his thoughts to unpleasant experiences in his life and unmentionable images: his pants falling down in Mrs. Jensen's second grade class, the smell of the swamplands in August, and road kill. It took quite a while, but finally the pressure started to go down. At least for the moment…

Mona stepped out of the bathroom in the sexiest dress she owned. It was a simple black number with spaghetti straps but the overlay was a floral, form fitting lace that hugged her in all the right places. Ever since she got pregnant, her breasts had almost doubled in size and she filled out the outfit in a whole new way. Of course, the other side of that was she looked thicker all around but nobody was going to notice unless she turned sideways. The Spanx were to thank for that. "How do I look?" Mona asked, twirling once for dramatic effect.

All the hard work Reno had been doing to take the edge off went right out the window. Mona's hair was piled atop her head in a towel to dry, she had a robe over her shoulders, and not a single stitch of makeup on…and she'd never been more beautiful. "Great," he squeaked. Without delay, he grabbed the first outfit he could find and dashed into the bathroom for a very long, very hot shower. It wasn't Reno's proudest moment but he craved release. It was only natural. He was a much gentler, more relaxed man when he finally stepped out of the shower forty-five minutes later.

Mona was just finishing her hair when Reno stepped out of the bathroom in a cloud of steam. "You look nice," she whistled. He was dressed in all black from his slacks to his button down. In Mona's opinion, there was just one thing missing. She stood, walking over to his suitcase and pulling out one of the bowties. "Trust me." To her great surprise, he didn't even protest. Setting the kelly green accent around his neck, she smoothed his collar. "Perfect! It completes the whole outfit."

"Thanks, pumpkin." Reno glanced at the clock. "We should go soon if we want to make it on time. Traffic at this time of night isn't always the easiest to navigate."

With a quick spritz of perfume and a smear of lip-gloss, Mona was ready to go. She opted for a simple black clutch tonight that contained only the essentials: phone, wallet with dollar bills, and her hotel keycard. Slipping into a pair of shiny black patent leather heels, she followed Reno out the door.

The valet pulled the car around and Reno opened the door for Mona. Once she was settled, he hurried into the driver's seat. This time, he didn't need the GPS to get home. It was second nature finding the side streets that would bring him right to his front door. As he parked along the grass in front of the house, he turned to her. "If you need me for any reason, just call and I'll be there as soon as I can."

It meant a lot to Mona that Reno was looking out for her. "I'm sure I'll be fine." She squeezed his hand gently. "And if *you* need anything, I have my phone on me too." He moved to get out of the car but she held fast. "Reno? Don't be too hard on Ray. He's a good kid," she warned. "Lizzy loves him and she loves you too."

Reno's eyebrows flew up in surprise. It was no secret he wanted to get to know Ray tonight and find out what the boy's intentions were with his sister. The protective instinct wasn't entirely rational about his baby sister's virtue. Mona's gentle reminder snapped him back into the moment. "Fine," he muttered. "But if he starts something, I'm going to finish it."

"I wouldn't have it any other way," Mona smirked. They exited the car and walked up the front steps side by side. Reno opened the door and she could see the women were meeting in the kitchen while the men were in the den. "I guess this is where we part ways…"

"Yeah." Reno found himself wishing that wasn't the case. "Have a good time tonight, pumpkin."

"You too." Mona brushed past him into the house. The moment she stepped inside, she was swept into an excited mess of young women. Lizzy had clearly been drinking before she arrived and hugged Mona tightly. The enthusiastic bride was slurring her words while introducing the bridal party: her college roommate Danielle, her high school best friend Charlotte, and a sour-faced girl who was identified as Ray's cousin Mia. Elina, Lisa and Meghan were also present for the festivities.

"Before you young ladies go out for a bit of fun, I'd like to make a toast," Martha called over the noise. Champagne was handed out. "To a wonderful hen party."

"And to enjoying your last night of freedom!" Meghan crowed.

Giggles and cheers erupted as everyone—except Mona—downed their glasses. She casually poured hers into the sink before being ushered out to where a big white limousine was waiting for them. She cast one last glance at Reno in the living room before the door swung closed behind her. Tonight was going to be a night she wouldn't forget.

Reno watched Mona go and he felt disappointment fill him. The stag party was much calmer. For one thing, Raymond was surrounded by Lizzy's brothers. Mark, Luke, Stephen, Rob, and Reno chatted quietly with one another. The groomsmen Lionel, George, and Frederick were stuffy country club types. It was an odd mix of men in the room. Luke, ever the ambassador, opened up and shotgunned a beer; it earned him an appreciative chuckle and the attention of the group. "Tonight we celebrate Ray's wild bachelor night. Let's have some fun, boys!"

A second black limo was waiting in the driveway and the men filed outside. Reno pinched the bridge of his nose as he found himself sandwiched between Ray and Stephen. It was going to be a long night…the sooner he started drinking, the better.

Chapter Ten

It didn't occur to Mona that Gwen wasn't present until suddenly she was.

"Sorry I'm late!" She hurried into the room, pausing to kiss Lizzy on the cheek. The wine bar was only a short walk from the hotel, which made it easy for Gwen to join them after she finished up at work. She'd changed into a skintight dress sewn in shimmery white fabric. It was clearly designer, unlike the department store polyester/cotton blend dress Mona was wearing. The difference between them was striking.

Vibrant chatter filled the air. Mona had been in the midst of a nice conversation with Meghan about her work as an ICU nurse. She was honestly impressed the woman managed to hold down a career while raising two kids and a husband. Mona wasn't sure she'd have the energy for all that. Once Gwen walked in, the whole dynamic of the room changed.

Meghan, Lisa, and Elina were whispering something Mona could only assume was about the strippers tonight. Lizzy and her bridesmaids finished their expensive wines and switched to mixed drinks, complete with penis-shaped straws. There was no one for Mona to talk to except Reno's ex…

It wasn't fair how pretty Gwen was up close. Her skin was flawless, not a single blemish or pore, and she clearly spent a lot of time at the gym. Was it too much to ask that she would be a huge bitch? Mona supposed it was, because Gwen seemed to get along with *everyone*. She struck up a conversation with Mona and it was as if they'd known each other for years.

"Mona, darling, you are I are so alike!" Gwen speared a forkful of salad, washing it down with a dainty sip of white wine. "I can't tell you how nice it is to find another woman who can't stand romantic comedies!" She shook her head. "You know who does love them?"

Mona didn't even need to think about it. "Reno's obsessed."

"I mean, what man's favorite movie is *Pretty Woman*?" The more she drank, the shriller Gwen's voice became and she signaled the waiter for another glass. Swaying slightly, Gwen leaned in and rested her hand on Mona's shoulder. "I think it's so sweet what you're doing for him, you know. I can just imagine how hard it would be for him to come back for his sister's wedding alone." When she smiled, all of her perfectly white teeth shone in the dim light of the restaurant. "You're a saint, Mona."

Pasting on a phony smile, Mona casually shrugged Gwen's hand away. She definitely wasn't a saint, especially since she was on the brink of biting Gwen's Barbie Doll head off. "Excuse me, I need to freshen up." Standing abruptly, Mona stalked to the bathroom and settled down on the toilet seat to unwind. When she finally gathered the strength to step out of the stall, Mona found Lizzy waiting for her. She washed up her hands, glancing sidelong at the girl as she rocked back and forth on her heels. "Are you having fun?"

"Yes," Lizzy chirped. Suddenly her face fell. "I don't

know…" Exhaling sharply, she turned slightly toward the mirror, running her fingers through her wavy blonde hair. "Mona? Can I ask you something?"

There was a small love seat on the far side of the bathroom and Mona sauntered over there, patting the seat beside her. Lizzy dashed over, plopping down next to Mona without hesitation. "What's on your mind?"

"It's Mia. I can't stand her!" Lizzy huffed. "She's surly and rude. I try and include her in things and make her feel welcome but she just walks around with that terrible screwed up pig face! It's driving me crazy!" She whimpered. "I only wanted two bridesmaids, you know. I told Ray, just two each and we'd have a nice small wedding party but *no*." She folded her arms over her chest and pouted. "He had to have his three best buddies, which meant I had to choose between a huge pool of good but not 'best' friends or choose someone from Ray's side of the family. Mia was the logical choice but she's horrible, Mona. I don't want her in my wedding!"

Tears shimmered in Lizzy's eyes and then began to fall. Mona wrapped an arm around her shoulders, brushing away a strand of honey blonde hair. "Hey, it's not so bad. So you have one bridesmaid you don't care for. You don't have to deal with her for much longer."

Wiping the moisture on her cheeks, Lizzy snuffled. "That's the thing, I've been drinking since breakfast and…I kind of just kicked her out of the wedding party. And the worst part is that's the first time I've ever seen Mia smile." She began to wail. "What am I going to do?

I am getting married in a week and I'm missing a bridesmaid! I need someone who'll fit in her dress and shoes and who won't drive me crazy! Where am I going to find someone like that, huh?"

"Shh," Mona soothed, rubbing Lizzy's back in gentle circles. "Mia's pretty average sized. It won't be hard to find someone to fit her dress. And the shoes aren't such a big deal either. You can always substitute something in a similar color. Everyone is going to be looking at you, Lizzy, not at your bridesmaids' shoes."

Almost as quickly as the tears came, they dried up and Lizzy was perky once more. "Mona, you're a 12, aren't you?"

Mona nodded, although she was inching closer to a bigger size thanks to the baby stretching her waist.

"You *have* to be my bridesmaid!" She gasped. "It'll be perfect! I bet the dress is going to look amazing on you. You have the right figure to fill it out. I knew you were the person to talk to about this!" Bouncing up from the love seat, she pulled Mona up with her. "Come on! We need to tell everyone!"

Mona's mouth opened and closed in shock. She couldn't form the words to stop Lizzy from announcing to the room that she was going to be the newest member of the bridal party. Danielle and Charlotte were clapping and cheering. Everyone seemed excited by the news, even Mia. Mona felt unsure. She'd come to Boston to be Reno's plus one. She was supposed to be quiet and stay in the background…and yet somehow she found herself a bridesmaid in the wedding and the center of attention. It was all very disorienting.

"Alright ladies, I hope you've eaten your fill because we're on to our final destination!" Danielle announced. Within minutes, all the ladies were packed back in the limo and headed deeper into the heart of Boston.

Mona found herself in the middle of a bunch of tipsy women. She hadn't had a single drink herself but she felt hazy nonetheless. Her vision blurred in and out and the heat and the crush of bodies overwhelmed her. It was a relief when they pulled off onto a side street and into an oil-slicked parking lot. Mona instantly knew where they were.

"What's a bachelorette party without...STRIPPERS!" Charlotte cried.

There was a neon sign guttering atop the building, burnt out and broken in several places. Mona couldn't tell what the name of it was. When they stepped inside, the club was poorly lit, which was probably a good thing considering how dirty the floors were here. Mona couldn't help but frown as they stepped into the venue and she was immediately assaulted by the smell of sweat and corn chips. She forced herself to move with the group toward a private back room, pausing as they were led to a long table directly in front of a rickety stage.

Mona picked up a menu, her stomach lurching at how sticky it was. She grabbed a napkin, trying to get some of the residue off. It was all she could do not to roll her eyes when the first notes of AC/DC's Big Balls started blasting over an ancient sound system. Mona really wished Reno was here; she needed him to save her from this nightmare.

A plume of dry ice filled the stage and Mona's stomach ached. Squinting at the stage, she watched three men step out from the back. They weren't abysmal dancers, as far as she concerned. She'd seen better, but she'd also seen a lot worse. Charlotte, Lizzy, and Danielle were hollering and throwing dollar bills. Elina couldn't stop giggling and Lisa was right there with her. Hell, even Gwen looked like she was having a good time. Mona couldn't fake it. She folded her arms across her chest and stared down at her phone.

The music changed over and the three stooges disappeared again. Bon Jovi's Wanted Dead or Alive opened and a tall, dark, handsome man stepped out in a G-string and cowboy hat. Before Mona realized what was happening, he had jumped off stage and was grinding right in her face. Turning her head away, Mona dug a dollar out of her purse and slipped into the garment he was wearing. "Alright," she warned, "The bride's over there." Peeling several more dollars off the roll, she inclined her head toward Lizzy. "Go on. It'll make her night."

"Mona?"

Focusing harder, she stared up at the man's face and froze. "*Mitch*?" She'd have recognized him anywhere; he had tightly curled black hair, cocoa colored skin, and the bluest eyes she'd ever seen. Before she could even fully comprehend his presence here, he was seated in her lap with his arms wrapped around her. Mona laughed, hugging him tighter. "What the hell are you doing in a dump like this?"

The music cut off a moment later and Mitch smiled so all his teeth were showing. "After I left NOLA, I hitched my way to Alabama. Do you know how hard it is to be a gorgeous gay black man in the deep South?" He shook his head. "I was nearly lynched three times before I decided to get out. Do you remember Warren? Well, she's Willow now. We've got a crappy little apartment down the road." He slapped his hands enthusiastically. "She is going to *die* when I tell her you're here!"

"I'm in town for a few days. Let's make plans for this week." Mona was acutely aware everyone was staring at her as she caught up with her dear old friend Mitch.

"I am going to call that bitch up immediately, sweetheart. It's a date!" Mitch gasped. "And by the way, you look sexy with a capital S. Did you have the girls done?" Mitch swung his leg over her, not waiting for an answer. "You just hold on a hot second. I'm going to get Lance. If your little bride wants to get hot tonight, she will not be disappointed."

"You're the best," Mona called after him. Gwen's voice stabbed through her subconscious and she immediately tensed.

"How do you two know each other?"

It was a loaded question. Mona opened her mouth to

explain they'd both lived in Louisiana when Lizzy's overdramatic reaction to seeing Lance for the first time interrupted. If she thought Mitch was tall, Lance made him look like a munchkin in comparison. He gyrated with expert skill. It made Mona laugh at how excited Lizzy got, she was throwing dollars around enthusiastically. It was a sight to see. With so much activity and noise, Mona was saved from having to answer Gwen's question…at least for the moment.

Twice she looked up and caught Gwen staring, but didn't say anything. Tonight was about Lizzy, not about her. The more Mona got to know Gwen, the less she liked her. At first the woman seemed sweet and sunny, but Mona was getting the impression there was something darker lurking under the surface. She needed to watch her back.

As Lizzy downed another shot and sloppily laid across her friends' laps, Mona exhaled. She really hoped Reno was having a better night. One of them deserved to have fun, at least.

* * *

The world's most awkward bachelor party started off with steaks at a place Luke read about in the Post. Reno's meal was well seasoned and the old fashioned he ordered was perfectly executed. What should've been a tasty meal was colored by awkward silence and palpable tension.

Reno glanced around the table. Luke kept checking his phone compulsively; he didn't leave Lana often and even though Martha and Richard were watching her, he was still a mess. Mark was three sheets to the wind but that surprised no one. Stephen was intensely focused on making a pyramid out of toothpicks. Clearing his throat loudly, Reno leaned in. After his fifth drink, he was finally feeling loose enough to break the silence. "Raymond." The boy had the good sense to stop speaking and sit up straighter. "You're marrying my sister next week..." There was an intentional curve to his lip that hinted the younger man might not make it that long. "Why don't you tell me a little bit about yourself?"

"I-I..." Raymond stuttered, gripping his snifter of bourbon closer. "There's not much to tell, I guess?" He cleared his throat. "I, um, I got a job working as a teaching assistant at Brighton Academy. I'm also working on my masters in education..." Of all Lizzy's brothers, Reno scared Ray the most. Not only was he physically imposing, but he was also closest to Lizzy. Ray desperately wanted to make a good impression.

"How much does a teaching assistant make? Enough to support a wife and family?" Reno narrowed his eyes.

"Christ, Vince," Mark guffawed loudly. He was suddenly wide awake now and leaning over the table. "I know Lizzy's your little princess but by her age, mom already had two kids."

That thought made Reno even angrier. Lizzy was in the prime of her life. She just graduated college last May and was a paralegal in a busy law firm. She had her whole life ahead of her and he didn't want her throwing it all away for this little punk. Reno glared at Mark.

"That's my point, jackass. You never know when you're going to end up a daddy. What're you going to do then, Raymond?"

Ray's eyes were wide as saucers. "I—"

Mark stood all the way up. "His father's loaded. Lizzy doesn't have to work a damn day in her life and neither does he." He lumbered around the table. "Don't blow this for her."

Silence hung over the table after Mark lumbered to the bathroom. Reno furrowed his eyebrows. "You've got money and you still work?" Ray couldn't seem to stop nodding. Reno sighed. "Well, I'm glad you aren't some lazy slob."

"Vincent, let's get another drink." Luke tugged his brother up, pushing him toward the bar.

The bartender was a gorgeous brunette with dark hair and a great rack. On any other day, Reno would've been all over that. Right now, he could only think about all the ways she didn't compare to Mona. As if on cue, the bubbly blonde waitress who'd taken their order popped behind the bar next; her too wide smile and overpainted lips made him think of Gwen. Both women were pretty, he'd happily sleep with either one, and now he was even more confused than he was before. "Shit…" He grunted. "Tequila. Straight up, three fingers." Reno turned to face Luke who looked bewildered for a moment. "And one for my brother," he ordered. Exhaling sharply, he leaned on the edge of the bar. "What's wrong with him, Luke?"

"Ray?" Luke sniffed his tequila cautiously. "Nothing as far as I can tell. He's a smart, well-read, respectable kid who's crazy about Lizzy. I like him, Vince. He'll be a good husband." He patted Reno on the shoulder, leading him further away from the table. "Speaking of husbands…you want to tell me a little bit more about Mona? I got the impression you two were together and then I overheard Elina talking about how you went out with Gwen last night."

"News travels fast in this family," Reno replied gruffly. He wasn't really angry, especially not at Luke. Another mouthful of tequila helped exponentially. "Mona and I work together. She's been helping me run the club since I bought the place. I thought things were just platonic between us but honestly, after the last couple weeks, I'm starting to realize it might be something more…"

Luke's face cracked into a wide grin. "That's great news! You deserve to be happy, Vince."

Reno shook his head in annoyance. "But then Gwen shows up in my hotel room and asks me out for drinks. She's been giving me all sorts of signals since then. She led on that she might want to get back together…or give it a shot, at least." He dragged a hand over his stubbled chin. "I'm so confused."

The smile faded a bit as Luke peered down at the opalescent tequila in his glass. He tipped his head back, taking a sip and coughing at the burn in the back of his throat. "So who do you want to be with?"

"That's the problem. I have no freaking clue." Reno was sick of watching Luke lapping up his tequila and grabbed it, downing the rest in one go. Motioning to the bartender to make them another, he stared into the two empty glasses in his hand. "Mona drives me insane. We can hardly go through twenty-four hours without getting into a fight but I still keep going back for more. Gwen and I have history. She's the girl I used to picture growing old with…"

A long silence hung between the brothers. Luke didn't speak until Reno looked up at him. "Everything that's happened in your life has made you who you are, Vincent. If Gwen never broke up with you, maybe you would've studied harder and become a wealthy man and given her all the things she wants out of life." Luke folded his arms over his chest. "Or maybe you would've been miserable, broken, and died in a gutter."

Reno furrowed his eyebrows. "Tell me this is going somewhere."

Luke gave Reno a one-fingered salute before clasping him on the shoulder. "What I'm saying is there's no way to know what could've happened. Mona is great. So is Gwen. They're both pretty, smart women who are somehow attracted to you…" He ribbed Reno gently. "There's no use living in the past. It's time to start thinking about what you want your future to look like."

"That's…*really* good advice."

"You don't have to act so surprised," Luke groused.

This time, he was the one who took the drink out of Reno's hand and finished it in one gulp. "I love you. I want you to be happy." Inclining his head toward the table, he smirked. "And cut Ray a little bit of slack. He's in love with Lizzy. He's marrying her. Even if he's a bit of a spineless weasel, we need to give him the benefit of the doubt. Better to start things off on a good foot. He'll be family soon."

Grumbling in annoyance, Reno reluctantly agreed. He didn't want to be nice to the kid or give him the benefit of the doubt. Unfortunately, better judgment won out— equal parts tequila and Luke's guiding hand. Moving to the head of the table, Reno smirked. "So, are we actually going to have fun tonight or what?" He clapped Ray on the shoulders. "Come on. We're getting you liquored up." He turned to Lionel who seemed the most mischievous in the group. With three more drinks in him, Reno was starting to feel languid. "Tell me the truth, did you hire a stripper?"

Ray sputtered and coughed. "No! No strippers!" He shook his head exaggeratedly. "Lizzy will *kill* me!"

Stephen snorted loudly. "My wife texted me and said they went to the Raging Bull after the wine bar tonight. If you think they're not getting freaky over there, you're dead wrong."

"There's only one thing to do then." Reno grinned darkly. "We're going to crash. Come on!" Maybe it was the liquor on board but he wasn't taking no for an answer.

Champagne was chilling in the back of the limo and Reno poured everyone a glass before taking a long swallow from the neck of the bottle. He would remember none of this tomorrow, and that was just fine with him. They had just pulled into the parking lot when Reno rolled out of the limo with the groom-to-be in tow. Poor Ray had to jog to keep up or risk being choked by the hand clasped around the collar of his shirt.

At first, the bouncer at the Raging Bull stopped Reno but a hundred dollar bill slipped into his pocket greased their way in the door. In a single file line, the boys crept along the side of the club to the staging area where Lance was currently strutting his stuff for Lizzy and the girls. Ray's mouth was opened in horror, his cheeks flushing red at the sight.

Gwen was sitting primly in her chair, occasionally throwing a dollar onto the stage as if she was tossing a penny into a wishing well. Mona, on the other hand, was facing a man who looked like he'd been perfectly sculpted out of clay. He had his hands on her thighs, leaning in close as they talked over the music. White-hot jealousy stabbed through him. The little voice in the back of Reno's head that regulated things like his temper and kept him from making bad decisions had been drinking on the job. He strode over to Mona with his fists clenched tight. "Hey pumpkin," he slurred, possessively placing his hands on her shoulders.

Mona was in the process of making plans with Willow and Mitch for Tuesday. It seemed like a good day since Mitch got off the night shift at seven and Willow didn't work until noon. It took a little bit of coordination but

Mona had herself a brunch date. She was honestly excited to catch up with the two of them somewhere other than this noisy, dirty club. Besides, Reno was going out with Gwen that day and she'd welcome the distraction.

Just when she thought things were settled, Reno busted into the conversation and he looked pissed. Mona narrowed her eyes. "Reno, this an old friend of mine. Mitch, this is Reno." It was obvious to her he wasn't listening. There was something so sinister about the way Reno looked right now. Instinct kicked in and Mona stood up, giving Mitch the signal. "It was good to see you. I can't wait for Tuesday."

"See ya later, sweetheart." Mitch twirled to standing, striding to talk to the manager with his hips swinging. He glanced back, winking cheekily.

Reno smelled like tequila and steak. It didn't surprise Mona in the least that he had been drinking tonight but if he didn't back off, he was going to add in the stench of regret. "That was rude." She glowered. "What are you doing here? Are these the only strippers in Boston?"

"Ha ha," Reno scoffed dryly. "I didn't think it was fair you girls are stuck watching these weird guys stripping. I think you deserve something a little better."

Before Mona knew what was happening, Reno dragged off his bowtie and threw it at her. Her eyes widened in horror as he clambered up onto the stage, wobbling slightly from the booze. He started convulsing like an epileptic at a discotheque. Everyone was staring at him with wide eyes and she was fairly certain she saw Stephen pull out his phone to film this disaster.

"Reno," Mona warned. "Reno, get down from there!" He was a hot mess, struggling with the buttons on his shirt and cussing bitterly while he did it. Three times, Lance tried to get him down but it was no use. This was Reno's family, those who loved him the most…and the people he'd never be able to escape as long as he lived.

Mona knew what she had to do.

It took a little doing to climb up the stage. She grabbed Reno but he was still squirming around trying to disrobe instead of ignoring her demands. Mitch popped his head out from behind the curtain and she signaled him. "You remember my song?"

"Honey, how could I ever forget?"

Heavy guitar thundered over the stereo system as American Woman began to play. Mona knew these moves better than she knew her own name. She walked in time with the beat, dragging a chair over and pushing Reno down into it. Suddenly, he wasn't trying to tear his clothes off…he was silent and watching her, enraptured.

Mona became one with the music. She spun, catching the pole between her legs. Dark hair swept the stage, her jade eyes twinkling in the light as she gyrated. Everything else in the room died away except the beat of her heart keeping time with the music. It had been a while since she'd been up here but she still remembered her rhythm. As the song ramped up, so did Mona. She dipped and twirled and flirted, every movement perfectly calculated. For the big finale, she climbed to the very top of the pole and slowly slid down, ending with her arm outstretched as the final chord hit.

Pregnant or not, Mona tore it up out there. She was slightly out of breath when she finished. Lizzy was bouncing up and down as she clapped. Reno's brothers looked like they'd swallowed their tongues and their wives were just as shocked. Gwen, on the other hand, looked like she'd taken a bite out of a lemon. Mona took a quick bow before she grabbed Reno by the wrist and hauled him off the stage. "Well, this has been fun but I think we're both really tired. We'll call a cab—"

"No need. I want to get my husband home as soon as possible." Meghan fanned herself exaggeratedly. Although she was the only one who said it, it was clear that Lisa and Elina were thinking the same thing. Besides, Lizzy needed to be tucked in before she passed out. Ray hugged her tightly, rubbing her back as he helped Danielle lead her out of the strip club.

Mona pasted on a smile, keeping Reno close to her as they headed out to the limos. He was all over her, but that wasn't much of a surprise. He always got that way when he was drunk. By some miracle, Mona pulled him into the limo and settled herself beside him. Within minutes, his head was on her shoulder and his hands were wrapped around her hips. She elbowed him none too gently. "Hands off," Mona warned. "You're drunk.

You might not remember this in the morning but you *will* remember the black eye I give you."

Gwen was sitting across from them, nestled between Lisa and Luke and Stephen and Meghan. A frown marred her features. "He's just being affectionate."

"Yeah well, if I don't put a stop to it now, he'll be *affectionate* all over my cocktail dress before we even get back to the hotel." Mona turned her attention to Gwen. "Something bothering you?"

"No."

Mona chuckled derisively. "Bullshit."

A look of shock and dismay replaced Gwen's indignation. "Excuse me?"

"You've got a problem. You wanna share with the class or am I going to have to guess?" Mona glared at her. Reno leaned in, nuzzling her neck and she pressed her hand over his face. Gently, her thumb smoothed over his cheek and he stopped making advances, closing his eyes to take a nap instead. Gwen still wasn't talking. "You aren't going to get an answer if you don't ask the question."

"How do you know random gay strippers and how the hell do you know how to dance like that?" Gwen gasped.

Just because someone had schooling didn't mean they were smart. Clearly. "I met Mitch in New Orleans. We were both working at this club called the Gypsy," Mona explained. "I've been stripping since before I was old enough to vote."

Gwen reacted as if Mona told her the world was ending. She covered her mouth with both hands, gasping like something straight out of a telenovela. "Oh my goodness!" She grasped her sweater tighter around herself as if she would catch something being in the same space as Mona. "Does Reno know?"

Mona gritted her teeth. Reno was out cold now and blissfully unaware of the third degree she was getting. Not only was Gwen staring her down but Lisa, Luke, Stephen, Meghan, and Danielle joined in. It made her jaw tick. Eventually, she decided to be honest. "Reno and I share everything. There's nothing he doesn't know about me..." Except for the baby, but that was different.

It was a blessing when the limousine pulled back up in front of the house and saved Mona from any further conversation on the subject. She reached into Reno's pocket, dragging the keys from its depths. He shifted, murmuring something garbled but decidedly nasty. Mona shook her head, poking him straight in the chest. "Time to go, Casanova."

Reno opened one bleary eye. She climbed out of the car and he followed her blindly. Gwen brushed past them, tight lipped and angry as she stomped toward the house. Mona pushed Reno into the car and quickly shut the door so he wouldn't end up with an arm or a leg in the way. He slumped against the window, half-asleep.

When she slipped into the driver's seat, she leaned over him and clicked his seatbelt into place.

Navigating Boston in the dark was a little nerve-wracking. Mona had to turn on the GPS and she still ended up taking the long way around, not that she minded. Reno was sleeping and going out for a drive always helped clear her head. Yes, she was angry he got drunk and belligerent. They were definitely going to have words about that tomorrow…but she'd also been invited into Lizzy's bridal party and felt like she bonded with Lisa and Meghan. Gwen was uppity and rude, but Mona couldn't take it personally; it was just her personality. All in all, tonight was a wash.

By the time Mona dropped the car off with the valet and got Reno upstairs to bed, she was too tired to worry anymore. He grunted and turned onto his back, snoring heavily as he burrowed under the blankets. Mona poked him until he rolled over and the room was quiet once more. Her head was aching and her stomach was a little off center, but the exhaustion won her over. Within seconds, she was out cold. They could deal with the fallout tomorrow.

Chapter Eleven

Mona had been sleeping soundly when suddenly her stomach lurched. She rocketed out of bed, nearly tumbling over Reno's discarded shoes as she dashed for the bathroom. She barely made it to the toilet before the vomiting began. Mona wretched until nothing came up but bile. She was left weak and teary, curled up beside the tub.

The door was still open a crack and she could see Reno, sleeping like a rock. It wasn't fair! He'd been three sheets to the wind when she got him back to the room yet somehow she was the one with her head buried in the toilet, praying to the porcelain gods that this was the last round of puking.

Every time Mona tried to sit up, she got dizzy. She was forced to slide up against the cool tile of the wall to keep herself upright. Obviously, something she'd done last night hadn't agreed with her, but she couldn't figure out what. She hadn't eaten much, only a finger sized spinach and artichoke bite, a square of pizette—which was a glorified piece of pizza—and a small salad with olives, and mozzarella. She'd opted against the goat cheese because the doctor mentioned limiting soft cheeses in her diet. Mona was doing everything right and being careful, so why was she being made to suffer for it?

The nausea began to wane around the time Reno got up. Her stomach was calmer but the dizziness persisted. Mona eased her way into the living area, opening up a can of ginger ale and taking a sip. She stiffened when Reno plodded into the bathroom. He peed with the door wide open, muttering obscenities the entire time.

Mona rolled her eyes, but it simply brought on another wave of vertigo. She inhaled slowly until the sensation faded again. Reno dug through his bag, pulling out an entire box of Alka-Seltzer tablets. He tossed two into a glass and poured water over it, closing his eyes as the concoction began to fizz. Even from her position on the couch Mona could see Reno's eyes were bloodshot. She had no doubt he was hurting today and he deserved every minute of it. On any other occasion, Mona would've blasted him for what he put her through last night. Unfortunately, she didn't trust her own voice. Getting agitated and upset would only make it more likely that she'd get sick again. Instead, she turned her head and ignored him entirely.

Reno was mortified. Getting wasted and belligerent was one thing; doing it in front of his friends and family was quite another. Last night was not the drunkest he'd ever been. He kept having flashes of showing up at a nasty club and forcing Mona into dancing. It was no wonder she was giving him the silent treatment. He'd shored up his defenses for her screaming at him until she was hoarse…this reaction was a thousand times more unsettling.

Tiptoeing toward the couch, Reno drank in the sight of her, pale and off center. Her arms were wrapped around her stomach, one hand resting over her mouth. "Mona?" She wouldn't even look at him. His heart sank. "I'm going to grab coffee. You want anything?"

Still nothing. Shit, Reno was in the doghouse.

Since he was already fully dressed, Reno put on his sunglasses and headed down to the lobby. There was complimentary coffee and tea for hotel guests. Sounds and smells assaulted his senses and he cursed. With coffee in hand and a cup of tea for Mona, Reno turned toward the elevator but making a clean break wasn't in the cards. Gwen was standing right in front of him with her hands resting on her hips. "Hey," he grunted. "I was just—"

"A stripper, Vincent? You brought a *stripper* home to meet your family?" Gwen hissed. She kept her voice soft as to not make a scene in the lobby. He grimaced, shifting his weight from one foot to the other. She grabbed his arm and pulled him away. There was an empty room on the third floor and she swiped in with her personal keycard.

Reno was in no mood to deal with Gwen this morning...but getting lambasted by her was infinitely preferable to Mona's terrifying silence. He took a slug of the coffee, not caring that it tasted both bitter and sour at the same time. It was caffeine and that's all he cared about. He pinched the bridge of his nose. "Gwennie—"

"Don't!" Gwen stomped her foot and pointed an accusatory finger at him. "You were so drunk, you were getting up there to take your clothes off and before any of us could figure out what was happening your date was humping the pole like a whore!" She shook her head. "I have never been so shocked or embarrassed in my life. Is this the kind of company you keep, *Reno*?"

Anger quickly replaced apprehension. He knocked back another long drink of coffee before setting aside the cups he'd been holding. "Mona is not a whore! Yeah, she's a stripper. Used to be, anyway." He furrowed his eyebrows, though the aviator sunglasses on his face mostly obscured his expression. "She didn't even take her clothes off…" He paused. "Did she?"

Gwen let out an indignant cry. "No! Of course not! I just thought you had better taste than that." She turned her back. "I know what I said the other day about seeing each other again but now I'm not so sure. I feel like I don't know you at all."

"You're right. You don't," Reno countered. "I'm not the same stupid kid you knew in high school, Gwen. I'm all grown up." Back then, he'd have cowered away from a fight in the fear that she'd break up with him. Their relationship had always been a weapon she could hold over his head. Reno was done with it. "I own a strip club called the Watering Hole. Mona has worked there since long before I bought the place and she's been a huge part in making the business a success. I couldn't do it without her…and if you can't handle that, I think we'd better go our separate ways now."

Reno was halfway to the door when Gwen grabbed him. "Wait!" She cried, her blue eyes shimmering with tears. "Vince, I didn't mean it. I'm sorry."

He blinked at her. Was it really that simple? Reno was ready to walk out of here and write Gwen off forever.

Then the moment he got tough with her, she mellowed right out. Why hadn't he thought of that back when he was still in high school? Sighing heavily, Reno just nodded. "Look, it's almost ten and I need to get showered and get over to my mom's for brunch. We can continue this discussion later. Are you coming?" She was oddly calm now, her hands folded and her expression blank.

"Sure. Do you want to ride over together?" Gwen asked hopefully.

"Yeah." It didn't matter to him who drove over. They were headed the same place anyway. Besides, Reno was still scared shitless of Mona and having a buffer there would be a welcome relief. He booked it back upstairs to get ready as fast as humanly possible.

The room was pitch dark when Reno returned. He was surprised to find Mona curled up in bed again. Damn it, he'd forgotten her tea but he was sure his mom had some at the house. For now, they were running short on time. Reno ignored his thundering headache and took the world's fastest shower, changing into a pair of jeans and the blue button down Mona picked out for him. She was still snoozing when he got out and he walked around the bed. Mona was unnaturally pale. Bluish-purple stains were heavy beneath her eyes. Gingerly, he slid a hand over her hip. "Pumpkin, you've got to get ready. My mother will kick my ass if we miss brunch."

Mona was half-delirious with exhaustion. She couldn't open her eyes or risk the room spinning again. "Reno,

I…" Her throat felt bone dry and she couldn't moisten it. It took all her strength to roll onto her back. "I don't feel good."

Disappointment seared through him. "You can punish me later. Everyone's expecting you and I promise, you'll have fun. Come on, Mona, Gwen is waiting for us downstairs."

"Well, you better not keep her waiting then," Mona snarled. This time, she resisted the urge to keep her eyes closed and she sat up. It was not a good decision. Her vision swam again and she gripped the sheets tighter to anchor herself. "What the fuck are you waiting for? Beat it!"

Reno took a step back, his face burning with shame and embarrassment. "Fine!" He stomped toward the door, glancing back at her. "You know what? I'm not bringing you back anything either! You can sit here and mope." Muttering obscenities under his breath, he stormed out of the room and let the door slam behind him. It was bad enough to deal with Gwen and her histrionics but then to add Mona's sullen moodiness on top of it? Reno couldn't stand it. Why did he even bother with women anyway? They only made him miserable. He stormed into the lobby, heading straight for the door.

Gwen jogged to keep up, dogging Reno's every step as he rushed outside. He was barking orders at the valet, demanding his car be brought out immediately. The kid scrambled to find the keys and she offered him a gentle smile. Later on, she'd apologize fully. Right now, Reno needed to let off steam and it was better if she wasn't the target. Gwen cleared her throat. "So, where's Mona?"

"She's not coming," Reno snapped. He left it at that. As soon as they brought the car around, he was in the driver's seat and he wasn't stopping for anything. Gwen wasn't even buckled in when he peeled out of the parking lot and aggressively drove to the house. The ride was silent and he didn't bother opening the door for Gwen when they arrived.

Luke and Lisa were cozied up on the couch. Stephen and Meghan hadn't arrived yet and neither had Ray or his parents. Poor Lizzy was curled up in a ball on the armchair, wrapped in a blanket. Reno settled in beside her, his poor mood lightening only slightly when she whimpered and snuggled against his shoulder. "I'm never drinking again," she whined.

Reno pressed a gentle kiss to her forehead before he rested his chin atop her head. "Me either…"

Sensing Reno's need for space, Gwen went into the kitchen to help with breakfast. Martha was disappointed Mona wasn't around and Gwen tried not to take it personally. Martha just had the wrong impression of the relationship between Mona and Reno. Besides, it wasn't as if she had time to dwell on it long. Ray and his parents arrived shortly thereafter with a store bought coffee cake and the fixings for mimosas. Hand rolled cinnamon buns, bacon, sausage, fruit salad, and hash browns were arranged on the table around the coffee cake Gina brought. Carafes of coffee and tea were being kept warm on the stove.

Rob and Karen finally arrived with their children in tow and everyone helped themselves to the delicious spread. It was the first time they had all been together and Reno found himself wishing Mona was here. She would've loved Elina's story about their family trip to Jerusalem and Lana kept asking where her 'new auntie' was.

Reno's anger started to wane as he mingled with the family. He was swept up in getting reacquainted with his brothers and shoveling delicious food into his face. Plus, the mimosas were doing wonders for the hangover he was nursing. By the time the second round of food came out—which included cold cuts, rolls, salad, and chips—he was almost back to normal.

"So," Mark cleared his throat, halting Reno mid sentence. He had been talking to Rob and Luke about the club when their big brother interrupted. "Let's be serious. Did Mona dump your sorry ass last night?"

Reno furrowed his eyebrows. "Why would you think that?"

Mark snorted loudly, grabbing his phone out of his pocket. "Are you kidding? You were a dipshit of epic proportions last night. She totally swooped in and saved you before you showed your ass to your entire family. Then you passed out and she had to drag you home." He shook his head. "*I'd* have dumped you."

"Luckily Mona has more sense than you," Reno fired

back. He stared at Mark's phone as he pulled up the video for Reno to review. The music began to blare, Mona's flawless form coming into view. He groaned when she pushed him back into a chair, taking the heat off him. No wonder she was so pissed. Scrubbing a hand over his jaw, Reno made a promise then and there he'd find a way to make it up to her… Reno set aside his mimosa with a sigh. "Mona and I are solid, okay? She was tired this morning. It's not a big deal."

It was clear Mark wasn't buying a word of it.

Excusing himself, Reno padded into the kitchen to get himself a cup of coffee. He whipped out his phone, pressing the speed dial he had assigned to Mona, and waited. It rang a few times before her voicemail picked up. He tried again a few minutes later. Voicemail again.

Cursing bitterly, Reno shoved his phone back into his pocket and made himself a sandwich. Much to his relief, his mother and Richard were tied up talking to Gina and Tom Lawrence. He had no idea what the topic was, but he overheard Gina gushing about how Martha and Richard just *had* to come by the country club the weekend after the wedding as their personal guests, of course.

Ray and Lizzy were sitting together now and he was rubbing her back. He was gentle with her, brushing the wispy blonde strands that had come loose from her bun. Lisa and Luke were standing in the corner opposite Karen and Rob. Both men had their arms around their wives, smiling and chatting. Even though Mark and Elina were in the other room, Reno caught the loving glances they shared. It just wasn't fair. They were all so happy and he was so damn miserable.

The buzzing of his cellphone drew Reno's attention and he stared down at it. It wasn't a number he recognized, but it had a Boston area code. Usually, he'd have let a number like that go to voicemail…but something told him he needed to pick up. "Hello?"

"Mr. O'Keefe?" A breathy voice echoed on the other line.

Reno frowned, "Whatever you're selling—"

"Sir, my name is Amanda. I'm a secretary in the emergency department at Brigham and Women's Hospital. We have a Mona Gallo who was brought in this afternoon. She asked that you be notified as next of kin."

"What!" Reno wobbled on his feet. "Is she okay?" His heart was in his throat. "I'll be right there!" When he turned to search for his keys, he found every family member he had staring at him. "Mona's in the hospital. She wasn't feeling well this morning and I…" His voice cracked. "I have to get to her."

Reno was fast but Richard was faster. "You're in no shape to drive. I'll take you." All rational thought was gone from Reno's head and he was solely focused on getting to Mona. It didn't occur to him that his entire family coming along for the trip might be a bad idea. Instead, he sat in the passenger seat lambasting himself for not realizing she was sick earlier. She had been pale and weak this morning. Instead of asking her if she was okay, he'd yelled at her and been an absolute jackass.

Descending into a string of curses, Reno gripped the dash. Richard put his lead foot to good use, but Reno wasn't satisfied. As soon as the Brigham came into view, his seatbelt was off. They screeched up to the emergency room entrance and he into the emergency department. Reno nearly knocked over a little old lady and narrowly avoided slamming into a stretcher. Thankfully, he made it to the registration desk in one piece. "I'm Vincent O'Keefe. I'm looking for Mona Gallo?" He was breathless. "Please tell me she's okay!"

It seemed to take twenty years for the stoic receptionist to open up the chart. "They've just transferred her upstairs." Before she even finished talking, Reno was jogging down the hall. "I'm trying to get to Mona Gallo. She's—"

"Right this way." The guard stood. His badge was on a pulley and he swiped it before the elevator opened up. They rode up in dead silence. Reno didn't breathe until they were walking again. The security guard led him down the hallway and pointed. "The nurse's station is there."

Reno was getting seriously agitated being bounced around like this. "I'm here to see Mona Gallo," he demanded of a young Asian woman wearing a pair of powder blue scrubs. She jumped right up and checked the board before leading him down the hallway. "Thank you," he breathed. His throat was bone dry as she knocked and pushed the door open.

Mona was sitting up in bed, staring out the window. There was a mess of IVs running into her veins and machinery humming all around her. As soon as the door opened, she turned and her breath caught in her throat. Reno jogged over and she threw her arms around him; tears of relief burned down her cheeks. "Reno," she croaked.

"Holy shit, pumpkin, I thought you were dead." Reno inhaled the scent of her hair and absorbed the strength of her embrace. He didn't even mind when she gently slapped him and then dug her hands into his shirt.

"Why would you think that? I asked them to call you, Reno. How could I do that if I was dead?" There were tears in her eyes but she was suddenly smiling at how ridiculously he'd reacted. Exhaling sharply, Mona rested her head against his chest. "I started throwing up really early this morning, I couldn't keep anything down and I was dizzy…I must've passed out because the next thing I knew, I was in the emergency room." Mona cleared her throat. "The doctor said I'm dehydrated. I haven't been eating or drinking enough. So they admitted me to give me fluids and watch my blood pressure."

Reno glanced down at her. "You had that dizzy spell at the club a couple weeks back too." He traced the dark circles under her eyes with his thumb. "No more bullshit. You're sick, aren't you?"

Lying back against the pillow, Mona turned her gaze

back to the window again. "I'm not sick exactly. I just…" She floundered, searching for the words. "You know how Kyle and I broke up a few weeks ago?"

"Did he give you something?" Reno gritted his teeth.

"Kind of." Mona chuckled, but it was not a happy sound. "I'm pregnant, Reno." She waited for him to panic and spontaneously combust. Instead, he just sat there with a blank expression on his face. Mona shifted nervously, her nails digging into her palms. "Did you hear me?"

Reno was having a terrible time trying to process the new information. Everything was starting to make sense. "You're pregnant." He repeated. "You are *pregnant*." Standing up from the bed, he began to pace the length of the room. "You're—"

"*Pregnant*." Mona sat up a little straighter. "Now you're catching on."

"And you just found out?"

Nervously tugging at a string on the hospital sheets, Mona averted her eyes. "I've known for a while now. I'm fifteen weeks. In normal people time, almost four months?"

"*Four months!*" Reno exploded. "You're four months pregnant and you didn't *tell* me?" He demanded. "What the hell, Mona?"

Sorrow burned in her chest and she covered her face to stem the flow of more unwelcome tears. "I was scared, alright?" She couldn't look at him. "I was more afraid to tell you than I was to tell Kyle!"

The hospital bed seemed far too big for Mona, or perhaps she just looked small sitting there hooked up to a million different tubes and wires. Reno stopped to really look at her and his heart sank. The IV was replacing fluid she desperately needed. She had leads on her chest and abdomen monitoring her heart rate. Around her waist was a strange disk that looked like a CD player stuck to Velcro that was attached to a device that was spitting out thin strips of paper. He'd seen this machine once before…it was strikingly similar to the one that was measuring Lizzy's heart rate while his mother was in labor. Suddenly, it struck him that the machine was probably doing the same for *her* baby.

"What the hell are we going to do?" Reno asked, collapsing into a chair beside the bed.

Mona wasn't sure she heard him right. "What do you mean?"

"I mean you're having a baby, Mona!"

"Yes, *I'm* having a baby." Mona swallowed hard. "I made the decision to continue this pregnancy even though Kyle didn't want to be involved. It's not going to be easy but…Reno, if I waited any longer, I might not be able to have kids at all. This might've been unplanned but as far as I'm concerned, it's a happy accident." Leaning back in bed, she choked up again. "I want this baby so much."

Reno grabbed a box of tissues at the bedside, handing them over to her. He stared at her for a long time, watching her wipe away her tears and blow her nose. A nurse came in to put up a new bag of saline and to offer support. "Mona, your family is downstairs in the reception area. They're all really eager to see you but if you're feeling overwhelmed, I can ask them to go."

"Thanks," Mona replied, smiling gently at the young nurse. They weren't her family, they were Reno's, and she couldn't bring herself to face them right now. "Give me a little more time." The nurse didn't seem to mind at all; she headed back out of the room and closed the door quietly. Silence hung between them until Mona couldn't take it anymore. "*Say* something, please?"

"I don't know what to say." Reno's mind went from thinking the worst to suddenly shutting down all at once. "You're pregnant, you hid it from me—"

"I thought I was going to lose my job," Mona interrupted.

Reno nearly fell out of his chair. "Why the hell would you think that?" he snapped. "You know I've been nothing but supportive of Liberty raising her kids and when Rita was working with us? I was ready to bring her back after maternity leave but she decided it wasn't right for her!" His heart was thundering in his chest again. "You mean more to me than either of those girls! I would never fire you, especially not for getting pregnant!"

"How the hell was I supposed to know that?" Mona cried.

"YOU COULD'VE TOLD ME!" Reno hollered back. Silence filled the room again. Mona rested one hand on her belly, gingerly rubbing the small bump there. Reno had no idea how he'd missed it before. Even under the loose hospital gown, he could see the definition of it. Some of this was his fault too…

The sun was starting to dip lower in the sky and sunlight streamed through the window, warming the blankets. Mona ended up kicking them off. The TV attached to the ceiling was on but she had it muted. The only sound in the room was the ticking of the clock on the wall. It was maddening.

With all the fluids running into her, Mona found she had to use the bathroom. She gingerly rested her feet on the floor. Pulling the IV pole around the other side, she carefully got up. Mona felt steady but Reno was right there the instant she stood. He didn't wait for her permission, but wrapped his arm around her waist as he helped her into the ensuite. "I can take it from here," Mona replied lightly.

Reno cracked half a smile. "Good. I'll be outside if you need me."

Thankfully, she didn't. Mona took her time washing her hands and splashed a little water on her face. She still looked pale but she was already starting to feel stronger. The doctor said she wasn't getting enough iron, so he was going to give her a supplement to go home with. He'd also called Dr. Harris to get a copy of her most recent labs and vitals. Mona felt they were doing everything to make sure she and the baby were okay.

When she opened the bathroom door, Reno eased her back into bed. He started to move away but she held fast.

"I don't trust people. I'm stubborn and I..." Mona glanced away from him. "I've been hurt before, Reno. I couldn't take it from you."

"I really wish you would've just told me. I'm still pissed at you for that," Reno narrowed his eyes. "But knowing you're actually okay is such a relief. I don't even know how to explain it." Leaning in, he pressed a kiss to the top of her head. "I just want you to be okay."

"I'm fine. *We're* fine," Mona qualified. "I thought the morning sickness was done but then with jet lag and everything, it screwed me up. I'll be okay." She just needed to eat better and drink more water for the baby's sake. "I'm more worried about the fact that your family is downstairs. What the hell are we going to tell them?"

Reno shrugged. "We tell them you're having a baby. I mean, if you're ready to tell people?"

Mona frowned deeper. "I like them all so much. What'll they think of me?"

"Hey," Reno soothed. "They are still going to love you. You don't need to worry about what anyone is going to say. And if they have a problem, they can take it up with me."

"Thank you, Reno." Mona whispered. All the stress of the day plus getting so sick for most of the wee morning hours and into the afternoon took its toll. She began to fade, yawning deeply.

Reno waited until Mona was asleep. He slipped out and found the nurse to inform her he'd be back shortly. Taking another elevator down to the lobby, Reno was immediately bombarded by his loved ones. Martha threw her arms around him, hugging him tightly. Richard was not far behind. Lisa, Elina, Lizzy, and Mark were sitting in the waiting room. Meghan had gone to the chapel to light a candle.

"Mona is okay," Reno offered. All the words he'd prepared on his way down died in his throat, replaced by a lump he couldn't seem to swallow.

Martha hugged her son tighter. "What happened? Did she slip and fall? Was there an accident?"

"No, nothing like that." Reno explained. Martha and Richard breathed a heavy sigh of relief. "She just hasn't been feeling well. She wasn't drinking or eating enough and had low blood pressure. They're giving her fluids and watching her overnight." He forced a smile. "She's fine." There was a pause and he dragged a hand over his jaw. "The baby's fine too."

"I knew it! Didn't I tell you, Richard? I have such a sense about these things. " Martha clasped her hands together, tears gathering in her eyes. "Oh, Vincent, you are going to be such an amazing father. Congratulations." She was weeping openly now. "We've all waited so long for you to find the right woman."

Reno was so stunned by his mother's reaction, he couldn't bring himself to correct her. She was beaming with pride and gushing about all the joy a new baby would bring him. Richard was pounding him on the back in congratulations. Lizzy threw herself into his arms, chattering about how exciting it was to have a new niece or nephew and making plans to come visit. Even Mark seemed pleased. He didn't have a single sarcastic comment to make—a first for him.

Reno had come down here with every intention of telling his family the truth about Mona and their relationship. Instead, he found himself grinning and thanking everyone for their support. Long after they left, he sat in the chair at Mona's bedside, still in shock. He replayed the day's events over and over to try and find clarity but he kept coming up empty. Reno realized what he'd done…he'd claimed her baby as his own. And since he had no intention of actually being a father to this child, there was only one way this could possibly end: *badly*.

Chapter Twelve

Mona was discharged from the hospital late Monday afternoon. The doctors worked her up completely to ensure there wasn't something else triggering her nausea and weakness. She spent an hour in the lab doing a glucose tolerance test, which Dr. Harris had recommended prior to her next appointment anyway. Then, Mona had an ultrasound. Finally, she finished off the day with a full pelvic exam, one more urinalysis, and the blessing of the entire gynecological staff at the Brigham and Women's Hospital.

After several bags of IV fluids, Mona felt like a whole new woman. She was given instructions to follow up with Dr. Harris when she returned to Carson City, and filled the script for iron on their way out of the hospital. Just after five o'clock, they arrived at the hotel.

When Mona and Reno got back to the room, she was shocked at the massive amounts of flowers and cards waiting for her. Martha had purchased a teddy bear and it was sitting idly on the bed. "Your family went a little overboard with the presents," Mona breathed. "I don't know why they felt they needed to do that."

"Because they care about you, Mona," Reno replied with a shrug. The news of her pregnancy spread like wildfire throughout the family. It wasn't just his brothers and sister who knew, but everyone who was coming into town for the wedding…and they all thought she was having his baby. Instead of trying to control the damage, Reno decided ignoring it was the best way to go. Maybe if he waited it out, the problem would resolve on its own…

Mona took a shower and washed the smell of hospital off her. When she returned, Reno was still incredulous he hadn't noticed the baby bump before. Even in her stretchy yoga pants and tank top, her rounded belly was visible to the naked eye. He watched her hawkishly as she padded over to the fridge and searched inside.

"We have all the ingredients for a pretty awesome frittata. And I'll make some garlic bread since the loaf we bought is probably pretty stale by now. What do you think?"

Reno frowned at her. "The doctor said you needed to rest."

"He also said I can resume all normal activities," Mona countered. "I've been laid up since Sunday. I need to *do* something. Besides, cooking isn't that strenuous." Nevertheless, Reno dogged her every step as she began pulling things out of the fridge.

His mouth started to water when the scent of fresh veggies mingled with butter and garlic. Mona seemed less stressed while she was flitting around the kitchen, which put him at ease too. "That smells amazing."

A smile tugged at the corners of Mona's mouth as she added eggs to the pan and sprinkled them with a little bit of pepper and salt. It took all her concentration to flip the frittata without breaking it into pieces, but she managed it with relative grace. With garlic bread toasted up and frittata finished, she carried the loaded plates over to the table.

"You want something to drink?" Reno asked, nervous she was going to get dehydrated again and have to go back into the hospital. "You should have some water."

Mona wasn't thirsty but she accepted the bottle of water gratefully and took a small sip to appease him. Reno had been amazing over the last two days. She urged him to go back to the hotel and rest but he hadn't budged; he stuck by her side the entire time. All the nurses thought he was adorable and several had mentioned how lucky she was to have a boyfriend who was so involved. Mona just smiled and nodded; she didn't have it in her to explain to every one of them that Reno was her boss. For the moment, she was content to play along.

Reno devoured his portion and helped himself to another serving. "This is so much better than hospital food," he said through a mouthful of garlic bread.

Mona chuckled, "Tell me about it. They wanted me to eat but then served me cold, tasteless crap. I'm so glad to be out." Reno was giving her that look again and she picked up the water, taking in a good amount before setting it back down. "Reno, there's something I want to talk to you about…"

Rubbing the back of his neck nervously, he nodded. "I've got to tell you something too."

"Oh." Mona tucked her legs beneath herself, motioning for him to speak. "You go first."

"You sure?"

Mona was nodding and Reno exhaled sharply. "I…" He let out a shaky breath. "I fucked up." He couldn't look at her right now, especially when she was so close. "When I found out you were in the hospital, I lost it. When I found out you were pregnant, I was in shock. I wasn't thinking clearly and…I may have led my family to believe that's my baby."

Mona didn't move.

Reno groaned into the palms of his hands. "Everyone was so happy. They were hugging me and congratulating us. I didn't know what to do…so I let it happen." He glanced up at her. "What could I have said?"

"How about telling them the truth?" It wasn't an accusation. Mona was genuinely curious. "It's not that complicated, Reno. My long time boyfriend broke up with me because I got pregnant, so I decided to raise the baby on my own. I'm sure your family would've understood. You didn't have to lie to protect my virtue. They already know I'm a stripper, adding an unwed pregnancy to the mix couldn't possibly tarnish my reputation any worse in their eyes."

The explanation made total sense now, of course. What bothered Reno more was the fact that he hadn't just lied to protect Mona, but also because he welcomed the love and attention. His mother had been so happy to learn he was finally going to be a father and he couldn't bear to dash her hopes. "I just…I was thinking it'd be easier to tell them after we get back to Carson City. I know my mother was really looking forward to having another grandchild. I don't think I can look her in the eye when I tell her the truth…"

If Reno stabbed Mona straight in the chest right then, it probably would've hurt less. Her throat tightened and she drank more water just to keep the tears at bay. "You're asking me to lie to your family. More than I already have?" Reno was quiet then. She laughed bitterly. "You know, I'm starting to understand why you haven't been back to visit in a decade." Dragging a hand through her dark hair, Mona leaned back on the couch. "I didn't have a family like yours growing up, so excuse me if I'm off base but aren't these people supposed to love you no matter what?"

"It's not that simple," Reno huffed.

"Then explain it to me because I don't get it!" Mona fired back. "I understand you didn't want to go to a wedding alone. And I should've told you I was pregnant before we left. It wasn't right to keep that from you when I knew we were going to be spending time with your family…but I wasn't the one who told them you're the father, Reno." She slung an arm over her belly, cradling the tiny life inside of her. "Did you ever stop to think how this would make me feel?"

The wheels in Reno's head turned and a frown marred his features. "Why do you care? They aren't your family…you never have to see them again."

Anger replaced the sadness Mona was feeling. "*Why do I care?*" she thundered. "I'm supposed to let you take responsibility for my baby, play along, put on a grand old show for a week and then what? Turn off all my emotions and all the things I'm afraid of and all the things I want just because we're not in Boston anymore?" Standing straight up, she paced the length of the room. It was suddenly stifling in here. "Do you want this baby?"

"No."

It was an automatic answer. Reno couldn't keep a houseplant alive, let alone be responsible for another human life. Mona and her little one deserved the best and he wouldn't saddle them with his inadequacies. How could he be a good father to this baby?

At the very least, Reno didn't tiptoe around the truth. That was what Mona took comfort in when she went to the closet and dragged out her suitcase.

"Mona, come on. Where are you going?" Reno bolted off the couch, walking over to where the suitcase was. "You need to rest. You shouldn't be working yourself up like this!"

"I'm not working myself up. *You're* working me up!" Mona snarled at him. "It's fine you don't want the kid but then don't stand there and act all concerned for it either."

"Just because I don't want to be a dad doesn't mean I don't care! I want you and the baby to be okay," he countered. "It's getting dark. You're not going to find a room here because Lizzy blocked them off for the out of town family coming in...and I have the car keys!"

Murder flashed in Mona's green eyes. "That's the angle you're going to play? You have the keys so I have to stand here and take your bullshit?" She pushed him hard. "What the hell kind of idiot do you think I am?"

Reno stumbled back, his jaw ticking angrily. "I didn't mean it like *that*! I just don't want you to go!"

"Yeah, well we don't always get what we want, Reno." Throwing everything she owned into the suitcase haphazardly, she had to push hard to close the zipper. Stomping into the bathroom, she gathered up her toiletries and threw them into another bag, tucking it under her arm. Reno moved to try and help her take her suitcase off the bed but she elbowed him hard in the ribs. "Stay the hell away from me."

"Mona, *please*." Reno had tried being tough, but he was going to lose his mind without her. Tears burned in his eyes, his heart pounded, and his stomach hurt. "I'll do whatever you want. I'll sleep on the couch. You won't even know I'm here. If you go somewhere else, how am I going to know if you're sick again?" His voice cracked painfully. "Don't go."

Mona froze. She'd never seen Reno this emotional before and even though she hated it, he affected her. Every part of her wanted to storm out and leave Reno broken in her wake...except her heart. Only a few hours ago, he'd kept vigil at her bedside and held her hand through it all. Her eyes fluttered shut, blocking out the sight of him. "You're playing with my emotions and it's not fair."

Closing the distance between them, Reno pushed Mona's half-zipped suitcase away and threw his arms around her. She struggled for only a moment before burying her face in the crook of his neck. "I'm not trying to play with you. I'm just..." *Selfish*, the little voice inside of his head whispered. "I'm going to do better, okay?"

Mona inhaled the scent of Reno's soap and cologne. She'd have to do better too... Mona had been too open, too acquiescent, and too softhearted. She should've known better than to let him get to her. Gathering up her strength, she tugged away from him and stared down at the haphazardly packed suitcase. "I'm going to take a walk and pick up some overpriced chocolate. You mind getting rid of some of these flowers? It's a little overwhelming."

"Yeah, sure," Reno replied. His family had gone a little overboard with everything. While she slipped on her shoes, he bustled around the kitchen. Mona was almost out the door when he cleared his throat. "What were you going to say? Before I..." he glanced away, "Ruined everything."

"It doesn't matter." Mona opened the door and pulled it closed behind her. Instead of heading for the elevator, she wound her way down the stairs. It felt good to stretch her legs and she just needed to be away from everyone for a moment. The door to the outside was propped open and she stepped out into the hazy evening. The last rays of sunshine were fading from orange to soft purple. All around her, the world turned. She heard children laughing, couples arguing, horns blaring, the thumping of bass on a sound system, and birds chirping their evensong.

Fifteen years ago, Mona left New Orleans in search of better things. Now that her dreams had crumbled to dust, maybe it was time to try again in a new place. It didn't have to be Boston, though she enjoyed the vibrant city. Maybe she could go to Atlantic City or Los Angeles. There had to be someplace she could apply her skills as a stripper and an assistant manager in some capacity. Perhaps she'd finally get her GED and start taking night classes to do…*something* with her life. Certainly, it would help to have people Mona could rely on, especially with the baby coming but it wasn't a necessity. Once again she realized the only person she could count on was herself.

Mona couldn't believe she'd been so stupid. For a few hours, she actually thought Reno wanted this baby. It was a stupid fantasy. How could she have let herself fall again? How could she open herself again knowing full well it could only end in disaster? The only comfort she had now was knowing where Reno stood. He didn't want her and he never would. Time to move on.

It was dark outside when Mona finally slipped back inside. She made a quick run to the hotel shop, charging several packages of peanut butter cups to the room. By the time she got back Reno had cleaned up from dinner and unpacked her suitcase again. She didn't say anything as their eyes met. There were no words left.

Although it was still early, Mona hadn't slept well last night. Nurses had kept coming in and out of the hospital room to take her vital signs or draw blood or check the fetal monitor. She'd napped on and off, but it was hardly a solid rest. Now that she was back in a familiar environment, she was looking forward to sleep. Curling up in bed, Mona read until her eyelids started to droop. With a yawn, she set her e-reader on the nightstand. Reno had been watching television but as soon as he saw she was trying to rest, he turned it off. As she pulled the blankets around her, she heard his quiet voice: "Night, pumpkin."

Exhaling sharply, she let her eyes flutter closed. It was almost a full minute before she rolled onto her side. "Good night."

Mona's response wasn't warm, but at least it was something. While she was gone, Reno had paced the room a thousand times, finding any menial task to keep himself occupied during her absence. No matter how hard he tried, panic filled him. If Mona hadn't come back when she did, he'd have sent a search party out after her.

Reno wished he could go back to the way things were before this trip, before she told him she was pregnant. Things seemed simpler then. Over and over, his mind turned until he was numb. Mona was sleeping now but despite his exhaustion, he couldn't do the same. Sometime after midnight, he stopped trying.

Reno pulled out his computer and started searching anything he could find about pregnancy. Minutes ticked away into hours until the sun began to rise in the East. His eyes were bloodshot and his head, pounding. Reno was midway through an article on the importance of paternal support during pregnancy when his body gave out. The computer slid onto the floor and his limbs hung limply over the cushions on the couch. Maybe when Reno awoke again, the world would be at rights and Mona would forgive him.

A man could dream.

Chapter Thirteen

Breakfast with Mitch and Willow was exactly the distraction Mona needed. She got up long before Reno stirred and quickly prepped for the day. When she arrived at the quaint little apartment in a quiet section of town, just down the road from the Raging Bull, Mitch was returning from a late shift high on adrenaline and caffeine. Willow was dressed in scrubs and ready to leave for work later on. It was the perfect amount of time to catch up.

On the way over, Mona stopped and grabbed muffins and coffee. Mitch made a fruit salad and they relaxed and talked about everything and nothing. Mona hadn't seen Willow since she transitioned and it was wonderful how comfortable she finally was in her own skin. Mona wished she could find the same sense of peace. Unfortunately, there were factors outside of her control at work. For example, Reno woke up and panicked at her absence. He'd texted her no less than thirty times in the last five minutes. Mona did her best to ignore it. Then he started calling her…

"I need to deal with this. Give me a minute." Mona grabbed her phone out of her pocket, and fired off a text assuring Reno she hadn't run off.

Mona (08:21am): I'm at breakfast. Stop calling me, I'm fine. See you later.

"Sorry about that," Mona apologized. Pasting a smile on her face, she took another swallow of tea. "What were we talking about?"

"Was that your man?" Mitch asked, resting his chin on his knuckles. "Baldy? The one who couldn't keep his eyes *or* his hands off you at the club last Friday?" He grinned broadly, tilting his head to better absorb the gossip. "Come on, girl, spill!"

"Leave her alone," Willow scolded. "If she wants to tell us, she will." Standing up, she freshened Mona's tea and helped herself to a bit more fruit. "Is he the father?"

Mona's hand rested over her belly. She'd told them about the pregnancy early on in the visit. Since Reno knew, it seemed right to get everything out in the open but it still wasn't easy to talk about. "No," she admitted. "I was seeing this guy Kyle. We were together five years but when I told him, he said he wanted no part in it."

Willow hurried over, wrapping Mona in a tight hug. "Honey, I'm so sorry," she murmured. "You deserve so much better."

It felt good to be with friends, especially ones she'd known since she was fifteen. They fell out of touch for a while but now that they were reunited, it felt like no time had passed at all. "I was coping fine with doing this on my own. I'm excited, I want to be a mother…but then Reno came in and confused everything." Staring into her steaming cup of tea, she found herself sighing again. "He told his entire family he's the father of this baby."

Mitch grasped her hand gently, smoothing over her

knuckles with the pad of his thumb. "That bothers you?"

A lump was starting to form in Mona's throat again and she coughed to clear it. "When we got back from the hospital I asked him if he actually wanted to be involved and he made it very clear he doesn't." She pushed her plate away, her appetite suddenly gone. "It *shouldn't* bother me. I made the decision to have this baby on my own. I don't know why I'm so broken up over it…"

"Mona, it's okay to be confused. You've got a lot going on," Willow soothed. Gingerly, she stroked Mona's dark hair. "I'm sorry you have to do this on your own. If there's anyone that deserves to be happy, it's you."

Mona forced herself to look up, although her instinct was to hide her face. "He asked me to pretend the baby's his for the week. He wants his family to see him as this successful businessman who's also a loving boyfriend and father during all the wedding activities. Then once we get back to Carson City, it'll be business as usual." She glanced down again, her focus landing on her belly once more. "I don't get it. They're amazing people who love him no matter what. Everything he has is what I've dreamed about my whole life…and he just takes it for granted."

Willow and Mitch shared a look. "I wish I had better advice for you, honey. This isn't something Will or I have ever experienced," Mitch murmured. "What I do know is that you survived almost three years at the Gypsy. You pulled yourself up by your bootstraps, got out of the bayou, and made a life for yourself. I'm sure there were a lot of people who thought you'd never make it." He could tell by the expression on Mona's face that had certainly been the case. "But you did. You can do this too. And as for Reno, he's clearly got some issues of his own—"

"You have to do what feels right to you," Willow broke in before Mitch dug himself into a hole. She smiled gently. "Just know that we'll be here to support you no matter what."

A genuine smile ghosted over Mona's lips as she reached out to hug them both. "I love you guys. Thank you." It was such a twist of fate she'd found them here in Boston of all places. With promises to see each other again before Mona went back home, she said her goodbyes. Mitch needed to get to bed and Willow couldn't be late to work.

Even though the visit had been short, Mona felt stronger now. Willow and Mitch were right. She couldn't live to make others happy. She needed to do what was right for her and the baby with or without Reno at her side.

* * *

Reno had been on the brink of a meltdown when he woke up and Mona was gone. Yes, all of her things were still there but he wasn't exactly thinking rationally. Running on less than three hours of sleep was clearly affecting his brain...or maybe he'd lost his mind long ago. It certainly felt like he'd blurred the lines between right and wrong lately.

Reno knew he'd hurt Mona and the realization burned in his gut. Over the last five years, he'd never seen her as broken as when they got into it last night. He wasn't sure where to go from here; the only thing he was sure of was that he cared for her deeply.

Having kids was something Reno always assumed he'd do. Coming from a family like his, it was expected that someday he'd settle down, get married, and pass on the O'Keefe name. But Reno wasn't like his brothers. He was the reckless one, the adventurer. He'd never be content with a nine to five job, let alone a white picket fence. Then again, over the last few years, Reno was starting to wonder if there was more out there than one night stands. Could he be happy with just one woman for the rest of his life? If that woman was Mona, he was starting to think the answer was yes...but what if he was wrong? What if he screwed up and let Mona down? Now, there was a baby in the mix and everything was infinitely complicated.

What it all boiled down to was the fact that Reno was afraid. He was irresponsible, unreliable, and unprepared for fatherhood. He convinced himself pushing her away was the right thing to do. It was better for all of them. Hurting her a little bit now was infinitely preferable to miserably failing her and the baby later on. Someday she'd thank him...

Today was not that day.

When Mona finally texted him back, she informed him in no uncertain terms that she could go wherever the hell she wanted, whenever the hell she wanted and owed him no explanation. The truth hurt. Reno wanted it both ways. He wanted to spend his time with her, protect her, and be there when times got tough…but he didn't want the responsibility that accompanied that. It was a tough spot to be in.

A knock on the door shattered Reno's thoughts and he gritted his teeth in annoyance. He was certain Gwen coming to give him an earful about lying to her again. Maybe if he pretended not to be in, she'd go away…

The knocking became more forceful and Reno huffed in annoyance. "Just a second!" He tidied up the couch, tossing the blanket back onto the bed. Striding over to the door, he braced himself for Gwen's ire…but it wasn't her at the door, it was Ray. Raising an eyebrow at the nervous groom, Reno motioned him into the room. "You lost, kid?"

"I was looking for Mona…" Ray paced the length of the room, lacing his fingers together nervously. "Is she here?"

"Not right now." Reno folded his arms across his chest. "Why don't you talk to me instead?" Ray's expression went from concerned to terrified, as if Reno had suggested he walk into a burning building. "Forget I'm Lizzy's brother for a minute. We're both men. Whatever it is you're worried about, I'm sure I've been through it before."

Ray hesitated. "When is Mona going to be back?"

Reno scoffed. "Sit down!" He ushered Ray to the couch

before perching next to him. It irked him that everyone seemed to prefer Mona over him. His mother was enamored of her, Lizzy had put her in the wedding party, and now Ray needed her advice. "Come on, kid, what's the matter? Did something happen between you and Lizzy?"

"No." Ray put up his hands in mock surrender. "Everything is fine. I can't wait to get married to her. I just...I..."

"Spit it out!"

"I'm a virgin!" Ray squeaked and buried his face in his hands. "I went to an all-boys private school and...let's just say sex education was very low on their to-do list. I met Lizzy on our first day of college and I've never wanted to be with anyone else. She wanted to wait and I'm fine with that. But now I'm getting married next week and I'm panicking! I want her first time to be good and I have no idea what I'm doing!" He dragged in a shaky breath, reaching for his inhaler and taking a long puff.

Damn.

Reno pinched the bridge of his nose and tried not to lose his temper. Of course he knew Lizzy would eventually have sex. He also knew that losing it to her husband was absolutely what he'd have expected of her. Abstractly, he understood sex was a vital part of any relationship...but the thought of her having it made rage burn in his gut. After a long silence, Reno shook his head. "I think you're right...we should wait for Mona. Do you want something to drink?"

Ray nodded eagerly. He gripped the edge of the couch while Reno dug through the fridge and came back with a couple of colas. Handing Ray one, Reno cracked open his soda and took a long drink. "So, how about the weather?"

"Oh, the weather is great!" Ray replied enthusiastically.

It was a blessed relief when Mona walked through the door twenty minutes later. She stared at the two of them, sitting awkwardly on either end of the couch. Reno stood up as soon as she got in and she froze. "What's going on?"

"Ray needs to talk to you," Reno announced. He couldn't put into words how glad he was to see her at this very moment. "And I need to take a shower. You two have fun!" Without waiting for her response, he grabbed clothes and hightailed it into the bathroom.

Well, that was bizarre, Mona thought to herself. After setting her purse down, she smiled gently at Ray. His face was red and his eyes were full of panic. She reached out, resting her hand on his shoulder. "Take a deep breath," Mona urged. "You look like you're going to explode."

Ray exhaled sharply; his entire body seemed to sag with the weight of his relief. "I'm going to be married in less than a week and I don't know anything about sex," he babbled. "I mean, I know the basics. The Internet is an informative place but…I didn't know who else to go to. I want to make Lizzy happy. She deserves a husband who knows how to please her."

Mona almost laughed. Ray's anxiety about losing his virginity was certainly normal, although he was quite a bit older than she was when she'd lost hers. "You're in a unique situation where you and your wife are both virgins. That's a really special thing, Ray." She resisted the urge to smooth his hair like he was a small child. "You won't know what Lizzy likes the first time because *she* doesn't know what she likes. My best advice is to listen. You'll be able to tell if she's enjoying herself or not."

"How?" Ray pressed, leaning forward to catch every word.

"Believe me, you'll know," Mona soothed. "There's a learning curve. The first time you have sex might be a little awkward but keep at it. You'll be an old pro in no time." She smiled comfortingly. Mona had no doubt Ray was going to be a fine husband. Anyone who cared enough to ask for help from a family member—even a fake one, like Mona—was clearly willing to do anything for his wife. "Does that help?"

Ray threw his arms around Mona's shoulders and hugged tight. "I knew you were the right person to talk to!" He pulled back, looking sheepish. "I also wanted to congratulate you and Reno. You're going to be an amazing mother." Not wanting to overstay his welcome, Ray stood up and headed for the door. "I'm sure you want some time to relax. Thanks again for your great advice and I'll see you tonight at the barbecue!"

Mona closed the door behind Ray, dissolving into a fit of giggles once she was sure he was out of earshot. It felt good to laugh after the seriousness of the last few days.

Reno peeked out from his hiding spot. "Is he gone?" He glanced around the corner.

"You're safe," Mona replied, her mirth dissipating a little bit. Licking her lips, she putzed around the room tidying up. Reno looked like he wanted to tell her the housekeeping staff would do that, but he wisely kept his mouth shut. After a while, she was starting to feel a little caged. "I'm going to take a walk and explore, maybe grab some lunch…"

"Do you want company?" Reno asked, looking up from his phone.

"Don't you have your big date with Gwen this afternoon?" Mona asked, raising an eyebrow at him. "Or did she cancel when she heard you knocked me up?"

Reno shrugged. "I haven't heard from her so I'm assuming she's done with me for good." He paused. "I'd rather spend time with you anyway." He regretted it the moment he'd said. Mona rolled her eyes at him and he didn't blame her. "Look, we've been friends for a long time. I don't want this trip to ruin everything we've built. That's why I've decided I'm going to tell everyone the truth at the barbecue tonight."

Mona stopped what she was doing and turned to look

at him. "What exactly are you going to tell them?"

"That you're an amazing friend who came with me on this trip so I wouldn't feel out of place at the wedding. I'm going to tell them the baby you're carrying isn't mine and I was wrong to lead them to believe it was." Reno sighed heavily. "You were right, Mona. My brothers are all happily married men with beautiful kids. That's how my family has always measured success. I guess I wanted to live up to that for once…" He hung his head. "I dragged you into it and I'm sorry."

Leaning against the wall, Mona's heart twisted. He was sincere; that was never in question. "You were right about something too. I don't know what it's like to grow up in a family like yours. I don't know what it feels like when your parents have expectations of you." She didn't have the strength to look him in the eye. "If you want to pretend for the rest of the week that you're the father of this kid and we're some power couple, I'll be okay." She rested a hand on her belly. "We're friends, Reno. I want us to stay that way."

A sense of relief washed over him and Reno eagerly agreed to her terms. "So…do friends take walks and go in search of food, because I'm starving."

Mona couldn't help but grin. Reno always had a way of lightening her up, even when it seemed impossible to do so. There was still a hint of uneasiness as they headed out into the heart of Boston.

As they sauntered down the sidewalk side by side, the conversation turned to mundane topics like sports and

Mona's current cravings. After a while, it almost felt like things were back to normal. Reno and Mona stopped by the park to soak up some sunshine and grabbed lunch at a deli nearby. When they returned to the hotel later that afternoon, both of them were feeling much better. Maybe this wasn't going to be as hard as Mona thought...

Chapter Fourteen

Driving up the private lane that led to the Lawrence family home made Mona feel uneasy. Reno warned her this was an upscale area and people weren't always friendly. Being from the South, Mona met every stranger with the same enthusiasm as if she were greeting her oldest friend. In this neck of the woods, people skittered away without making eye contact and kept to themselves. It was oddly disturbing.

Unlike the warmth of the O'Keefe homestead, the Lawrence Estate was two million dollars of sturdy brick mansion that didn't appear to be lived in at all. Every plant was perfectly manicured, the whitewashed porch was pristinely swept, and if not for the dozens of cars parked in the driveway, Mona would've sworn the place was uninhabited. She was afraid to touch anything as they were ushered into the house and out to the massive backyard.

The kids were laughing and playing in a large in-ground pool behind an enclosure. Luke was in the water too, keeping an extra close eye on Lana as she splashed about with her cousins. On the opposite side, a palatial patio was covered with tables and chairs galore. Lizzy and Ray sat on the edge of the stone wall, greeting guests and accepting congratulations. When they saw Reno and Mona walk in, they stopped to wave hello.

Every inch of decor exuded affluence and splendor. Mona had a hard time believing Tom and Gina were 'hamburger and hotdog' people, but the scent permeated the outdoor space. Mark, Rob, and Stephen were gathered around the grill, supervising as one of the caterers flipped the meat. Even though she and Reno had a pretty big lunch, Mona's mouth was already watering.

A bartender had been hired for the event, of course. Mona ordered a glass of lemonade; Reno thought about getting a beer but after Friday night's antics, decided against it. He felt validated when Mona smiled at him and they clinked their glasses together. Gingerly, he wrapped an arm around her waist and headed to where Richard and his mother were perched. They were chatting to his great Aunts Millie and Sophie. The twin sisters were in their eighties and clearly overjoyed to see Reno; the moment he got within reaching distance, he was dragged close and showered with kisses.

It took all Mona's strength not to laugh at Reno's rosy cheeks. When his aunts turned to chatter amongst themselves, Mona pulled a piece of tissue from her purse and helped him clean off the aftermath of bright red lipstick. The soft look he gave her in return made her toes curl. It wasn't real, she knew. He was just putting on a show because his parents and family were standing right there. It was for that very reason she didn't push his hands away from her when he tugged her against him, his warm palm resting possessively over her belly.

"Mona, we're so glad you're feeling better," Martha gushed, reaching out to grasp her hand. "I lit a candle for you at church on Sunday and you've been in my prayers every night." She squeezed tighter. "When I was pregnant with Reno, I had the worst morning sickness. I knew he was going to be a troublemaker before he was even born!" She smiled knowingly. "I'm certain Vernon was just as attentive as Vince. You know, there's one surefire way to make sure the rest of your pregnancy goes smoothly…"

"What is it?" Mona pressed, not knowing what she was walking into.

"Regular sex, of course," Martha replied, her expression level.

Reno spat out the mouthful of lemonade he had in his mouth. "Mom!" He coughed, trying to clear the liquid he'd surely inhaled into his lungs.

"Vincent, control yourself," Martha scolded. "I have six children. I know these things. My first pregnancy, I was so concerned being intimate with my husband would injure the baby but then a lady at church let me in on the secret. She's also the one who told me about taking a bit of castor oil if you're over your due date. It worked like a charm when Luke didn't want to come out!"

Mona was eager to learn all the secrets from Martha. "I feel like I should be taking notes." She grinned wider. "I would love to pick your brain. I've been reading everything I can get my hands on but I still feel unsure."

Martha inclined her head in reply. "Your instincts are good, Mona, you just need to listen to them." She smiled. "Don't let anyone tell you what you do for your children is wrong. All of my kids are different and I've learned how to deal with each of them in their own way. You'll come to know what's best for your baby too. You were born to be a mother. It takes one to know one." Martha glanced at Richard with love sparkling in her eyes. "The other thing you need is a partner. I've been so fortunate not only to have had the time I did with Vernon but I was able to find my soul mate." Richard bent down, kissing her ardently in response. They snuggled in each other's arms, looking natural and comfortable.

Reno could feel Mona stiffen in his arms and his heart sank. It was bad enough they'd fought about this very topic just last night, but now it was getting thrown in her face. Guilt gnawed at his insides and he jumped in to put an end to the conversation and her suffering. "Didn't you say you had to use the restroom? I think I see a sign for it. Come on, pumpkin." He grasped her elbow and ushered her away from his mother.

Mona's face was burning as she stalked down the hall and pushed her way into the bathroom. To her surprise, Reno followed her in and locked the door behind them. She stared incredulously at him. "What the hell was that?"

"I was rescuing you?" Reno offered, looking appropriately sheepish as he dragged a hand over his bald head.

"I wasn't aware I suddenly turned into a damsel in distress," Mona replied coldly. "I was actually looking forward to talking to your mother about some things." She folded her arms over her chest. Today, she'd decided to wear the stretchy black dress with the emerald bodice that hugged her curves and accentuated her jade eyes. She'd turned a few heads today, pregnant or not. "My mom's dead…and even if she wasn't, I wouldn't take parenting advice from her." Mona narrowed her eyes. "I want to be a good mom and yours is the best. I want to learn from her." She exhaled sharply. "I don't need to be rescued, Reno. Least of all by you…"

As hard as Reno tried to do the right thing, he kept screwing up. This was just another sin she could lay at his feet. "Maybe it'd be better if I gave you some space. I'll hang around the grill with my brothers and you can talk to my mom or spend time with the girls?" He shifted his weight from one foot to the other. "I'm not trying to make this harder on you, Mona…"

"I know," she whispered. Mona glanced around the bathroom, shaking her head at how lavish it was. This half-bath was bigger than the living room in her condo. "It's fine, the baby's pressing on my bladder anyway." She opened up the door and shooed him out. Once he was gone, Mona plopped down on the lid of the toilet and covered her face with her hands. She took a long moment to compose herself before washing her hands and heading back outside to mingle.

Martha was helping the wait staff put food out; they kept trying to get her to relax but she was adamant. Mona gravitated toward the pool and eventually found herself sitting on the edge, dipping her feet in the water. Luke swam up, grinning. "You want to come in? The water's great!"

"I didn't bring my suit." Mona grinned. "Besides, I don't want to be mistaken for a beached whale."

"Aw, come on," Luke huffed. "You can barely tell you're pregnant. You look awesome and I hope my brother is telling you that every day. If he's not, I will kick his ass." He shot a glance to Reno, giving a wave before he hopped out of the pool and settled himself across from Mona. There wasn't anyone around except the two of them, and the kids were engrossed in playing. Luke cleared his throat. "I just want you to know, Reno told me the truth about your relationship. I am guessing he didn't know about the baby at the time…"

Mona's cheeks burned. "Yeah." She stared into the dark blue water and wished she could simply disappear into the depths. "It's complicated." Reno hadn't told Luke the baby wasn't his, it seemed. "Right now, I'm just focused on making sure we stay healthy. We had quite a scare there. I don't want a repeat of that."

Luke pushed the wet hair back from his eyes, molding the dark strands in place. "When Lisa found out she was pregnant, I was scared out of my mind. I couldn't eat, I could hardly breathe most of the time…I read all the books, I did webinars on baby care, and I got certified in first aid and CPR." He chuckled. "My perspective changed a lot when Lana was born. I just loved her so wholly and completely, all my fear went away." He beamed. "It'll be the same for you and Vince, trust me."

Trust. Mona wasn't sure she had it in her to trust

anymore. Luke was Reno's brother and she didn't feel like she should burden him with her uncertainty. Instead, she continued to fake a smile and nod along. Lana swam over to say a watery hello and Luke jumped in to save Mona from getting soaked. She waved enthusiastically to the child before deciding to rejoin the adults.

Getting up from the edge of the pool took a little doing given her shifting center of balance. Mona was grateful when Reno wrapped his arms around her and pulled her up. She turned to thank him and her words died in her throat when she realized it wasn't Reno…the man who'd touched her so familiarly was in his early thirties and wore a three piece suit. His blonde hair was cut close to his head and his chin had a perfect dimple in the middle of it; he was almost painfully handsome. Mona was instantly uncomfortable. "Thanks…" She brushed invisible dirt off her dress. "I'm Mona Gallo."

"It's a pleasure to meet you. I'm Benjamin, Ray's much better looking cousin. I'm just kidding…about the handsome part, anyway." He laughed, but there was something in his tone that betrayed he wasn't entirely joking. "Don't tell me you're one of Lizzy's sisters-in-law?"

"Not exactly," Mona replied with a shrug. She glanced over to where Reno was standing and found him glaring daggers at her. Benjamin's palm was still resting against her arm. "I *am* here with Reno, though. Vincent, I mean." She nonchalantly took a step backwards to dislodge the unwelcome hand.

A single eyebrow arched upward as he glanced across the patio. "Ah, that must be the overgrown frat boy who's trying to kill me with his mind." Benjamin gave an overzealous wave before turning back to Mona. "Can I get you a drink?"

"I'll go with you," Mona offered. She didn't trust him not to slip something in her drink; it was a holdover from her days at the Gypsy. After getting her hands on more lemonade, she smiled as Benjamin clinked his beer bottle against her glass. "Cheers."

He took a small sip, frowning at the people milling around. "I've got to say, I wasn't expecting to see anyone as hot as you at my little cousin's pre-wedding barbecue."

Taking a long drink of her beverage, Mona turned and faced him head on. "You can cool it with the flirting. I'm not interested." She watched his expression change and he took a slight step to the left. At least he was starting to get the hint. She took a casual sip of her lemonade. "You're Mia's brother?"

"*Half*-brother," Benjamin replied coolly. "She was incredibly relieved you took her place in the wedding party, by the way. She can't stand Elizabeth."

Anger flared up in Mona's chest and she furrowed her eyebrows. "Why? Lizzy is the kindest, sweetest girl I've ever met."

"You don't understand. She's not like the girls we grew up with." Benjamin inclined his head. "Take a look at the difference between the way Lizzy's mother carries herself and the way my mother does." He motioned to a rail-thin woman who'd clearly been worked on by multiple plastic surgeons as she walked stiffly around the patio with a glass of champagne in hand.

"Are you trying to say you think your mother is better than Martha because of the way she walks?" Mona finished her lemonade, setting the empty glass on a tray. She was going to need both of her hands free if this uppity jerk made one more stupid comment. Mona folded her arms across her chest. "I'd probably walk that way too if I had a stick jammed up my ass."

Benjamin's mouth gaped open. "You know, now that I think about it, Raymond *did* mention you. You're the dirty skank who decided to get up on the stripper pole at a bachelorette party?"

Mona gritted her teeth and grinned predatorily. "I *am* a stripper. I'm pregnant too," She added for good measure. "Ben, I'm glad you got all the looks in the family because you clearly got shafted when they handed out common sense." She took a step away from him. "Thanks for the drink. Enjoy your evening." Mona stomped over to where Reno was standing, her heart pounding angrily and her cheeks flushed.

"What was that?" Reno asked, his brows knitted with worry. He glanced back to where Benjamin was gripping his bottle of beer, muttering curses under his breath as he turned his attention to Gwen, who had just walked in. Reno didn't even care. He was focused solely on Mona. "Did he make a move? I swear to God,

I will kick his—"

"Jealousy isn't a good look on you," Mona scoffed. "Benjamin was concerned this family isn't high class enough. I let him know just how deep the barrel goes." She saw Reno's fist tighten and she stepped into his arms to keep him from making a mistake. "There are always going to be jerks, Reno. I took care of it." Placing her hand against his cheek, she forced him to look at her. "Stop scowling or people are going to think we're fighting."

It was hard to stay mad when Mona was standing this close to him. He wrapped his arms around her, cuddling her as he rested his forehead against hers. They remained entangled for quite some time. Reno glanced out over the crowd, catching his mother's approving gaze. He smiled back and pressed a kiss to the top of Mona's head. "The food will be served soon."

She let out a soft moan. "Good, it smells amazing and I'm starving."

Concern speared through Reno and he tightened his grip. "Why didn't you tell me before?"

"Reno, it's just an expression," Mona soothed. She gazed into his warm brown eyes so he'd hear what she was saying fully. "I feel really good right now. I had a huge lunch just a couple hours ago, if you'll recall. Plus, I had several cups of lemonade. I'm hardly wasting away." It touched her how worried he seemed for her wellbeing. "I promise you, I'm okay." Mona smiled at him tenderly and grasped his hand. "I think there are enough guys manning the grill. You want to grab a seat?"

Reno didn't need to be asked twice. He headed to the table near Lizzy and Ray. Pulling a chair out for Mona, he helped her to get situated comfortably before he settled beside her. Lizzy hurried over as soon as she could break away from the crowd of well-wishers. Tears shimmered in her eyes as she hugged Mona tightly. "Congratulations! I am so happy my brother has finally found someone as amazing as he is." Lizzy choked back tears. "I can't believe we just met because I feel like I've known you my whole life. And you're going to be in my wedding now, too. I'm just so happy!" She wailed.

Before Reno knew what was happening, Lizzy and Mona were both blubbering. He wasn't sure who to comfort first and his heart started to pound. Thankfully, Ray hurried over and rubbed Lizzy's back. Reno followed the younger man's lead, gingerly tracing circles over Mona's spine. The girls dabbed at their eyes, laughing over a shared moment of emotion. Reno would never understand women as long as he lived...

The tears dried almost as quickly as they came. Mona and Lizzy were back to giggling a few minutes later. Reno looked around, watching as the staff started to put out the food and family members started taking their seats. There was a pretty clear divide between the Lawrence family and the O'Keefe-Sunderland clan. For one thing, the O'Keefes outnumbered the Lawrences two to one. Gina had a sister, who couldn't make it to the barbecue but would attend the wedding. Tom's brother Hunter and his children Benjamin, Mia, and Harriet were in attendance, along with his newest wife, who didn't appear to speak English. Several more of Tom and Gina's friends had attended but mostly the grounds were overrun with the ever-growing brood of O'Keefes.

Reno insisted on making Mona a plate, even though she was more than capable of standing in line for food. He served her twice as much as any normal person could've eaten and seemed disappointed when she couldn't eat a hamburger and a hot dog, pasta salad, potato salad, beans, corn, potato chips *and* the multiple slices of watermelon he obtained. "Uncle," she moaned. "I can't eat another bite!"

"Are you sure?" Reno frowned slightly. "I want to make sure you're taking in enough." He was still reeling from their hospital trip. His instincts told him Mona was fine but he hadn't realized she was sick the last time. He glanced down at her half-eaten plate with concern.

"Believe me, I'm stuffed," Mona chuckled. "At this rate, I won't fit in my bridesmaid dress." She meant it as a joke but Reno looked upset.

He scoffed at her, his hand hovering just above her belly. "You've always been pretty, but that baby inside of you makes you even more beautiful. Anybody who thinks otherwise is an idiot. You're perfect, pumpkin."

Mona was glad she hadn't been standing up, because she might've fallen over in shock. Reno looked so sincere. When she glanced around, she noticed Elina and Meghan giving her such warm looks. Reno once accused her of putting on a show but he was the real master. Worst of all, she almost believed him. Two could play at that game…Mona leaned in, pressing her lips to his softly.

Reno was momentarily taken aback as she leaned into him. His tongue darted out, tasting the sweetness of her mouth. He hadn't even realized anyone was watching until she pulled back and he heard the flutter of gossip ripping around the table. If it wasn't for the clamber of voices around him, Reno would've been swept away. Mona was gorgeous but there was something so alluring about her right now. He'd never believed pregnant women had a 'glow' about them until her…even more so when she was flushed from his kisses.

"If I can have everyone's attention please." Richard clinked his fork against a water glass. "I just want to say on behalf of my family, a big thank you to Tom and Gina for hosting this shindig." Clapping and cheering resounded in the patio area. "Congratulations to my daughter, Elizabeth, and her fiancé Raymond. I wish you many happy years together as you start your new lives as husband and wife."

Martha stood up beside her husband, pecking him gently on the lips. "We are blessed to be adding a new son to our family. I'm also very pleased to announce, we'll also be adding another little one to our brood this coming February. Mona? Vincent? Give a wave you two!"

Mona flushed and Reno groaned. "Ma, this isn't about us!" he called to her. "It's Lizzy's day." Standing up, he rested a hand on Mona's shoulder. "Here's to the bride and groom!" Glasses were raised and clinked together. Mona smiled at Reno as he settled beside her. "I'm sorry. I didn't know she'd make an announcement like that." He dragged a hand over his chin. The sun was starting to dip lower in the sky and the outdoor lights were turned on, including hundreds of twinkling strands that illuminated the backyard.

"It's okay," Mona offered. She was still floating from the kisses they'd shared. If the sky were to fall right now, it wouldn't bother her in the least. She snuggled against Reno and chattered with the people who sat at their table. Conversation flowed pleasantly and cake was served shortly thereafter. Even though she was full up, Mona managed to make quite a dent in the huge piece Reno served her.

Most of the older couples went home after dessert, including Benjamin and Gwen, who snuck out the back. Martha and Richard said their goodbyes as they shepherded the great aunts to the car. Luke carried Lana out while Lisa said their goodbyes and helped Karen shepherd her brood into the minivan. The younger crowd started up a fire in the pit, couples snuggling beside each other as marshmallows were roasted and stories were swapped.

Mona was having a great time. She was laughing at Lionel's ridiculous antics and gossiping with Lizzy about hairstyles for the wedding. They were going to go to the salon and try out looks after the fittings tomorrow morning.

Sometime later in the evening Frederick tried to light a cigar but Reno glared at him until he thought better of it. Reno wasn't going to let anyone smoke around the baby…he'd also gone the entire night without even wanting a drink. It was a big win for both of them.

Eventually Mona's back started to ache from sitting against the rock wall. Reno must've realized because he instinctively moved behind her. Mona leaned against him as they lounged by the fire. It didn't bother her at all when his arm wrapped around her waist and his hand splayed over her belly. It felt natural to be sitting here like this.

Reno wasn't sure why he did it. Mona kept shifting and he knew she had to be sore. As soon as she settled herself against him, he instantly relaxed. He was content to sit there, chatting with George about what it was like to open up a club and occasionally rib Ray as he recounted horror stories from work. As hard as he tried to fight it, Reno's hand was drawn like a magnet to Mona's stomach. Her tummy was firmer than he expected and he marveled at how perfectly the swell fit in his hand. Fourteen weeks was a little too early to feel the baby moving, but he still found himself imagining what it would be like to feel those first flutters. The instinct to protect and provide flared to life inside of him, taking hold of his good sense.

Sometime after midnight, Mona yawned and Reno knew it was time to go. "Come on, pumpkin, we have a bit of a drive back." There was no argument from her.

After doling out hugs and firming up plans for tomorrow, they headed to the car.

It was a pleasant drive since there was barely anyone on the road. Moonlight illuminated the pavement and lit the world around them. Mona glanced over at Reno, smiling gently. "I had a really good time today," she said softly. "Thank you."

"Thank *you*," Reno grinned back at her. "I couldn't have done this without you. That was the happiest I've seen my family in so long. Even Rob and Karen looked like they were having fun, and they don't seem to like anything that isn't directly related to Jesus in some way."

"That must've been the person I heard muttering about premarital sex when Martha announced my pregnancy to everyone." They shared another laugh at that. Mona leaned back in her seat. "I had a nice talk with Luke today too. He mentioned you told him the truth about us. Except not the whole truth…"

Reno tensed. "I must've told him on the night of the bachelor party. It was before I knew about the baby." He peered over at her, filled with apprehension. "I hope he didn't give you a hard time."

"Not at all," Mona clarified quickly. "It made me feel a little guilty, actually." She licked her lips. "I know you were really excited about giving it another go with Gwen—"

"No," Reno interrupted. "I mean, yes, I *was* but…I've

been thinking a lot about it and it just wouldn't work out. I'm in a different place in my life. My club is in Carson City, my life is out there." Silence hung between them for a moment. "Gwen and I are completely different people. She's been married and divorced and now she's looking for more. She wants commitment and I'm not interested in giving her that." He scratched at the back of his neck. "I forgot how uptight she can be sometimes…"

Mona laughed uncontrollably. "Understatement of the year?" She shook her head, wiping the moisture that had collected beneath her eyes. "Thanks. I needed that."

"Happy to oblige." Seeing Mona like this put Reno in such a good mood. He shrugged one shoulder before tossing his keys to the valet. With the keys safely tucked away and his arm around Mona, they headed upstairs to the room.

Once they were in for the night, Reno pulled off his shirt and pants, leaving him in only his boxers. He went in search of the blanket he'd been using on the couch last night when Mona stepped out of the bathroom. He nearly fell over at the sight of her in a black, silky nightgown. "Holy shit," Reno gasped.

"What?" Mona tensed.

"You can't wear that," Reno demanded.

She glanced down at herself. "Why not? It's just a nightgown…"

"For God's sake, Mona! It's bad enough you're gorgeous and we are sleeping in the same room. Then you go and wear something like that. I'm not a saint, you know!" Reno ached. He gritted his teeth.

"Underneath this stupid nightgown, it looks like I'm trying to smuggle a melon. I've got several stretch marks coming in that are quite unattractive and the veins in my chest look like something out of a horror movie." Mona laid back on the bed, huffing in annoyance. "It's hard for me too, you know. I'm horny as hell right now, but you don't see me losing my mind over it."

Reno groaned loudly. "Don't tell me that! It just makes me want you more!" He was pacing the room now in a vain attempt to burn off some steam. "We've already royally screwed up this fake relationship. The last thing we need to do is complicate it more." His mouth was moving, but his libido was not listening at all. "Although, my mother did say that having regular sex is an important part of a healthy pregnancy…"

Mona crossed and uncrossed her legs, green eyes flashing with excitement. "What are you suggesting?" Her tongue darted out to wet her lips.

"You've done so much for me over the last couple weeks. Maybe it's time I do something for you…" Reno closed the distance between them. There wasn't a single drop of alcohol in his system, yet when he kissed her he felt like he'd finished off a whole bottle of tequila. Mona overwhelmed his senses.

Reno gently pressed her against the mattress as he crawled in beside her. His thick, warm fingers curled over her hip as he gently broke the kiss. "I want you, Mona..." His voice was low and gravelly. "But if you don't want to do this or you're not ready, just say the word."

Breathlessly, Mona shook her head. "I need you. *Please*," she begged. With her hormones in overdrive and Reno offering himself so sweetly, she was powerless to resist. It didn't matter that things were complicated or that this could mess up everything they'd been working toward. She didn't care that it was the exact opposite of every promise she made to keep him at arm's length.

Tonight, Mona Gallo was going to sleep with Reno O'Keefe and damn the consequences.

Chapter Fifteen

Reno's fingertips ghosted over the creamy expanse of Mona's thigh and her breath hitched in her throat. Dark hair fanned out over the pillow as she dipped her head back, shuddering at his gentle touch. Her eyes were dilated nearly black with pleasure, only a ring of vibrant green catching the light as she gazed at him with heavy-lidded desire. Mona was so beautiful his chest ached.

Despite the overwhelming desire thundering through him, Reno found himself lost in the memory of meeting Mona for the first time. Their introduction came at a time in his life when he was lost and searching for something. When he walked into the Watering Hole and saw this woman dancing on the stage, he knew he'd found it. Reno was instantly mesmerized; every movement Mona made drove him mad. He'd have done anything to have her, even spend his entire life savings on a crumbling strip club. If she showed him even the slightest bit of interest back then, it would be *his* child in her belly. Of that, Reno had no doubt.

Fingernails trailing down the bareness of his shoulder snapped Reno back to the present. Five years he'd waited for a shot with her. Five years he'd never been fully satisfied. That was all about to change.

Every inch of Mona felt like it was on fire. Her cheeks were flushed, her skin electrified, and the space between her thighs already overflowing. Reno had barely touched her and she was already lost to him. Warm, rough fingertips skimmed her flesh and a moan emanated her that felt like it originated in her toes.

Much to Mona's dismay, Reno's touches were feather light. He seemed determined to drive her mad as he sought to learn every curve of her body. On another occasion, she would've enjoyed his tender ministrations, but right now it felt like torture. "Enough of the foreplay," she whimpered. Mona's nails bit into his shoulders as she tugged him toward her. Dragging his mouth to hers, she drank in the sweetness of his mouth.

Maybe it was the hormones or perhaps Reno simply had powers beyond her comprehension, but electricity crackled in Mona's veins. He hovered over her, the warmth of his flesh mere inches from her. Suddenly, the pretty black nightgown she was wearing was nothing but a barrier between them. Mona reached for the edge, breaking the kiss just long enough to pull the garment over her head.

Gooseflesh erupted over her skin as she wrapped herself around him, desperate to feel the warmth of his body against hers. Mona kissed him again, growing bolder with each moment that passed. Yet the more she pressed, the more Reno seemed to pull back. At first she thought it might be the way he was sitting, but when she saw the uncertainty in his warm brown eyes, she could tell he was stalling. Mona pulled away from him, her heart beating faster as she prepared herself for rejection. "Reno, what's the matter?"

Mona knew him so well, it was frightening sometimes. Exhaling sharply, Reno sat back on his heels and glanced into her vibrant jade eyes. Dark hair tumbled over her shoulders and her lips were slightly parted and swollen from his kisses. She was beautiful…and she was pregnant. He settled beside her, dragging a hand across his face.

Martha assured them both that having sex would be fine, she even recommended it. The doctor at the Brigham had been clear as well that sexual intercourse was perfectly fine. There was more to his concern than her physical condition. What they were about to share was incredibly intimate and she was already vulnerable. He couldn't bear the thought of damaging their relationship beyond repair. "Mona, I don't want to hurt you…"

"You won't," Mona pressed. "I trust you." She truly did. Reno had become such an integral part of her life over the years. They worked together and although he might not have realized it, he was her very best friend. She didn't trust easily and she had learned long ago how to push people away. Reno never let her…he always pushed back, he always returned, even after their worst fights. Mona and Kyle never fought. It wasn't healthy. It wasn't right. And it was the reason Mona didn't even miss Kyle…but she could never live without Reno.

Cuddling beside him on the bed, Mona rested her head against the pillow. "There aren't any secrets between us anymore, Reno. I'm not going into this blind." She slipped her hand into his, gripping tightly as she inched toward him. "It doesn't have to be anything more than tonight. I want you…and I know you want me too…"

Reno needed no further encouragement. Settling his hands against her hips, he dragged her against him. Her skin and hair had absorbed the scent of wood smoke and mingled with the lilac scent of shampoo. He was going to devour her.

The scruffy five o'clock shadow was a delightful pain-pleasure as it scraped across her sensitized skin. Mona was completely bare to him, open and ready to receive everything Reno had to give. He inched down, growling low in his throat as he knelt between her thighs. She dipped her finger into the waistband of his boxers, tugging them down his hips. She hid her smile as she wrapped her hand around his bare length and was rewarded with a growl.

"You keep that up and we'll be finished here before I even get started," Reno warned. He was already was on the brink of explosion and he'd barely warmed her up. He intended to make sure she had a good time. Mona wasn't some bimbo he picked up that he didn't intend to call again; she deserved to be thoroughly pleased.

Gingerly, he slid his hands up to brush over her breasts. They were much heavier than he expected and her nipples were darker than he'd ever seen. She hissed slightly when he touched them and he chewed his bottom lip, "Sore?" Mona nodded but locked her legs around his hips to keep him from pulling away. "I'll be gentle," he murmured.

Mona couldn't help but smile. He always had a way of reading her mind. The warmth of his breath fanning over her skin was enough to send her into overdrive, when his cheek brushed over the sensitive orb she nearly ratcheted off the bed. Reno didn't stay there long, since it was clear he was concerned about hurting her. Instead, he eased downward, trailing kisses over her breastbone and then lower. He paused at the soft arc of her belly, his fingertips tracing the roundness there.

Tears sprang to her eyes as Reno bent, peppering kisses over the sacred space where her child slept. It was a simple gesture but to Mona, it meant everything. A sly smile ghosted over her lips. She slid her thighs around his waist. "I'm ready, Reno. You've had me hot and bothered all afternoon. I don't want to wait." Already he was swollen and twitching between her thighs. Delicate fingers slid up his chest. Her nails dug slightly into the flesh of his pecs as she kissed down the contour of his neck. When she hit his collarbone and he growled, she knew she'd hit the sweet spot.

As Reno pressed her back against the bed, their lips met again but this time, there was an urgency he couldn't ignore. All the years of pent up frustration and fear and longing were suddenly gone. He aligned himself with her center, their eyes caught and held as he slid inside of her. White heat enveloped him and set his soul aflame.

Mona dragged air into her lungs, gasping at the relief of being filled. Reno was perfectly in sync with the rhythm of her body and waited only a moment before he began to move. He rocked, slowly at first but then increasing with intensity until she was sure she was beyond the brink of insanity.

Reno was infinitely careful not to put too much pressure on Mona. He suspended himself above her, arms tight as he made love to her. With each stroke, he was rewarded with another whimper and it kept him running on pure adrenaline. Knowing he could bring Mona this kind of pleasure was power beyond anything he'd ever tasted.

The first wave that slammed through Mona's core knocked the air right out of her lungs. She arched upward, her mouth opened in a silent gasp. Almost as quickly as it had gone, her breath returned and Reno's name tumbled from her lips. Their hearts beat in time as need crested inside her, tight and hot. Moments later, the dam burst and she spasmed around him. Reno was powerless to resist her and unleashed himself within the occupied depths on her womb.

Although he ached to collapse, Reno rolled to the side and pulled her against his chest. Mona tangled her legs with his, needing to be close to him after such an intimate moment.

It took a while before Mona could catch her breath enough to speak. "Why the hell did we wait five years to do that?"

"You're asking the wrong guy," Reno replied cheekily. He pressed a gentle kiss to the top of her head. "You sure I didn't hurt you?" One arm was wrapped around her shoulders but the other instinctively cradled the swell of her belly. He meant to check for injury but it felt more intimate than that. The soft, loving look Mona gave him in reply tore a hole in his chest. All the fear he'd been holding onto dissipated and he tugged her closer to hold onto the afterglow of making love.

If it weren't so late—or early, Mona would've been up for round two. Unfortunately, she hadn't slept well last night alone in this big, lonely bed. With Reno's arms wrapped around her, she quickly fell into a peaceful slumber.

Although he was exhausted, sleep eluded Reno for a time. Mona's breathing was soft and even, her cheeks still flushed, and her hand covered his as it curled protectively around the baby. Rolling halfway onto his back, Reno stared up at the swirls in the plaster on the ceiling and asked God to give him some clarity. He adored Mona and was coming to terms with the idea of there being a baby…but he was also terrified of what it would mean to be part of this little family.

Reno's brothers were happily married and had children of their own now. He was constantly bombarded with proof they were the very best husbands and fathers anyone could ever ask for. But Reno didn't have Mark's fierce determination, Luke's tenderness, Stephen's levelheadedness, or Rob's faith. How could he be worth anything to Mona without at least *one* of those qualities?

Even if he wasn't a complete failure at being a husband and father, there was one niggling thought at the back of his mind. What if she didn't love him back? Mona tolerated him, of course. He used to think that was enough…but could it ever be more between them? As he glanced over at her, asleep in his arms, Reno sighed.

Mona stuck by him through thick and thin. She didn't leave when he bought the club. Instead, she put up with his crap until he wised up and realized how much he needed her insight into the business. It had been Mona who finally made him quit smoking. He could actually walk up the stairs to his apartment without feeling like he was about to die now. She drove him home when he was drunk and making bad decisions. When he needed new clothes, she took him shopping and didn't let him bullshit himself about what size he needed. There was no judgment, just the facts. Most of all, Mona was there when he was frightened and when he needed to be held…

Didn't she deserve the same from him?

Reno wished the answer was simple, but it was far too much to tackle tonight. His eyelids were already starting to droop and he was quickly losing steam. Tomorrow, Mona would be occupied with the fittings for the wedding and spending time with his sister. There was also something Reno had been putting it off since he arrived. It was high time he swallowed his fear. With his plans made for tomorrow and Mona in his arms, Reno fell into a deep, dreamless sleep.

Chapter Sixteen

Mona was startled awake by the sound of her phone falling off the nightstand. She realized it was buzzing and managed to migrate all the way to the side of the table. Suddenly, Mona sat bolt upright and rubbed her eyes. She had six missed calls and just as many voicemails from Lizzy. Oh crap. She had overslept.

"Reno!" Mona gasped and elbowed him in the ribs. "It's ten o'clock! Everyone is waiting for me downstairs!" Scrambling for her missing nightgown, she kept coming up empty. Cursing a blue streak, she felt a wave of nausea pass over her and stilled for a moment, perching on the edge of the bed as she waited for it to subside.

To his credit, Reno managed to fall out of the bed with as much dignity as possible. He glanced over at Mona and his throat tightened. "Are you okay, pumpkin?" She looked green and he was certain she was going to throw up. An angry knock on the door paralyzed him for a moment as he turned to stare. Mona was in no shape to get the door and the person was clearly not going away. Reno grabbed his boxers off the floor and pulled them on. "Just a minute!" he groused. The pounding continued and he finally stomped over, throwing it open.

"Reno, I'm not dressed!" Mona hollered just as the door opened. She dragged the blanket over herself just in time. Her cheeks flamed as a very agitated Lizzy appeared in the doorway. At first, it looked like the petite blonde was going to yell...then she began to giggle uncontrollably. It took her a full minute to control herself and she leaned against the doorjamb.

"Wow…" Lizzy was grinning like a fool. "Take your time, Mona. We'll be downstairs when you're ready. I'm sure the shop won't mind if we're a few minutes late." She covered her mouth with her hand to stop a new fit of laughter. "Vince, I have no words…"

"Beat it, squirt!" Reno huffed. Shooing her out of the room, he closed the door and rested his forehead against it. This was not good at all. He gathered his strength and prepared to face Mona's ire, but when he turned around, she was laughing almost as hard as Lizzy had been.

What else could Mona do? The situation was embarrassing, sure, but it wasn't the end of the world. Slipping out of the bed, she hurried across the room, unclothed. "I am going to take the world's fastest shower." Before she had a chance to think about what she was doing, she pressed a soft kiss to Reno's lips and dashed into the bathroom. As she stepped under the lukewarm spray of the shower, Mona was flabbergasted at how casually she'd kissed Reno, as if they'd been lovers for years. Last night was supposed to be about sex…but she felt closer to him than any other person in her entire life. Mona closed her eyes, focusing on the song that was stuck in her head instead of her overwhelming feelings. There would be ample time to berate herself later. Right now, she had to get ready and out the door as soon as possible.

For a long moment, Reno just stood there. He had to pinch himself to make sure he hadn't entered an alternate dimension. Mona was singing softly in the shower and it brought a smile to his face. Her voice was nothing short of terrible, but what she lacked in talent she certainly made up for in enthusiasm. Once he regained his bearings, Reno puttered around the room. He expected this morning to be awkward. Instead, Mona's soft kisses made him feel warm and fuzzy inside. As he leaned against the edge of the bed, he was starting to think making love to her was the best decision he ever made, instead of the worst mistake of his life.

Mona changed into a flowery blue sundress that stretched over her baby bump. With a black sweater, a smear of lip balm, and her hair hastily braided, she was ready to go. On the way out, she paused to glance at herself in the mirror. A smile slid over her features as Reno's arm snaked around her waist.

"Make sure you eat something," he chided.

"I will." Mona stole one last kiss. "I'll text you when we're on our way back. Have fun today!" Slipping on a pair of black ballerina flats, she hurried down to the lobby where Lizzy, Danielle, Charlotte, and Martha were waiting for her. She tightened her grip on the strap of her purse. "I'm sorry I'm late."

Martha smiled knowingly, wrapping her arm around Mona's shoulders. "No need to apologize, sweetheart." They headed out to where the car was parked on the street. As they piled in, Martha leaned closer. "I'm glad you're taking my advice. You're positively glowing this morning. And I'm sure you feel better too!"

Mona's cheeks flushed as the gaggle of girls around her began to giggle again. Honestly, she did feel better. A sense of calm washed over her. No matter what happened today, she felt prepared to face it. Serenity was a wonderful thing.

* * *

The bridal shop was a charming family owned business tucked in the middle of a small shopping plaza. A variety of dresses, new and vintage, hung in the window. Mona immediately felt at home as she stepped in the front door and the tiny bell chimed. A woman in her late sixties scolded Lizzy in Greek as she ushered the group to a back room for the fitting.

Norah, the owner and seamstress on hand, had several bags lined up and hung on a simple metal rack. "You change!" She commanded, clapping her hands and hurrying the girls along to find their items and so she could get to work.

Mona waited for the others to get their garments, so she'd know which one was hers. Once everyone was situated, she grabbed the one that remained and headed to an empty dressing room. It was like Christmas come early when she unzipped the black wrapper and saw the lovely gown beneath. The dresses Lizzy had picked were royal purple and beautifully simple. Dragging her fingers over the soft silk, a smile ghosted over Mona's lips. She changed quickly, eager to see how she'd look in the outfit. Unsurprisingly, it was a little snug in the bodice, but the empire waist hid her belly well. From the front, nobody could even tell she was pregnant. The side view was a different story…

As she stepped out of the dressing room, Mona joined the other two bridesmaids in front of a tall collection of mirrors. Norah clucked her tongue, making several markings on the dress in chalk and making notes in her booklet. "You don't worry," she soothed. "We take it out for you no problem. No one will know." The smile crinkled the corner of her eyes.

"I'm fairly sure everyone in the family knows," Mona chuckled, resting her hand over her belly. Still, there was a thrill of excitement that she wouldn't look so pregnant in the wedding pictures.

Lizzy began to sing the wedding march as she stepped out from behind the curtain. Mona couldn't stop the tears from her eyes as the crinkle of pristine white fabric swished with her every movement. The dress was a simple white scoop neck gown with an overlay of delicate, hand-sewn lace. Around her middle was a silky sash affixed with a jeweled brooch that rested against her hip. Unlike the modern wedding dresses Mona had seen, this one had a long train. It was so beautiful, she couldn't help but shed a tear.

Martha was right there with her, dabbing her eyes and offering Mona tissues. "Oh Lizzy, you look so beautiful." Her voice cracked. "I can't believe my little girl is getting married." She blew her nose before turning her attention back to Mona. "It's so different when it's your sons get married. A daughter is such a blessing." She rested her hand on Mona's forearm. "I hope I'll be around for the day when your babies are getting married."

Mona smiled through her tears. "I hope so too." She'd never been to a wedding where there wasn't at least one shotgun involved. Nobody was rushing to make this marriage legal, so they could take their time and savor the experience. Mona felt the love and excitement of everyone around her. She forced away the feelings of jealousy. Lizzy deserved to be happy. Mona, on the other hand, was just grateful to be sharing in this with her.

Norah continued to bustle to and fro. More measurements were taken before she finally clapped her hands. "I will get to work immediately," she announced.

Once all of the dresses were returned to their hangers, the girls met at the front of the shop. Mona paused in front of a small section near the back that had discounted gowns. She thumbed through the rack but she wasn't paying attention. The moment she felt Martha move behind her, she dropped her hand. "I was just curious…" She pasted a smile on.

"Well, they're all gorgeous." Martha smiled knowingly. "Why don't you try a few on?"

"Oh, that's okay…" Mona's throat was suddenly dry. She swallowed hard. "I want this to be about Lizzy." Glancing back at the girls, Mona felt bittersweet. They were each more than ten years her junior and had their lives ahead of them. Mona wished nothing but joy and happiness for each of them; she hoped they found loving partners, had children, and were content with their lot in life. It wasn't that Mona was unhappy with the hand she was dealt. Some days, she just wished her path could've been a little easier. When she glanced up again, she realized Martha was staring.

"You don't think my son is going to marry you?" Martha asked softly; a frown of concern crossed her careworn face.

Mona had no answer, at least not one Martha would be happy to hear. Thankfully Lizzy interceded. "I got a text from Vince asking if you ate yet?" She already knew the answer to the question and inclined her head. "Come on, there's this amazing little bakery next door. Let's get you something before my brother has a cow."

Martha grinned from ear to ear as the group filed toward the restaurant. The smell of fresh baked bread and cookies mingled in the air. It wasn't until that moment Mona realized she was really hungry. Ordering herself a cup of tea, she also splurged on a piece of raspberry danish before settling down across from Martha.

Lizzy was all smiles. "I'm going to run ahead to the hair salon. I need to get these roots touched up anyway. Then I'll try to pick out a hairstyle for the wedding!"

"Have fun, honey. Mona and I will be along in a bit," Martha called. Waving the girls off, she ordered a cappuccino and a cinnamon roll for herself. Her posture was relaxed, her hazel eyes sparkling with mirth. A comforting aura exuded from her as she gratefully accepted her plate from the shopkeeper. Martha took a single bite before launching right back into their previous conversation without missing a beat. "You see? My son wants to make sure you're eating well and getting enough rest. He cares about you two." She folded her hands on the table. "Vince has always been my most difficult child. Rebellious, argumentative…" Martha chuckled again. "He also reminds me the most of his father. I know the boys don't believe me but Vernon was a hell raiser in his day."

Chuckling softly, Mona chewed thoughtfully. "Tell me about him," she pressed. "I mean, if it's not too painful."

Martha shook her head. "Talking about him keeps his memory alive. One thing I always promised was that I would never forget the man I first loved. Richard understands that better than anyone." She sighed softly. "I met Vernon at a sock hop arranged by our local church. He was a few years older and it was clear he didn't want to be anywhere near that silly dance." She paused, her hand threading around a locket at her throat. "I always said God had a hand in our meeting. I was running late because my friend ripped her stockings and we had to stop at the drugstore to get a new pair. He was sneaking out when we were walking in and we crashed into each other." A sly grin crossed her features. "It was the first time he held me in his arms and I knew I'd met the man I'd spend the rest of my life with."

A lump formed in Mona's throat as she listened to Martha talk about how much she loved Vernon. The older woman's fingertips continued to stroke the precious chain that hung close to her heart. "Vernon had this convertible and a leather jacket. He smoked cigarettes and he had this air about him. I thought he was so handsome." A smile tugged at the corners of Martha's lips. "My mother couldn't stand him, of course. She thought he'd get me in trouble and I'd end up in a convent somewhere. I might've if Vernon hadn't proposed when he did. We couldn't keep our hands off each other." Martha glanced up again. "I see a lot of myself in you, Mona. You're strong, smart, and brave. There are a lot of women in your position who might've made a different choice…"

"It never crossed my mind," Mona said firmly. "Not for a second. I want this baby so much." A protective hand curled around her waist.

Reaching out, Martha grasped Mona's chin. "That's how I know you're going to be an excellent mother and a fantastic wife." She narrowed her eyes. "I know things are different these days but I also know my son. He'll do right by you…just give him time."

Mona forced herself to smile through the pain. No amount of time was going to change the reality of the situation. Reno didn't want to be a father, especially to a baby that wasn't his. Sleeping with him—even though it was mind-blowing, toe-curling, passionate sex—was not going to change his mind. Why would it? They agreed it meant nothing…

Returning her focus to the danish on her plate, Mona finished up the last few bites and her mug of tea.

Martha seemed content now that they'd gotten everything out in the open. She ordered the rest of her cinnamon bun wrapped up and soon, the two women were headed to the salon to meet up with Lizzy and the girls. It was an 'all hands on deck' situation when they arrived. There were tons of bridal magazines and flyers to go through. Mona joined the fray, picking up a thick booklet of wedding hairstyles. Throwing herself into finding the perfect look was just the distraction she needed. She couldn't fret about her relationship with Reno any more this week. It was time to focus on something else for a change.

Chapter Seventeen

After Mona took off for the fitting, Reno putzed around the empty room. He ordered himself some breakfast and took a long hot shower before heading out for the day. Nerves simmered in his veins the whole drive.

Reno pulled into the driveway and sat there for a moment. Several times, he reached for the keys—part of him wanted to back out at top speed and not look back, the other knew it wasn't an option. The door to his childhood home swung open before he was even halfway out of the car.

Richard grinned broadly, opening up his arms and enveloping Reno in a bear hug as he came up the front steps. "Come on in. I just made coffee, can I pour you a cup?"

Reno eyeballed him skeptically. Usually it was Martha who made the coffee and it was strong enough to grow hair on his chest. Still, it seemed rude not to take what was offered. He inhaled the heady scent and took a hesitant sip; to his surprise, it was actually good. "Thanks, this is great."

The two men walked to the den in tandem. Reno exhaled as he sat down on the old leather couch; it was always his favorite spot as a kid. The overstuffed sofa was at least as old as he was and had been the one and only thing Richard brought with him when he moved into this house. Martha still told the story of how she tried to make him get rid of it. He promised to take her to Ireland if she let it stay and she happily accepted the deal. It took them several years to save up the money but he eventually made good on that promise. Come to think of it, Lizzy had been born roughly nine months after that trip…but that was neither here nor there.

"I'm so happy you stopped by. I was going to call but then I realized I didn't have your new number," Richard started. He crossed his legs at the ankle and leaned back in his armchair. Holding his coffee mug with a firm grasp, he took a long drink and blotted the excess liquid that clung to his mustache with a napkin. "Your mother says you go by Reno now?"

"That's what they call me at work." Reno rubbed his neck. "You can still call me Vincent. Mona's just used to calling me by my nickname." He cleared his throat, averting his eyes. There was a long beat of silence before Reno spoke again. "Richard, there are some things I've been thinking about. I'm just not sure where to start."

"You can talk to me about anything, son…" Richard pressed. "What's on your mind?"

There was a note of hurt in Richard's tone, but Reno wasn't certain where it was coming from. He stared down at his hands, tracing his knuckles out of habit. "Before I start, I just want to make sure what I tell you will be kept in confidence. You can't tell anyone…especially mom." Reno looked up. He expected Richard to balk but the older man just nodded and motioned for Reno to continue. "Mona and I aren't exactly a couple. I mean, we work together and spend most of our free time together…but I asked her to come on this trip because I didn't want anyone to know I'm a miserable failure at dating."

Dragging a hand over his face, Reno shook his head. "It was actually Lizzy who gave me the idea. Mona drove me home one night and they ended up talking. I guess she made quite the impression. Mona was supposed to come here as moral support. Plus, I knew she'd be a blast to have at the wedding." He was well aware he was rambling now, but he couldn't stop the words from tumbling out. "Mona is perfect. She's smart as a whip, sexy, and she keeps me in line. I trust her with my life."

Reno wrapped both hands around his coffee mug, absorbing the warmth from the cup. "Of course I'm attracted to her. You've seen her…but it's more than that. She's beautiful on the inside, too." Richard was still listening silently, giving Reno the strength he needed to continue. "She was dating this other guy until recently. It's never been romantic between Mona and I…until now." He scoffed. "Or maybe not even now. I screwed up, Richard. I told everyone in this family she's carrying my baby, and then when she stood in front of me all scared and vulnerable, I told her I didn't want it."

"Oh dear…" Richard shifted in his chair. "I can see why you didn't want your mother to know about this. She's already started knitting Mona and the baby Christmas stockings…"

Groaning in aggravation, Reno buried his face in his hands. "I'm weak, Richard. I want her to be in my life but I'm not sure I can be more than we are now. Then I slept with her knowing full well it was going to make things harder." He fidgeted. "I've been breaking her heart every single day since we left Carson City and I can't take another second of it."

Richard waited an appropriate amount of time to make sure Reno was done speaking. "This is clearly taking its toll on the both of you." He licked his lips, leaning slightly forward as he weighed in. "We all saw how concerned you were when she was in the hospital. I have to say, I was personally very moved by your devotion to her and the baby." Richard crossed his arms and gathered his thoughts. "I've known you a long time, Reno. You're not going to convince me you don't love that girl."

"That's not it." Reno shifted uncomfortably. "*Mona* I could live with." He cursed softly, "Maybe, I mean. She's a tough nut to crack. Half the time I have no idea what she's thinking! I think she'll be fine and she freaks out. Then other times I'm sure she's going to murder me in my sleep and she takes it in stride. I don't understand her!"

"And you never will. That's how women are, son." Richard grinned cheekily. "So, you're concerned the baby isn't yours." He quirked an eyebrow at him. "What does the father have to say?"

"He tucked tail and ran the minute he found out she was pregnant. She was with the guy five damn years and he just walked away. What kind of lowlife does that to a girl? And to Mona of all people!" Anger was starting to creep up in Reno's chest. "I never liked that squirrelly bastard and if he were here right now, I'd kick his ass." He clenched his fist in anger. "She deserves so much better."

Richard smiled softly. "It sounds like you've put a lot of thought into what Mona deserves." The expression that crossed Reno's face validated Richard's assertion. "But you've decided you don't want to be the one to give it to her…"

All the blood drained from Reno's face and pooled in his chest. "No, that's not it!" His throat felt tight with emotion. "I'm not sure I *can*." Closing his eyes, he forced himself to take deep breaths. "Look at me… I'm almost forty, I've never been in a committed relationship except with my high school sweetheart—who I just realized cares nothing about me. And to top it all off, Mona's baby is going to need a male role model in its life." He opened his watery eyes and stared hard at Richard. "The real reason I came over here was because I have to know for sure." Reno laced his fingers tightly. "No bullshit. No lies. No judgment. I just…I need to know this and you're the only person I can ask."

Reno braced himself for impact. "Do you really love us? My brothers and I…do you love us as much as you love Lizzy?" He choked on his emotion. "Can you really love somebody else's child as much as you love your own?"

Richard stood abruptly and moved to Reno's side. "I love you every bit as much." His tone was level and his blue eyes shimmered with tears. "I'm sure you were far too young to remember when we met for the first time.

I'd been dating your mother for six months and we decided it was time to meet the family. You were this squirmy little terror who couldn't sit still. We were eating dinner, you finished your meatloaf and you asked your mom for some more. She said you could if you finished your peas. You've always hated peas…so when your mom wasn't looking, you scooted over to my plate and helped yourself to my portion." Richard laughed at the memory. "I didn't know what to do, so I picked you up and sat you in my lap and we ate the rest of that meatloaf together."

Dabbing at his eyes, Richard cleared his throat. "After supper, your mom was cleaning up in the kitchen. You crawled over and sat right next to me on the old sofa and you asked me if I was going to stay for a movie. I realized in that moment, I wanted to stay forever." Tears were rolling down his cheeks now but he kept smiling. "I proposed to your mother that very night. I didn't want to be apart from any of you ever again." He shook his head. "Blood or no blood, you're my family." He paused to blow his nose in a checkered handkerchief. "You used to call me dad…"

"You *are* my dad." Reno's voice was thick with emotion. "I just thought you'd be more comfortable with me calling you Richard since I've been away so long." Clearly he'd been mistaken. "I guess I always thought you would get sick of playing father to kids that aren't yours…"

"You couldn't be more wrong." Richard reached out, hugging Reno tightly. "You're my son and that'll never change no matter how long it's been. I love you." He exhaled shakily. "Trust me, when that baby is born and you hold him or her in your arms for the first time, you'll love him too. It won't matter whose blood he shares. Not one little bit."

Resting his chin against Richard's shoulder, Reno let out a heavy breath. "Even if I *can* love the kid, I'm still not sure I can be a good dad. I'm irresponsible. I get drunk and make an ass out of myself. I treated Mona like crap the day of the brunch and she was really sick...I should've known she wasn't okay! She told me she wasn't feeling well *point blank* and I ignored her. A baby can't always tell me what it needs. I'm going to fail miserably..." He swallowed hard. "I'm not sure I have it in me to be the guy she deserves."

Gently pulling out of the hug, Richard let his hand linger on Reno's shoulder. "Every new father has these fears. What if you aren't good enough? What if you drop the baby on its head? What if you screw him up for life?" A comforting smile crossed his features. "The difference between a real man and a coward is fighting through. I made mistakes as a parent. I have made a great many, as a matter of fact. Although, to this day, I've never dropped any of you kids on your head." He chuckled appreciatively. "What you need to do is decide if you want to try. Nobody can make that decision but you."

Richard's words put everything into perspective for Reno. It certainly didn't make the decision any easier, but at least he had new clarity about it. The soft buzzing of his phone drew his attention away. Mona texted him that they were on their way back. With everything that had transpired, Reno was eager to see Mona again.

"The girls will be back soon. I should get back to the hotel." Reno stood up, brushing invisible crumbs off his jeans. "Thanks for everything."

"Don't mention it." Richard smiled knowingly. "Leave your new number on the pad by the telephone. I want to make sure I have it before you go. And if you need anything, you know you can call me any time, day or night."

Reno closed the distance between them again and wrapped Richard in a tight hug. "Thanks, dad." It felt like a huge weight had been lifted off Reno's shoulders as he got back in his car and headed for the hotel. On the way in the front door, he bumped into Mona being dropped off. With a quick wave to the girls, he wrapped his arm around Mona's waist as they headed back to the room. "Did you have fun today, pumpkin?"

"A little too much, if you ask me." Mona lay back on the bed, stifling a yawn as she stared up at the ceiling. "Before you ask, I am feeling perfectly fine. I'm just a little tired because I didn't get much sleep last night." She flashed him a playful mock-glare. "I had breakfast *and* lunch *and* I drank plenty of water today." She let out a soft huff, but there was no anger in her voice or her posture. "Thank God the wedding is only three days away because any longer and that poor seamstress would have to take the dress out *again*."

Reno snorted and sidled over to where she was lying. Settling himself next to her on the bed, he rested his arms behind his head. "I wouldn't worry about it. You're going to look gorgeous, no matter what kind of getup

Lizzy picked out for you." Silence hung between them for a moment before he cleared his throat. "I spent the afternoon with my dad." He cleared his throat. "Richard, my dad…not my *dad*."

Mona nodded. "I knew what you meant." She rolled halfway onto her side, turning to face him head on. "How was it?"

"It felt good to clear the air. I needed to talk to him. God, I didn't realize how much I missed my family until now." Reno sighed heavily. "Dad's sage advice, my mom's enthusiasm and her cooking, my baby sister's energy and charisma, and the support of my brothers. Ever since I moved to Carson City, I put the past behind me and I shut my family out in the process. It was wrong." Reaching out, he rested his warm palm on the curve of her hip, right below where her belly swelled out.

Warmth coursed through Mona and a lazy smile slid over her features. She watched Reno silently for a moment before he leaned in and kissed her. There was no hesitation at all as she wrapped herself around him. This time when they made love it was slow and sweet.

When they finally broke apart, Mona rolled onto her side and Reno curled at her back. Within moments, she was sleeping deeply and he joined in, unperturbed by the demons that haunted him. For the first time in as long as he could remember, Reno felt at peace.

Chapter Eighteen

The rest of the week was a blur. Mona and Reno were the epitome of happiness and serenity. By day the family adored them and by night, they tore up the sheets. They were content to live in the moment and not worry about the future or what was to come.

In the blink of an eye, the rehearsal dinner was over and the wedding was upon them. At four in the morning, Mona and Reno slogged out of bed, showered, and hit the road. Mona tried not to doze on the way up, but failed miserably. Reno hardly minded. He'd been running her ragged every night, it was no wonder she was so tired. The thought made him smile as he followed the GPS to their destination.

Mona perked up as they turned onto a pristinely kept cobblestone drive. She couldn't believe the venue Lizzy had picked. It was no wonder she decided to take the first available date because it was a real life fairytale castle nestled in the hills of Massachusetts. Lush, green grass was neatly trimmed around massive old oak trees that looked mysterious in the silvery morning fog. Once they moved through the thicket, Hayden Castle came into view.

The massive stone keep wasn't built in the medieval times of course, but it definitely had that old-world feel. The building itself was six or seven stories high and carefully paved with stone. Ivy climbed the walls, adding a warm feel to the place. To the right of the castle sat a crystal blue lake with a small beach. They'd even added a little drawbridge, which would be perfect for taking wedding photos. Reno pulled to the left where the massive parking lot was located. Seeing such a large, asphalt structure was a little jarring after being enveloped by the scenery around them. Thankfully, it returned quickly as they walked to the darling little church where the wedding would take place.

Lizzy was a jittery mess of nerves. Danielle hadn't arrived yet and Charlotte was extremely hungover from last night. Martha was clearly overwhelmed. The minute Mona stepped in the room, everyone heaved a collective sigh of relief. A soft smile crossed her features. She turned to Reno, sliding her hands up his chest. "Will you do me a favor?" she asked softly.

"Anything." Reno's reply was automatic. "What do you need?"

"Coffee…and make Lizzy's a decaf." Mona grinned broadly. "Maybe pick up some bagels and fruit or something? The ceremony isn't until noon and we're going to be hungry." Mona meant her and the girls but it was clear from Reno's expression he was thinking about the baby.

"Of course." Reno leaned in, kissing her sweetly on her lips. "I can't believe I didn't think of it earlier. Probably because any earlier and it'd still be yesterday…" He exhaled sharply. "You girls need anything else?" Everyone was shaking their heads and he traipsed back to the car. Honestly, Reno was happy to have something to do. Mona could've grabbed a ride from his mom so he could catch a few more hours of sleep, but he wanted to be with her, even if it meant being at the church disgustingly early.

With Reno occupied, Mona turned to the bride to be. Lizzy was yammering like a madwoman again and she stepped over, resting her hands on the girl's thin shoulders. "Honey," Mona narrowed her eyes. "Everything is going to be fine." She brushed away a wayward strand of Lizzy's blonde hair and smiled comfortingly. "You are going to be a beautiful bride." Lizzy threw her arms around Mona and for the first time since she got up this morning, she relaxed.

When Reno got back with the food, the hairdresser and makeup artists were setting up shop. Mona was sitting on a chair beside Martha, chuckling softly at something they were talking about. As he snuck in the door, he was suddenly confronted by his baby sister in a snit.

"Don't you know it's bad luck to see the bridesmaid before the wedding?" she accused.

"I think that only applies to the bride, squirt." Reno smirked at her. He tried to peer around her to get a glimpse of the dress hidden beneath the fluffy white robe but Lizzy poked him square in the chest, putting on her best menacing face.

Lizzy scoffed and grabbed the bagels out of his hand. "Beat it!"

Well, so much for spending time with Mona. It appeared he was banned from seeing her before the ceremony, and it made him feel oddly nervous. He walked along the halls, pausing in front of the room on the other side of the church where Ray was sitting. His eyes were closed in a silent prayer.

Reno hadn't been a good Catholic in a long time. He didn't even go to mass on the high holy days anymore. Christmas and Easter tended to be big days for lonely strip club frequenters. Reno didn't mind working because he didn't have a family to entertain or to spend time with. Besides, he was a sinner at heart; God had probably written him off long ago. It wasn't until Mona ended up in the hospital that Reno found himself aching for mercy. He prayed for the first time in years and, surprisingly, those prayers had been answered.

Silently, Reno padded over and slid into the pew next to Ray. On bended knee, he prayed Lizzy and Ray would be happy in their marriage, his parents would be happy and his father's soul was peaceful in heaven. Finally, he thanked God for Mona and the baby being healthy and a part of his life.

When Reno had wrapped Mona in his arms this morning, he was filled with such adoration for her. Her cheeks were rosy and she glowed with happiness; she was the picture of health. After seeing her so weak and sallow during her hospital stay, he really feared he was going to lose her. Reno was lucky but more than that, he was blessed. Ray's gentle movement broke Reno out of his reverie. "I hope you don't mind I joined in. I just—"

"Not at all," Ray interrupted. "I'm glad you're here." Gazing up at the crucifix hanging on the wall, he grinned. "I thought I'd be nervous. Everyone I talked to, even my dad, said it was normal to be apprehensive. But that's not how I feel. I'm excited. I love Lizzy and I'm going to spend the rest of my life making her happy." He leaned back in his seat. "I just had to take a minute and say thanks."

"I know how you feel." Reno shifted gears slightly, staring down at his hands. "I'm sorry I gave you a hard time before. I love Lizzy and I want what's best for her." It wouldn't have been Reno's first choice but Ray went in for the hug and he patted the boy gently on the back "Don't get me wrong, if you hurt her I will hunt you down…but my gut tells me that's not going to happen."

Ray didn't intend on hurting Lizzy either, so there no was conflict of interest. Lionel popped in a moment later with coffee and doughnuts. Frederick had the tuxes all pressed and ready to go. Nips of whiskey were passed around to be added to coffee and it was a pleasant morning for all.

Breakfast and beautification were finished by ten o'clock. Lizzy's hair had taken the most time. It was a modern take on a 1930s classic hairstyle, with a dramatic part and soft, bouncy curls that framed her face. Mona and the other bridesmaids had their hair coiffed into a soft bun and several pieces had been curled and hung down beneath it. Mona was glad Lizzy had chosen this style since it kept her hair off her neck. Despite the chill in the air outside, it was warm in the church—or perhaps it was just her nerves.

Initially, Mona thought calling them all in at five in the morning was a little excessive, but time was flying.

Norah had her sewing kit at the ready, fixing a small tear in Martha's mother of the bride dress that had occurred when she caught the hem on her heel.

Mona was a little anxious about the fit of her dress, personally. She held her breath as she slid the fabric over her head. Turning her back, Martha helped Mona with the zipper. Much to her relief, the dress went on without issue and she didn't even have to suck it in. She twirled once in the mirror before grinning broadly. Mona couldn't wait for Reno to see her. He wouldn't be able to keep his hands off her tonight.

Shortly after the girls were dressed, the florist arrived with the bouquets. Mona was in awe of the beautiful simplicity. For the bridesmaids, there were three long stem roses surrounded by baby's breath; they were wrapped in royal purple that perfectly matched their dresses. Lizzy's dozen white roses were accented by with two gorgeous white lilies, all wrapped in cream satin.

Half an hour before the ceremony was set to begin, Father Flanagan rapped sharply on the door. He had to be in his late eighties and walked with a pronounced limp. Despite his advanced age, he had a full, curly head of white hair and a well manicured white beard. With horn-rimmed glasses sitting at the edge of his nose and a twinkle in his blue eyes, he put Mona immediately at ease. With his bible in hand, he grinned. "I have enjoyed the time we've spent in Pre-Cana. I know Raymond will make an excellent husband. I'd like to offer individual prayers as you embark on your lives as separate but unified souls. May your faith carry you through many happy years together."

Mona bowed her head as Father Flanagan prayed. She wasn't used to religion herself but the man's words seemed to bring Lizzy comfort. Martha crossed herself, holding tightly to a rosary that she kept gripped in her hand. Mona simply observed. She'd committed a myriad of sins in her life. Even a just and righteous God couldn't possibly forgive all she'd done…

Music reached their ears shortly thereafter. A harpist and an organist had taken their places the hall, welcoming guests with gentle melodies as they entered the church. It wasn't long before Lizzy was settling the veil over her face. Ray was already at the front of the church, his face in danger of cracking with how wide he was smiling.

When the familiar chords of Pachelbel's Canon began, everyone turned to stare. Lana played her role as flower girl perfectly, tossing flowers as she went before running to sit with her father. Charlotte and Lionel processed in next, followed by Danielle and Frederick. George took Mona's arm gently; he remained stoic as they walked down the aisle together. A blush crept over her cheeks as she caught sight of Reno sitting at the edge of the third pew. He remained focused on her even when the wedding march began and Lizzy processed up the aisle on Richard's arm.

Mona had never been to a Catholic mass before and the rehearsal hadn't made it seem this involved. There was more sitting, standing, kneeling, and organized prayers than she knew what to do with. Even with the missal in hand, she had a hard time keeping up. Every once in a while, she looked at Reno and he would comfort her with a wink and a grin. They were sitting through the homily when Father Flanagan hit his stride. It baffled Mona how well an elderly man who'd never been married summed up love and commitment so perfectly.

Finally, it came time for the vows and there wasn't a dry eye in the house as Ray and Lizzy pledged their lives to one another. An hour later, they had finally finished all the rites, blessings, and the good Catholics took communion. It didn't escape her notice that Reno chose to abstain. It seemed she wasn't the only one feeling like she was too tarnished by sin to be accepted here. Even so, it was a beautiful ceremony enjoyed by all.

When Father Flanagan finally told them the mass was ended and to go in peace, Lizzy cheered and threw herself into Ray's embrace. Laughter rippled through the crowd as they eagerly kissed. He swept her into his arms, holding her tight as he carried her down the aisle. The organ and harpist played on as they processed out of the church.

George played his part well, but as soon as Reno was at Mona's side, it was his arms wrapped around her waist. "You look beautiful," he whispered into her ear. Mona smiled, kissing him gently on the cheek. They remained entwined until she was called away to take photos with the wedding party. Reno went with them, simply because he didn't want her to be out of his sight for a moment longer than was necessary. By the time the photographer was done, Mona was looking forward to the reception.

Reno made Mona sit with her feet elevated while he fetched her a plate of appetizers and a bottle of water. The wedding party was at a table up at the front of the banquet hall, but Lizzy made sure Reno had a place next to Mona. She must have realized how inseparable they were…or perhaps she knew Mona might feel overwhelmed by the massive amount of family members cooing over her.

The O'Keefes were out in force. Great Aunts Millie and Sophie were tearing it up on the dance floor. All the aunts, uncles, cousins, and their loved ones they'd grown up with were all here. Ray's family, though not as tight knit, were there. The friends who Ray had grown up with and come to love like his own were in attendance. Everyone who mattered in their lives had attended the wedding and the love was palpable in the room.

Ray and Lizzy snuggled together, kissing and laughing with one another. Toasts were given, including a particularly moving one from Richard about what it took to sustain a marriage. Mona couldn't help but lean against Reno, absorbing his strength and taking comfort in his presence.

Dinner was served at seven. Mona had selected the chicken and Reno had selected the filet mignon; she ended up eating most of his meal and he was all too happy to let her. Every once in a while, the family would begin clinking their forks against their glasses and Lizzy and Ray leaned in to kiss. Reno found himself following suit, moved by the sweetness of the day. It may all have started as a charade to fool his family, but Reno knew his feelings for Mona had changed.

When the music kicked up again, Mona grabbed Reno by the arm. "Dance with me," she begged.

"Mona," Reno groaned…but he got up anyway. He was a terrible dancer but he wanted to make her happy. She was an animal, moving with the beat of the music as it flowed through her. Mona danced with him, his brothers, Lizzy and the bridesmaids, his great aunts, and strangers passing by. When a slow song came on, she happily accepted Richard's invitation to dance. Reno cut in halfway through, holding her close as they swayed.

"I wish this night would never end," Mona whispered against his ear. "I'm having such a good time." Reno just smiled and rubbed her back.

Tomorrow afternoon they'd be getting back on a plane for Carson City. Reno found himself wondering if anything would change. He and Mona were closer now, of course. He knew her as more than a coworker and certainly he couldn't put that aside. Then again, Reno still wasn't sure he had it in him to be what Mona needed. There were so many questions, he couldn't even begin to formulate an answer. The only thing he could do was close his eyes and sway to the music, hoping the moment would last forever.

At the end of the night, cake was served. Guests began to leave after that. Mona and Reno stayed until the DJ played the last song. It was well after midnight when they finally walked out to the car, with Mona's in her hand. When they got back to the hotel, Reno shepherded her upstairs. They had to keep prodding each other to stay awake while getting ready for bed. Finally, they both dropped onto the mattress and were asleep within seconds. Reno curled his arms around her, holding her and the baby tightly. Tonight, they were perfectly, wonderfully, blissfully happy.

There was no telling what tomorrow would bring.

Chapter Nineteen

It was bittersweet saying goodbye to the family on Sunday morning. Tears were shed, numbers were exchanged, and promises to keep in touch were made. Reno and Mona boarded the plane with heavy hearts and suitcases.

Mona slept most of the way home, much to Reno's relief. He wasn't ready to talk about what they meant to one another. It was coming, of course; eventually they'd have to define their relationship. Unfortunately, Reno still wasn't sure what he wanted to do. Even after an eight hour flight with nothing to do but think, he hadn't made a decision about their future.

After collecting their luggage and hiking out to the long-term parking lot, Mona and Reno left the airport at three in the morning. She settled beside him, bleary eyed and stiff from traveling. Not a single word was exchanged, even as he pulled up to her condo and carried her things upstairs. There was a moment Mona felt like Reno was going to lean in and kiss her, as he'd done many times over the course of their trip. Instead, he turned and slipped away. Wrapping her arms tightly around her waist, Mona headed for the bedroom and tried to ignore the hurt gnawing in her chest.

Reno didn't have it in him to say goodbye. Mona looked so soft as she stood in the hazy light of her living room; he wanted to sleep in her arms again, but better judgment prevailed. Or at least, that's what he told himself when he trudged into his cluttered studio apartment and plopped face first onto the mattress.

Even though Reno was wrecked, sleep didn't come easily. He missed Mona's soft breathing and warm body snuggled against him. He missed the floral fragrance of her shampoo and the clean scent of her skin. God, he even missed her elbowing him in the ribs and accusing him of snoring.

Eventually, Reno must've passed out because he awoke to the blaring of his alarm. Mumbling obscenities, he slogged out of bed, showered, shaved, and headed to the club. Despite all the uncertainty in his life right now, Reno felt a sense of peace wash over him as the Watering Hole came into view. It was good to be home. This was where he belonged...

As he stepped through the front door, Reno was greeted by cheers...or maybe those were for Mona. She walked in right behind him and all the girls rushed to give her hugs and inquire about the trip. Even in the black slacks and tank top she wore, her pregnancy was far more pronounced than it had been when they left. He was pretty sure his ears were going to be ringing for a week after Liberty found out about the baby. Reno glanced back at them, catching Mona's eye for just a moment before he headed upstairs.

Mona remained busy downstairs for as long as possible before she was forced to go to the office. She knocked on the wooden paneling of the doorjamb to get Reno's attention. He was sitting in his chair with his head in his hands... "I hope I'm not interrupting?"

Scrambling to sit up, Reno tried to make it look like he wasn't brooding. "No, I was just getting caught up on some stuff." He cleared his throat. "Is there something you need?"

"I just need to use the computer for a bit. We need to renew our liquor license by the end of the month and the taxes are due the fifteenth, so I want to make sure we have everything in order…" Mona stepped forward but Reno didn't move. She shifted uncomfortably. "You mind?"

"Oh! Not at all." Reno hurriedly stood up from his chair, motioning for her to take it. "Take your time. I'm going to run down to the kitchen and take stock." He was halfway to the door when he heard Mona curse under her breath. Shoulders tightening, he turned to face her again. "Are you okay?"

Mona leaned over the desk, her palms resting flat on the glass top. "*I'm* fine, Reno. *You*, on the other hand, are acting weird." She narrowed her eyes. "I can only assume this is because you don't know how to remind me about the conversation we had in Boston. The trip was fun, I will cherish the memories but I didn't forget I mean nothing to you." Reno's mouth dropped open but Mona held up her hand to silence him. "I don't need excuses. I just want everything to go back to normal."

If a wind happened to blow through the room at this very moment, Reno would've tumbled over. How could she think she meant nothing to him? "*Mona*…" She turned toward him but he couldn't find the right words to say.

Mona pasted on a smile that didn't quite reach her

eyes. "Didn't you have some inventory to do?"

If Reno were a better man, he would've told her right then that he'd fallen for her a long time ago. Instead, he tucked tail and ran. When he got back downstairs, he found Otis looking quite disgruntled. "What's wrong?" It didn't matter what it was. Any distraction was welcome at this point. He needed to keep his mind off Mona.

"That guy is back," Otis scowled. He inclined his head. "The suit that just walked in? He's been here every day demanding to talk to Mona. I don't like the look of him. He's squirrelly and he's been a real dick to the girls."

"I'll take care of it."

The man in question was indeed an odd looking fellow. He was leering at Liberty while she danced, his teeth a little too white and his hair plugs not quite realistic enough. Reno folded his arms over his chest, muscles bulging against the fabric of his t-shirt as he did so. "Excuse me. Can I help you with something?"

Snapping to attention, the man shuffled an envelope in his hand. "I'm Eric Sylvester. I'm looking for Ms. Mona Gallo. I was told this is her current place of employment." His Southern accent was thick enough to cut with a knife.

"What's this regarding?" Reno demanded. The man opened his mouth but was swiftly cut off by a very agitated Reno. "No, you know what? I know what this is about. Kyle Andreas can go to hell for all I care. Stay the hell away from Mona and the baby."

A confused look crossed the man's face. "I'm sorry, I'm not sure who that is…" He gripped his briefcase tighter. "This is a sensitive matter that I'd prefer to discuss with Ms. Gallo in person. Is she here or not?"

Reno hesitated but eventually decided Mona deserved the opportunity to handle this herself. He inclined his head. "She's upstairs." The man seemed pleased and nipped at Reno's heels as the two of them traipsed up the staircase.

Mona was printing out the schedule for next week when she heard footsteps. She furrowed her eyebrows as Reno appeared with a man in a fancy suit. "We ain't due for a health inspection for another year," she huffed indignantly. "Did Smith complain again?"

"Eric Sylvester," the man corrected. He stepped forward, extending a hand to her. "I'm not the health inspector. I'm a lawyer. I wanted to track you down regarding your father's estate…"

Mona's throat went dry. "What do you mean his estate?" She furrowed her eyebrows, inching toward the chair and settling herself down in it. "Are you telling me my father is dead?"

Reno froze, staring hard at the man who had stopped rifling through a mess of papers to glance up at her. "Ms. Gallo, your father died twelve years ago. I was under the impression you were aware." He swallowed hard. "I'm sorry…"

"How did it happen?" Mona blurted. "The last I knew, my daddy was serving a sentence at county for drug possession. That's what my mama always said." Her heart was pounding, the blood staining her cheeks. She simultaneously wished Reno had left the room and prayed he'd hold her in his arms. Thankfully, he did neither.

Eric hesitated. "Your father wasn't at county. He began serving a life sentence at Angola for triple homicide and home invasion in 1989." Since he had to be the bearer of bad news, Eric launched into the next part of what he needed to discuss without waiting for her to digest the news. "Six years into his sentence, he started complaining of headaches and pain. They treated him with basic pain medication and it improved. Then eight years ago, he had a seizure and the MRI revealed he had very advanced brain cancer. He died very shortly thereafter and his assets went to probate. A final decision was finally rendered in the case this year and I felt it was my duty to bring you the remainder of his personal effects."

Mona barely remembered her father…he had dark hair, was always unkempt, and he smelled like chew and booze. The only thing they had in common were the vibrant green eyes that stared back at her as she peered down at the glass desktop. "I…I don't know what to say." She swallowed hard. "Can I have them?"

"Sure, I just need to follow protocol…" he cleared his throat. "Can you provide proof that you are indeed Mona Renee Gallo, born March 15, 1982?" Mona nodded and he flashed her a comforting smile. "Can you tell me who your parents are?"

"Darla Gallo and William Pickett…" Mona shrugged. "My dad wasn't around much when I was a kid so I don't know anything personal about him." Why was she telling the lawyer all this? He didn't care. And Reno was still standing there with that stricken look on his face. It was all so overwhelming.

"You lived on Topsy Bel Road?"

Mona shrugged. "That's where the trailer park was but I didn't live there for very long. They repoed it when my mama died." She licked her lips. "With all due respect, you really travelled two thousand miles unsure that I was the Mona Gallo you're looking for?" She exhaled sharply. "Let's just cut the bullshit and get on with this…"

Eric nodded slowly. He pulled out a manila envelope and slid it across the table to her. "Enclosed are the items your father had on his person when he turned himself in to the police and the items collected from his cell after his death. His monetary assets, while small, were seized by the state upon his death to cover burial expenses. Everything else belongs to you." He stood up and reached into the lapel of his coat pocket. "Take some time and go through it all. Here's my card. I'll be in town through the end of the week if you need to get a hold of me regarding the estate." A soft smile crossed his face. "Or you may see me around…this is quite a club you have."

Reno stepped up, making it clear it was time for Eric to

leave. "Thanks. We'll be in touch if we need you." He walked the man to the stairs and made sure he was out of the club before turning back to Mona. "Are you alright?" he probed softly.

Mona glanced up at him. "I think so. I should probably feel sad but I don't…" she admitted. "I barely knew my dad. He was good to my mom and me when he was around." She found herself shrugging again; she'd been doing that a lot lately. "We were practically strangers." She tugged open the corner of the envelope and then ran her finger along it to loosen the adhesive. Once she could see the contents inside, she started looking for any excuse not to go through it. "I shouldn't be doing this at work. I've been away and there's so much to catch up on…"

Reno must've sensed her fear; this time, he moved to her side. "You can do this, pumpkin. I'm here for you."

Exhaling sharply, Mona dumped the contents onto the table. The first thing that plopped out was a half-used tin of snuff, which she promptly tossed into the trash. It smelled awful and turned her stomach. Next, she found a beat up leather wallet, stained with nicotine and ripped in several spots. Mona thumbed through it, pausing to look at her dad's license. He looked high in the picture; she had no doubt he had been. In another pocket was a business card for a local machine shop, a crinkled up receipt for the chewing tobacco she'd just tossed, and eleven dollars. Mona was about to toss the wallet aside when she noticed another compartment. She opened it, pulling out a faded picture. Her heart ached at the sight.

"Is that your mom?" Reno asked softly.

Nodding jerkily, Mona's fingers traced the edges of the worn photo. "When the bank came and repoed the trailer, they took everything. Clothes, knickknacks, all that stuff…I haven't seen a picture of her in fifteen years." Emotion was starting to build behind her eyes. Even if they found nothing else in the envelope, that one picture was priceless. Darla Gallo couldn't have been more than sixteen when the photo had been taken. Her dark hair curled gently over her shoulders and she was smiling shyly. It was a simpler time in the young woman's life. Darla didn't have a baby she never wanted or a drug habit she couldn't kick. She was young, carefree, and beautiful.

Mona took a moment to compose herself before digging through the rest of the items. There was a watch with a frayed Velcro strap that had stopped working a long time ago. The rest of the items had clearly come from William Pickett's prison cell. A pocket-sized notebook was nestled between drawings of people Mona didn't recognize. As she shuffled through them, a small key clinked on the desk; she picked it up, turning it over. It looked like it belonged to a safety deposit box and the document on the top of the pile confirmed it. The government hadn't seized the contents of whatever was inside, which made Mona curious as to what her father had been keeping there…

Palming the frayed notebook, Mona cautiously slid open the cover. It was filled with more sketches of strangers. They meant nothing to her until she found one of a tiny, cowering girl. Dark stringy hair hung down past the child's waist and her arms were wrapped around her knees. Mona had spent most of her childhood in that very position, terrified and small.

Slamming the book shut, Mona threw it aside. "I'm going to have to shower after touching all this stuff. It smells like a prison." It was a defense mechanism. She had to be hard or she'd surely fall apart again. The last few loose papers were William Pickett's death certificate and detailed explanation of where the remains had been buried in the potter's field at Angola. There was correspondence of how they tried to contact the family but were unable to reach her. By that point, Darla Gallo had been dead for a while.

"That's the last of it," Mona announced. There was relief in that. Pushing herself up from the desk, she cleared her throat. "Most of it's junk." She brushed a strand of dark hair behind her ear. "I want you to throw all of it out."

Reno raised an eyebrow at her. "Are you sure?" He picked up the picture of her mom again. "Even this?"

Mona stormed over, swiping it from his hand and sliding into her pocket. "Everything else," she demanded. "Burn it, for all I care." Anger was starting to replace the hurt in her heart. Her father hadn't cared about her one iota. If he had, he'd have protected her from everyone and everything that tried to hurt her.

"What about the safety deposit box?" Reno pressed. "There could be something in there worth having, right?"

"Do what you want!" Mona hollered, her grief spilling over into ire. "I don't give a shit! I'm not going to mourn for some murderer who got what he deserved!" Dragging in a shaky breath, she stalked to the door. She needed to get out of here and avoid Reno's concerned glances for the rest of the night. "I'm going to be late tomorrow. I have an appointment with Dr. Harris."

The room spun as Reno choked on his fear. "Are you okay? Is something wrong with the baby?"

Mona tensed. "The doctors at Brigham and Women's told me to follow up with my doctor when I got back into town. I called Dr. Harris and she wanted to see me tomorrow. The only appointment they had was at four." She licked her lips. "I don't think it'll take more than an hour. I'll come in an hour earlier the day after."

"That's not necessary. Your health comes first and—"

"I don't want special treatment!" Mona was in no mood to be coddled right now. She was keyed up, angry, sad, and hurt. It was a terrible combination. "I'm not going to screw around and shirk my responsibilities. With the baby coming, I can't afford to lose my only source of income."

Reno stared incredulously at her. "Jesus Christ, Mona. I'm not going to fire you because you have a doctor's appointment!" He took a step toward her. "And we will work things out when the baby comes. You can bring the kid here or…I can look into getting a person onsite. I know that'd make Liberty happy."

Mona's heart sank into her stomach. She glanced back at the desk, looking at that notebook with the little girl frightened of her own shadow. She thought back to the nights she'd spent crawling around on bar room floors. "I can't…" She choked out. "I can't do this."

"Can't do what?"

"I'm not letting my kid grow up like I did." Mona watched the horror cross his face and she turned away.

Panic seared through Reno's chest. "Mona, no! We need you." *He* needed her. "We can work this out. There has to be something I can do!"

"There isn't," Mona replied coldly. "I have to go." She turned on her heel, hurrying down the stairs. She drove home in silence, her knuckles white from gripping the steering wheel. Reno was calling her the entire way. As soon as she got in the front door, she turned the phone off and tossed it into her purse. Mona was at her worst tonight and she wasn't going to drag him down with her. For now, she needed to be alone with her emotions.

Reno cursed bitterly, hurling his cellphone across the room in anger. He couldn't let Mona quit. He ached to chase her but he knew if he pushed her too hard, he'd lose her forever. She needed to cool down…and so did he.

Tonight was a wakeup call. Reno started imagining the

club without her…which meant he had to start imagining what his life would be like without her. Suddenly, all the fears and doubts Reno had about being a father and a husband were inconsequential in comparison the terror of never seeing Mona again. He was nothing without her…

It was in that moment Reno accepted the thing that he'd been fighting for five long years: he was in love with Mona Gallo. She was the only woman who'd ever embraced him for who he was and stuck by him in spite of it. She was the only person in his life he trusted without question. She was the only one he could ever see himself settling down with and starting a family. Reno needed to make this right and there was only one way he knew how.

Love was finally conquering fear.

Chapter Twenty

Mona had a very rough night.

Her sleep cycle was all screwed up from traveling. There was also the crushing insecurity of realizing her child was going to grow up just like she did and her all her greatest fears were realized. Plus the fact she'd effectively quit her job last night…it created a vicious combination that left Mona feeling frightened and weak.

When she was finally able to drag herself out of bed, she showered and then started searching for openings in the area. Very quickly, she grew frustrated. Everyone seemed to want a bachelors degree for menial jobs; Mona didn't even have a high school diploma. How the hell was she supposed to support herself and a kid with no income?

Finally Mona came across a cashier position at a family run supermarket down the street. No degree was required and it paid decent enough. She'd have to tighten her belt but she was no stranger to frugality…

Mona decided to swing by the grocery store before her doctor's appointment. The owner offered her an interview on the spot but when she got into the manager's office, he kept trying to look down her top and hinted several times she needed to use all her 'skills' to get a job here. It wasn't her first time being sexually harassed by a morbidly obese redneck with a bad mustache but her threshold for bullshit was frighteningly low. Halfway through a long-winded speech about 'making sure the boss was happy', Mona stood up and walked out. Not only would she never work here, but she was never, ever going to shop here again. Stomping out to the car, she slid in the driver's seat and headed to the doctor's office.

"The last patient just cancelled her appointment. The doctor can see you now." The receptionist beamed when Mona walked in.

Well, at least that was one thing going her way. Mona got on the scale, ignoring the nurse as she kept ticking that agitating little bar in the upward direction. It was normal, she reminded herself. There was a whole new person inside of her that accounted for the weight...then again, some of it was likely chocolate.

Dr. Harris hurried in with Mona's chart clutched in her hand. "You gave me quite a scare last week. The Brigham faxed me a copy of your chart with blood tests and the ultrasound." Dr. Harris folded her hands. "Everything looks good but I'd like to do repeat blood work this week, just in case." She glanced at the data the nurse scribbled onto the file. "Your blood pressure is a little high." She grabbed the blood pressure cuff. "I'd just like to check it again to make sure. These things can be a fluke." She wrapped the cuff around Mona's arm and inflated it, resting the stethoscope against her skin. Slowly, she let the air out until it was all gone. "Still a little bit elevated, although better than before." The doctor made a quick note.

"Is there something I can do about it?" Mona asked, taking a deep breath to calm her nerves. Getting worked up couldn't be good for her blood pressure or the baby.

"I'm going to recommend you see me every two weeks for a while so I can keep a close eye on you. I also want you to watch the salt in your diet." Reaching into her desk, Dr. Harris pulled out a pamphlet. "Put your feet up periodically during the day and drink plenty of water. I'd also recommend walking or gentle yoga, it's important to get regular exercise." She patted Mona's shoulder comfortingly. "I'm not anticipating any problems with your pregnancy. You're a healthy woman, you're active, and you keep up with your appointments. I'd just rather be safe than sorry." There was a pause before Dr. Harris spoke again. "Mona, may I ask you something?"

Looking up from the educational materials the doctor gave her, Mona nodded nervously. This couldn't be good.

"You made mention of the fact that the father of your child doesn't want to be involved. However, when I received the materials from the Brigham, there's documentation about a Vincent O'Keefe who was present for your entire hospital stay…"

Mona shifted in her chair. "It's complicated." She stared down at her belly. "He's the guy I went to the wedding with. He's my boss…*former* boss…"

Dr. Harris furrowed her eyebrows. "Did he fire you?

"Not exactly. I kind of quit yesterday…" Mona wrapped her arms around herself. "It was stupid. I *need* to work. I need the health insurance…but I can't raise a baby at a strip club." She licked her lips. "You probably think I'm crazy."

"Not at all," the doctor soothed. "You obviously have a lot going on in your life right now. It's okay to feel overwhelmed." Dr. Harris folded her hands. "Pregnancy is a tumultuous time as it is and making big life decisions can be difficult." Reaching into her bag, she pulled out a card and scribbled a number onto it. "This is my cell phone. If you need anything, day or night, just call me. My advice is to talk to your boss. He clearly cares enough to stay with you at the hospital. Maybe the two of you can work something out."

Grasping the business card, Mona nodded. "Thanks. This means a lot to me." Her head was still swimming when she headed out of the office and nearly crashed into a man barreling in the front door. It took her a second to realize it was Reno. "What are you doing here?" Mona demanded.

Reno had showered and donned a pair of black pants and a crisp white button-down shirt. For good measure, he'd also put on just a dab of the aftershave she liked. He wanted to look his best for her. Much of the last half hour had been psyching himself up to walk in and sit down next to her while they waited for her to be called back. He was going to tell her he wanted to give things a try…but now he was disoriented and concerned he'd had the time all wrong. "Isn't your appointment at four?" he sputtered.

"They were able to see me early—" Mona shook her head forcefully. "What the hell are you doing at my

OBGYN office?"

"I wanted to be here." Reno licked his lips. "I've been thinking a lot about everything and…" His voice died in his throat. "Shit, this is harder than I thought it was going to be." He took a step forward. "Mona—"

"I've got to go. I can't be late to work." Mona interrupted. She was getting frustrated with his inability to form a complete sentence.

"I think the boss will understand," Reno teased, jogging to keep up with her. "Let me give you a ride and we can talk on the way."

Mona brushed past him. "I don't want to leave my car here. They might tow it." Digging in her purse for the keys, she glanced at him out of the corner of her eye and hurt crawled into her chest. "Reno, I appreciate you wanting to support me but I think it'd be better if we stayed out of each other's way."

"I don't *want* to be out of your way." Reno huffed. "I want to give this a try."

"Give what a try?" Mona opened her door, half-facing him as leaned against the frame of the car.

"This. *Us.*" Reno dug his hands into his pockets. "The last couple weeks with you have been some of the happiest in my life. I like myself when I'm with you, Mona. I want to see where this goes."

The more Mona thought about it, the more convinced

she was that Reno was only trying to win her back to the club. "Look, I won't leave my job. I'll figure out the logistics of it all and we'll come up with something." She paused, staring down at her feet. "You don't have to do all this just to get me to stay. I made a rash decision, which my doctor has advised me against doing in the future…"

Reno was glad to hear she wasn't quitting but that wasn't the point he was making. "I'm not doing anything I don't want to, Mona. I've been thinking a lot about you and me. Believe me, I was freaked out about the kid but…I had a really great conversation with my dad. Richard, my dad—"

"Reno, I know! You don't have to clarify that every time!" Mona was becoming exasperated. "Where are you going with this?"

God, she was infuriating sometimes. Reno was trying to open his heart and pour out his soul and she wouldn't let him get a word in edgewise! "I want to date you!" he blurted. "I have feelings for you, Mona. Would you at least consider giving you and me a try?" Mona blinked at him, her eyes wide and she didn't say a word. Reno waited…and waited…then waited some more. Finally, he sighed. "Say something. I'm dying over here!"

Mona snapped out of her momentary daze. "Sorry," she muttered. Wrapping her arms around her waist, she exhaled sharply. "We're a package deal, Reno. Me and the baby…" Still, she couldn't deny this was what she deeply wanted but was too afraid to hope for. "Can I think about it?"

"Do you want to think about it over dinner?"

Despite the tension of the moment, Mona genuinely laughed. "You don't give up, do you?"

"Not when it's this important," Reno pressed. "It's just dinner. What's the worst that can happen? You're already pregnant."

Mona elbowed him playfully. She felt lighter now; the laughter was doing wonders for her mood. "Okay. When?"

Reno narrowly avoided pumping his fist in triumph. "I'm going to do this the right way." He grinned. "Which means I'm going to ask you for your number."

"You already have my number." Mona thought he was joking but he kept waiting in earnest. Reaching into her bag, she dug around for a receipt and scribbled her cell phone number onto it. He slipped into his pocket, a giddy grin tugged at the corners of his lips. "You are so weird." Mona glanced at the angry red numbers on a sign across the street that told her time was running out. "I'm sorry to cut this short but I really need to get to work. My boss is a real dick sometimes."

"I hear you there. It was so nice to meet you, Mona. I'll call you." Grasping her hand, he bent and pressed a kiss to her knuckles. She rolled her eyes but Reno could tell she was hiding a smile. That's all he wanted. He'd seen her cry, put on a brave face, and frown. Now, he wanted her laughter, smiles, and love.

As soon as he got back to his car, Reno picked up his phone and pressed the number one on his speed dial. He watched Mona in his rearview mirror as she fumbled in her purse and brought the phone to her ear.

"Hello?"

"Mona, it's Reno…"

"I can still *see* you," Mona snorted.

"Well, that's a little creepy," he teased. "I was wondering if you'd like to go to dinner with me on Friday? A little birdie told me you have the night off."

A blush crept over Mona's cheeks as she turned to peer at him. "And memorizing my work schedule isn't creepy?" She ribbed him right back. "I don't have any plans so…sure."

Reno felt like he was walking on sunshine. "Great. I'll pick you up at six. I'm looking forward to it." With the date settled, he waited to make sure Mona got out of the parking lot okay before following her down to the club.

So much had to be done now that Mona and Reno were back, there was no time for awkwardness tonight. He ordered a ton of stuff for the kitchen, she fired Valentina for missing an excessive amount of work and forcing the other girls to cover her ass, and a very rowdy bachelor party was in full swing. By the end of the night, everyone was exhausted. Reno made Mona leave right at two, but he stayed until almost five in the morning cleaning and making sure they were ready for the weekend crowd. Even though he was exhausted, Reno couldn't stop smiling as he closed up shop for the night. No matter what happened, Friday was going to be amazing. He'd make sure of it.

* * *

Date night rolled around before Mona was ready. She ended up working late on Thursday because Reno disappeared sometime around midnight and he didn't return until she was locking up at quarter to four. He apologized profusely for his absence but Mona was far too tired to care. She simply drove home and fell into bed.

Friday was filled to the brim with grocery shopping—at the store across town, laundry, and tidying up the place. While Mona was rifling through some of the mail that had been delivered, she found a coupon for a manicure/pedicure special and decided that would be a nice treat. After all, she wanted to look her best. Once she tossed in the third load of laundry, she headed over to Get Nailed and settled in for a relaxing hour of pampering.

With fingers and toes painted a saucy pink, Mona headed back home to finish getting ready. She showered and swept half her hair up to create a curly, no fuss style that she let dry naturally with a bit of product. As Mona went through her outfits, she paused to glance at herself in the mirror. The dress she'd picked was the black and green stretchy number she'd worn to the barbecue. It was a little snugger than before but still breezy enough she wouldn't get overheated on this unseasonably warm autumn day.

Butterflies erupted in Mona's belly and she found herself rubbing the soft bulge there. Why she was nervous, she had no idea. She'd been out with Reno hundreds of times in the last few years. There were parties, quiet nights in with a movie and takeout, or just milling around the office doing separate things while just enjoying each other's company. Tonight was no different…so why did she nearly jump out of her skin when the doorbell rang?

"Just a second!" Mona hollered. It was only quarter to six; she had at least fifteen minutes to finish putting herself together. Why the hell was Reno so early? She hurried out of the bathroom, putting on her earrings as she went. "You should know better than to be early for a date. I'm not finished getting ready," she chastised. She threw open the door and froze. "Oh…"

"Sorry to stop over unannounced." The icy blue eyes of her ex-boyfriend narrowed as his gaze swept over her. "Is this a bad time?"

It had been months since she'd seen or heard from Kyle. The night he told her he didn't want to be a father, she turned and walked out of his life and never looked back. Honestly, she hadn't even missed him. "Yeah, I've got plans tonight," she replied coldly.

Kyle nodded and stepped past her into the house. "I understand you're pissed at me but I need to get this off my chest. I'll keep it brief—"

"Before you get up on your high horse and ride off into the sunset, let me make a few things clear." Mona cut him off brutally. "I *am* pissed. I'm pissed I fell for your bullshit for so long." She watched his handsome face go from stoic to shocked. "You never cared about me or wanted a future, but you were too chickenshit to say anything! You're a coward. I don't need that in my life." She glared at him. "So, if you think you're going to come crawling back here and we'll pick up where we left off, you have another thing coming to you."

"That's not why I'm here." Kyle frowned deeper. "I've been discussing things with a lawyer and…I'm willing to offer you a substantial fee in exchange for leaving my name off the child's birth certificate. I know that may be difficult but I feel it would be in our best interests. In the long run, you're really doing all of us a favor."

Mona took a menacing step toward him. "Keep your money. The only favor I want is for you to stay the hell away from us. You hear me? If I see you within a thousand feet of my child and *I'll* be the one needing a lawyer!" Her voice got louder as she stepped toward him. "Get the fuck out of my house!"

Kyle turned to run. He'd been on the receiving end of Mona's wrath before, but he'd never seen her this angry. In his haste to get away, he tripped and tumbled down the last three steps. His nose was bleeding and he'd ripped his expensive suit during the fall. He opened his mouth to complain but when he looked up, he found Reno staring menacingly at him. Scrambling up from the ground, Kyle broke into a dead run.

It took all the strength in Reno's body not to chase Kyle Andreas to his expensive sorts car. If not for Mona appearing in the doorway, he'd certainly have beaten that deadbeat to dust. Instead, Reno hurried up the steps and wrapped his arms around her waist. She wasn't crying but her breathing was jerky and labored. When he pulled away to comfort her, he realized she was laughing. "You are a very strange woman, Mona Gallo…"

"Did you see his face?" She held her sides, fearing they might split from the force of her laughter. This time when she leaned against Reno, it was because she didn't trust her legs. Tears ran down Mona's cheeks and she brushed them away. It took a while for her to regain control of herself and she let out a heavy sigh. "Oh man, I haven't laughed that hard in a long time…"

Reno rubbed her back soothingly. "You look stunning, by the way. I made us a reservation at a fancy restaurant with real tablecloths and candles and menus that are mostly in French…but if you want to stay in and order food and watch a movie, I'd be up for that too."

"You must've been reading my mind." Mona leaned in but then stopped. "Are you going to think I'm loose if I kiss you on our first date?" He leaned in, answering her with a swift, passionate kiss. Mona found herself smiling against his lips. "You're still going to pay for dinner, right?"

Reno feigned indignation. "Of course, I could no longer

276

call myself a gentleman if I didn't!" He pecked her on the lips once more before he tugged off his suit jacket. Next, he undid his cufflinks and rolled up his sleeves, then loosened the first few buttons at the neckline of his shirt. Last, but not least, Reno let his belt out a couple of notches and let out a heavy sigh of relief. Mona was smirking at him and he gave her a sheepish grin. "I guess I overdid it a bit in Boston...I'm going to have to hit the gym more now that we're back. People are going to think *I'm* the one who's pregnant."

"You were really going to suck it in all night?" Mona teased. "I'm a lucky woman."

In that moment, Reno grew serious. "I just want to make you happy, Mona."

"I want you to be yourself." Mona was touched by his vulnerability and sincerity She closed the distance between them again. "I care about you, Reno. I don't give a crap about your beat up car or your messy apartment or your love handles..."

Reno panicked for a moment, checking his reflection in the living room mirror. "I don't have love handles!" When Mona started laughing again, he dragged her into his arms. "You're going to pay for that." Kissing her swiftly, he marveled at how perfectly she fit against him. They were like two halves of a whole that had finally come together.

It wasn't until Mona's stomach growled that he pulled away. "You and the little guy need to eat. What're you feeling like tonight? Pizza? Chinese? Thai?" He started going through the drawer where he knew she kept the menus. "Barbecue?"

As usual, there was a twenty minute discussion—well, heated argument—about where to get food until Mona finally made the decision. They ordered an obscene amount of Chinese food before settling down on the couch. Reno picked out a nice romantic comedy for them, and they had a very pleasant evening. At the end of the night, he glanced at Mona who was snuggled at his side.

"I wish it could be like this all the time," Reno said softly.

"Yeah, me too," Mona admitted.

"You know, I can't think of a single reason why it can't..."

Mona turned to face him. "I thought you wanted to take this slow?"

"I don't," Reno exhaled sharply. "I want to be with you."

Shock coursed through Mona's veins. She had to face away from him in an attempt to catch her breath. Dr. Harris's words kept running through her head: don't do anything rash, don't make any big decisions without thinking about them first. Then again, Reno had been in her life longer than any person she'd ever known. Was it really rushing into it if she knew in her heart he was the one for her?

Mona's throat was dry as a bone. "I've been hurt a lot in

my life." She cradled her belly gently. "I learned the hard way that love isn't always enough." Reno's face fell and she grasped his shoulders. "No, let me finish," she begged. "I want you, Reno. I just need to learn how to open up…on my terms." Leaning in, she kissed him softly. "Please be patient with me."

Reno felt a little better that he wasn't being rejected outright. Still, it felt like they'd taken a big step backwards. "This is all new for me too, you know. Most of my dates start with getting wasted and end up in bed…" He dragged a hand across his jaw.

"Well, there's no booze around here." Mona's hand slid across his chest. "But you better take me to bed tonight. I haven't been watching The Notebook for an hour because it's a good movie…" She watched Reno's expression go from pouty to excited and she laughed again. "I just want us to be honest with each other."

Glancing back at the television for a moment, Reno flicked it off. "You have my word." He inched toward her. "And honestly? I want nothing more than to drag you off to bed right now."

"What the hell are you waiting for?"

Wrapping his arms around her waist, Reno pulled her into the bedroom. She fell against the mattress, moaning with pleasure as he knelt between her thighs and ravaged her until they were both spent. Long after they made love, Mona curled against him, sleeping soundly in the aftermath of their lovemaking. Reno settled beside her, happy as a clam. For the first time since they got back to Carson City, it felt like he was home.

Chapter Twenty-One

The late days of September bled into October. Before Mona could blink, it was November and she was in her third trimester. Over the last few months, she and Reno had fallen into a comfortable routine with one another. Nights were split between his apartment and her condo, he went to all Mona's doctor's appointments, and they decided to take a baby preparation and Lamaze class on Monday nights. Against all odds, things were going really well.

At first, Mona was concerned Reno might not want her as her pregnancy advanced. It wasn't so far fetched that he might not find her attractive when she was so heavily pregnant. It didn't take long to realize she had nothing to worry about. Reno was obsessed with her belly, especially once he could feel the baby kicking. He spent almost every night chasing movement until all three of them were exhausted. It was adorable.

There were still some times they slept apart, although it wasn't by choice. For example, they'd found out last week that Reno's great aunt Sophie passed away peacefully in her sleep. A day later, her twin sister Millie joined her. It wasn't entirely unexpected, since both of them were in their late eighties but it was a crushing blow to the family nonetheless. Mona desperately wanted to be at Reno's side for the funeral but Dr. Harris advised her it wouldn't be safe to fly. With her due date looming ever closer the family understood, but Mona was still upset.

A few days without Reno made Mona realize just how

much she'd come to rely on him and how deeply she'd miss him if he were gone. Needless to say, he was treated to a very warm homecoming. She rested her head against his chest, smiling as his fingertips traced circles across her belly. They'd been lying in bed for hours when finally she peered up at him. "Are you okay?"

"Yeah," Reno replied, a little too quickly. "I was just thinking about my aunts. Neither of them ever got married or had children, but they had each other. They couldn't live one day without the other…" He held her closer. "I feel the same way about you, Mona. If anything were to happen to you, I wouldn't survive."

"Don't say that." Mona sat up so she could look directly in his eyes. "Nothing's going to happen to me." She leaned in, kissing him softly. "Dr. Harris said she was being overly cautious. I'm fine, Reno. You don't need to worry."

Reno cupped her cheek tenderly. "I know, pumpkin. My point was, I realized I don't want to ever be apart from you again…" The ring he'd bought for her in Boston was burning a hole in his pocket but he needed to clear the air first. "There's something I need to talk to you about."

Nodding solemnly, Mona leaned against him. "What's on your mind?"

"You remember when that lawyer came into town to give you that stuff from your father?" Reno could tell by her expression the answer was yes, even though she didn't speak. "I met with him before he left. I was able to get information about the safety deposit box. It took a little doing but the contents arrived today."

Mona wasn't sure whether to be angry or curious. A little of both would do just fine. "Well? What the hell was in it?"

"A few coins that are worth a couple hundred bucks now and a pretty nice antique Colt. I'm guessing it's probably stolen. I'm surprised the state didn't take it when they seized your father's assets..." Reno chewed his bottom lip. "There was also a letter..."

"What did it say?" Mona pressed.

Reno shook his head. "I didn't read it. It's not my place." He grasped her hand tightly. "I know this feels like a betrayal and I honestly didn't mean to look at anything. I thought the bank would send the actual *box*..."

Mona chuckled. "You've led a sheltered life." She glanced around the room. "Is the letter here? I'd like to read it."

Reno rolled off the bed and padded over to the desk. Carefully opening up the drawer, he pulled out a long, slim envelope. "You don't have to open it now. I can put it away or I can hide it...whatever you need." He could sense her unease and he wished he could do something to make it go away.

"No," Mona grimaced. "I'm ready." When the lawyer first showed up, she'd been overwhelmed. She'd told Reno to throw everything out in a fit of anger. Thankfully, he hadn't listened and all that was left of her father was tucked away in a safe place. "Here goes nothing, I guess…" Mona took a calming breath before sliding a nail against the corner. The adhesive was so old it popped open without her having to tear into it.

Mona stared at the paper for so long, Reno was afraid she'd frozen in time. He reached out, resting a hand on her shoulder. "What's it say?"

"Dear Darla, I'm sorry. All my love, Willie." Turning the piece of paper over, she glanced into the envelope and found a simple silver band. It wasn't much, probably all he could afford. It had to have been purchased around the time he'd been incarcerated and it was obvious Darla never received the letter. Mona wasn't proud of her heritage or the way her parents lived but every second of it made her who she was today and led her to this very moment. She refused to be sorry for that. Leaning against Reno, Mona closed her eyes. "I know I don't say it a lot but…thank you. For being there when I needed you, for knowing when to give me space, and for stepping up. For everything." She swallowed hard. "I love you so much."

"I'm glad you feel that way, pumpkin." Reaching into his pocket, Reno pulled out a black velvet box and got down on bended knee. "Being away from you for three days was torture. I meant what I said before. I can't live without you…I hope I don't have to." He gathered up all his courage. "Mona Renee Gallo, will you marry me?"

Mona's mouth fell open slightly as she stared at him,

then down at the box in his hand. "Are you sure?" she blurted.

It wasn't the response he was expecting…then again, Reno never knew exactly what to expect from Mona. "I love you and the baby. I want to wake up with you every morning and be at your side every night. I never want you to doubt that I'm committed to you." He licked his lips. "I want everyone to know I'm yours." He frowned slightly. "So, let's try this again…will you marry me?"

Of all the reasons Mona expected, the ones he gave were incredible. Tears filled her eyes and she threw her arms around him. "Of course I will." Salty tears mingled on their lips as she kissed him fervently. It wasn't only Mona who was crying, though. "I can't wait to be your wife!"

Sliding back onto the bed, Reno smirked. The ring was a single karat and flanked by small, perfect emeralds in a princess cut setting. He'd searched high and low for the perfect one and was so glad when it slid onto her finger. Mona looked very pleased, which made his heart flutter. "I don't think we should wait. I invited my family up for Thanksgiving. I was thinking we could surprise them. If Lizzy can plan a massive wedding in six weeks, I think we can do a small one in two. Don't you?"

"They're coming here? All of them?" Mona scrambled to find a piece of paper and a pen. "There's so much to do! We need licenses and a venue and a caterer and you need to clean your apartment…"

"This is Nevada, sweetheart. We can get our licenses at any quickie wedding chapel of our choosing. As for the venue, I was thinking we could have the ceremony at the club." Reno smirked. "We can wrap ribbons around the poles and put cloth over on our usual tables. There's a kitchen, so whoever we hire can use our facilities and it'll reduce the cost. We can invite Liberty and Cadence and all the girls, and my family will be there." He dragged a hand over his chin. "And yes, I will clean the apartment before they come over, pumpkin."

Mona was slightly incredulous. "You've given this a lot of thought." She chuckled. "Honestly, as long as I end up your wife, I don't really care about the ceremony." She exhaled and flopped back onto the mattress. "I never thought I could be this happy," she whispered. "And I've never been this afraid."

Reno dropped a gentle kiss to the crown of her head. "You don't need to be afraid. I love you, pumpkin, and I can't wait to spend the rest of my life showing you just how much." His words must've placated her, because Mona pressed a soft kiss to his lips. It was already late and they'd had a long day at work. Leaning over, he flicked off the light. With everything out in the open and his ring on her finger, Reno was finally at peace.

* * *

"How the hell did Lizzy do this?" Mona lamented. She'd been running like a madwoman for two whole weeks. The family was set to arrive tomorrow evening and she still didn't have a dress. Between meeting with the caterer, picking out flower arrangements, choosing a DJ, getting the marriage license—which was in no way as easy as Reno said it would be—and finding a justice of the peace willing to marry them, Mona was ready to lose her mind.

Liberty looked up from the bridal magazine she was currently flipping through and shrugged. "It took me almost a whole year to plan my second wedding and I still felt like it wasn't enough time. You're crazy, that's all I have to say."

"Thanks, Lib, that's real helpful," Mona snarked. Reno was out picking up wedding china. They couldn't exactly serve dinner in the red plastic baskets usually reserved for chicken fingers and fries, although he'd suggested it numerous times. The wedding was a little rushed, but Mona still wanted it to be elegant.

She grunted slightly as she pushed herself up from the couch. At six and a half months pregnant, she was more cumbersome than she could ever have imagined. The baby gave a sharp kick to her ribs in protest, obviously disgruntled mommy had interrupted his nap. "I give up. I'm not going to find the perfect wedding dress in one of these magazines. I say we go shopping and maybe get something to eat. I'm craving fruit salad again."

Grabbing the keys off the desk, Liberty waited for Mona to use the bathroom one more time before they headed out. Liberty's vibrant red hair was swept into a ponytail, keeping it out of her angular face. She pulled open the door for Mona, smiling gently as they got settled in.

The first stop was a bridal superstore that seemed to

have everything a girl could ever want. The sales associate brought over every empire waisted gown she could find, but Mona didn't like any of them. They were all cut too low in the front and unflattering to her figure—what was left of it, that was. Liberty's brutally honest opinion was why Mona brought her along, and they both agreed this wasn't the place she was going to find her dress.

"Well, that was a bust." Mona sighed as they hurried back into the car. There were a number of smaller shops but it was getting later in the day and half of them were already closed. It was only a twenty minute ride to the mall, so they headed that way. "Maybe we should stop looking at traditional wedding dresses. I'm not going to fool anyone into thinking I'm a virgin. I don't have to wear a white dress…"

Sticking to the area maternity shops yielded no 'perfect dress' either. Mona was getting frustrated with the lack of selection. The girls stopped off at a frozen yogurt place and she felt a lot better after she ate a cup of fruit with vanilla custard on top. Liberty ordered a soda and they sat, watching the world go by. "Maybe we're looking at this the wrong way. We've been searching out new dresses but maybe we should look for older ones. There's a giant second hand store about ten minutes from here. It's where I got all my maternity clothes when I was pregnant with Gigi," Liberty suggested.

It certainly couldn't hurt to take a look. Mona was desperate at this point. If they didn't find something today, she'd end up walking down the aisle in yoga pants and a tank top—which was what most of her wardrobe consisted of these days.

The Salvation Army store was deserted by the time Liberty and Mona arrived. Heading in the side door, they weaved through aisles of electronics and into the massive collection of clothing amassed here. The entire place smelled like mothballs and hundreds of different kinds of laundry soap. Mona breathed through her mouth and followed Liberty to the back corner.

There was an entire section dedicated to wedding dresses, which surprised Mona. "People really donate this stuff?" she asked, thumbing through the selection for something that might fit her. "I guess it makes sense. You only wear it for one day and then it takes up space in the closet." All the idle chatter stopped when Mona's hand landed on *the* dress. Her mouth fell open slightly as she pulled it off the rack. "I really hope this fits!"

Liberty's eyes widened. "Oh Mona, it's perfect!" They hurried for the dressing room. It took a little maneuvering but with Liberty's help, Mona was able to slip the dress on over her head. To her surprise, it was actually a little bit roomy, especially in the bodice area. Whoever had worn this dress had obviously been chestier than her.

Dabbing her eyes with a tissue, Liberty took a step back to admire the dress. "It's perfect..." The dress was a shade of white that complemented Mona's porcelain complexion without washing her out. The fabric was buttery soft silk and cut so it had a sweetheart neckline without revealing too much cleavage. Although the dress itself was sleeveless, there was a lacy sweater with little cap sleeves that covered her shoulders and added elegance to the simple gown. What Mona loved about it most, though, was the price tag. "Fifty bucks? Liberty, you are a genius."

Since the wedding dress had a pink dot on it, it was an extra 10% off. All told, she bought her wedding dress for less than she'd spent on her last tank of gas. Liberty was beaming with excitement as they got back in the car. "And don't worry about the alterations. I know a guy. He'll have the dress dry cleaned and taken in well before the wedding tomorrow."

On the way back into town, they dropped off the dress with Liberty's dry cleaning guru—who also happened to be her first ex-husband. Everyone was content by the time they headed back home.

Now that the wedding dress had been acquired, Mona felt a new sense of calm wash over her. Reno already had his tux picked up—not that it was difficult to find a rental place around here. The menu had been finalized, all the flowers would be delivered to the club, the DJ was paid in full, and their marriage license was waiting to be signed at the ceremony tomorrow. With all the details in place, Mona could finally rest.

Reno worked late that night. Once they closed down the club for business, he brought in a cleaning crew to scour every inch of the place. The Watering Hole was always well kept but they didn't get a chance to clear the cobwebs on the vaulted ceilings all that often. With the wedding tomorrow and his family coming into town, he wanted everything to be perfect. Tito and Otis updated the website to inform customers the club would be closed for a private function. They also printed and posted signs to that effect and had been telling the regulars all night.

Cadence threw herself into decorating with gusto. The minute she heard about a wedding taking place in the club, she'd been like a kid at a candy store. She bought white and green ribbon, wrapping up the poles and making them look like statuesque pillars around the room. White tablecloths were arranged neatly over newly washed wooden tables and she used the same ribbon to tie around vases where flowers would be placed once they arrived. She bustled around, chattering to anyone who would listen about how amazing it was that there was going to be a wedding.

Reno couldn't help but smile as he arranged tea lights around the arches of the doorway and threaded them around the support beams of the ceiling. Everything was going to be perfect on Mona's special day. Finally around five in the morning, they were all finished.

Reno slogged home, collapsing in bed beside her. Mona rolled over and he smiled. In a few hours, she was going to be his wife. His entire family was coming in at four, then by the time he got them out of the airport and over to the club, it'd be nearly six. They'd have a wedding, a grand dinner, and a massive party to celebrate it all. Reno was suddenly energized. He waited until Mona went to the bathroom again before sneaking downstairs to make her breakfast. When she came down, wrapped up in his robe, he smiled. "Happy Wedding Day, pumpkin."

Padding over, Mona kissed him sweetly on the lips. He went back to flipping pancakes and she started the kettle for tea. Reno began singing some silly love song and she couldn't help but laugh. He was ridiculous and dorky and he was all hers. She really was the luckiest woman alive. Mona couldn't wait to be with him for the rest of her life.

Chapter Twenty-Two

Mona had almost forgotten how overwhelming Reno's family was and she wasn't even at the airport when he picked them up. Since the O'Keefe-Sunderland clan arrived, Lizzie had texted her no less than fifty times. Mona had also heard from Elina, Luke, Ray, and Meghan. It was hard to keep up with last minute wedding details while making sure she didn't give anything away. Eventually, she had to tell a bit of a white lie about taking quick nap before they got in; playing the pregnant card was the only thing that worked.

Finally setting the phone aside, Mona turned to stare at her reflection in the mirror. She'd been a stripper since she was fifteen years old, she knew her way around hair and makeup…but it didn't prepare her for the day when she'd have to decide on a style for her own wedding. Liberty offered to spring for a professional stylist but Mona wanted to keep things simple. Today was about friends and family, about pledging her life to Reno, not about her hair and makeup.

After a bit of a debate, Mona decided to let her dark tresses curl over her shoulders. To add elegance, she tucked a single white daisy behind her ear. With a quick swish of mascara and a smear of lipstick, she was ready. The fabric of her gown rustled slightly as she stood up. It was a miracle what Liberty's tailor had been able to accomplish in less than twenty-four hours. The dress was pristinely white and unblemished by the hands of time. With the bodice taken in, the silk cradled her curves like a lover's hand. Mona felt like a princess despite being seven months pregnant.

"You look beautiful," Liberty sniffled. She'd been weepy since Mona started getting ready but now that they were so close to the wedding, she was practically inconsolable. Pulling more tissues out of her purse, she blew her nose loudly. "I'm sorry. I am just so happy you two finally realized you're perfect for each other."

"What do you mean?" Mona raised an eyebrow at her. "Was it obvious?"

Liberty snuffled and nodded enthusiastically. "You'd have to be blind not to notice! Reno's been smitten with you since the day he walked in here…we all had bets on how long it would take ya'll to figure it out."

Mona's stared at her incredulously, folding her arms across her chest. "Well, who won?"

"Yeah, about that…"

"Liberty!"

Reaching into her bra, she pulled out several hundred dollar bills. Liberty kissed the pack goodbye before extending the wad to Mona. "Here…consider it an investment in your future."

"I don't want your money, Lib. Put it in your Disney fund," Mona chastised. "I'm just surprised. You're not usually the gambling type."

"I only play it when I know I can win," Liberty winked.

"This was a sure bet."

Mona huffed. "In the beginning, all I remember is fighting with Reno and spending long hours trying to teach him how to manage his own club and his life. We got into some pretty big fights, Liberty."

She moved behind Mona, delicately fixing a wayward curl in the back of her hair. "The minute he walked on the scene, it was always *Reno and Mona*. You couldn't talk about one without the other." Leaning against the makeup table, Liberty found herself grinning again. "I never thought it'd last as long as it did with Kyle. I always hoped you'd wake up one day and realize Reno was in love with you..." She sighed. "The two of you are stubborn, that's all I can say."

Chuckling softly, Mona slid a hand across her rounded belly. The baby within her leapt at the intrusion, enthralling her with a series of fluttering kicks. "We certainly are. That's how I know we're going to make it. Neither of us are willing to give up, no matter what." A soft chime from Mona's phone alerted her that Reno had arrived with his family in tow. "They're here," she announced excitedly.

"That's my cue!" Liberty hurried upstairs to let the staff know it was time to get this show on the road.

The music kicked up from the sound booth and Mona felt her heart begin to pound. She and Reno had decided not to find out the sex of the child but the swift jab to the ribs confirmed her suspicion he was a boy. No little girl would be so disenchanted at the prospect of a wedding. Mona had to laugh at the absurdity of that, but she believed it nonetheless. "Here we go," she whispered to the baby.

Drawing a breath deep into her lungs, she carefully ascended the stairs. Lizzy's signature squeal of excitement filled the room and Mona felt laughter bubble up inside her. Martha was instantly misty eyed and had to be helped to her seat by Richard, who was grinning wider than she'd ever seen. Even with all the family members and friends in the room, Mona found herself focused solely on her husband-to-be.

Reno pulled on his tuxedo jacket, adjusting the lapels so they would lay flat. He'd been waiting for this moment all day...hell, he'd been waiting for it for his entire life. Knowing Mona was down at the other end of that makeshift aisle filled him with pride and joy. He couldn't wait to be her husband. When she finally came into view, Reno had to pull his handkerchief out of his pocket to wipe away the tears that collected at the corners of his eyes. Mona was the most beautiful woman he'd ever known. Seeing her in that white dress, knowing she'd soon be standing at his side and sharing his life forever, it was all too much to take in.

Mona was nearly up the aisle when she let out an indignant cry. "Reno O'Keefe, don't you start!" She choked on the emotion in her throat. "I won't be able to say my vows!"

"I can't help it!" Reno took a step toward her, reaching out to take her hand. "You're so damn beautiful, I'm the luckiest man in the whole damn universe, and I can't believe you're mine." He sniffled, wiping his face. "How about you hurry up before we're both a mess?"

Family and friends laughed at the exchange. Mona picked up the pace until she reached the spot where the justice of the peace was standing. "Let's get this show on the road," she urged.

"Dearly beloved, we're gathered here today to celebrate the union of Vincent 'Reno' O'Keefe and Mona Renee Gallo." The man presiding over the ceremony was in his seventies with ivory white hair and a kind face. He turned to each of them. "I've had the pleasure of getting to know the two of you a little bit over the last couple weeks and I've never seen a couple so well suited." He grinned. "The love Mona and Reno share goes beyond the legal bounds they are now entering into. It is part of their being, body and soul." Stepping back, he motioned to Reno. "The couple has chosen to share their own vows."

Reno had words written down on a piece of paper in his pocket but didn't need them now. When he gazed into Mona's green eyes, he was speaking straight from the heart. "Five years ago I was an aimless, uninspired, overgrown frat boy. I was searching for anything to fulfill me and I came to this club looking for it. It was the best decision I ever made. It may have taken me five years but I've found what I've always wanted: *you*." He inhaled shakily. "I thought for so long it was the club that saved me but it wasn't. It's always been you, Mona." Reno squeezed her hands tightly. "I love you. I can't wait to spend the rest of my life with you…"

It took all of Mona's strength to hold back her tears. "You're still an overgrown frat boy," she added cheekily. Reno smirked and the crowd around them chuckled appreciatively. "I could spend forever talking about how much you've come to mean to me and what a great father you're going to be to our baby. You really are the most amazing man I've ever met…that's not to say you're without your flaws." A smile ghosted over her lips. "It drives me nuts the way you constantly hover like I'm made of glass. You're awful at putting the toilet seat down. I won't even mention how embarrassing it is when you have to save me when I've fallen in." Reno snorted and Mona squeezed his hands again. "Worst of all, you never, ever let me stay angry at you. Just when I think I'm going to get a chance to stew, you do something so sweet, I just can't help myself." Mona's belly bumped against his as she leaned into his embrace. "I've never had anyone in my life who knew me so well or loved me so much. I never though I'd have someone who could put up with everything I am. I love you with everything I've got."

The exchanging of rings was supposed to come next but Reno didn't care about the order of the ceremony. He leaned in for Mona's lips in a moment of blissful passion. He was lost in her and the sweetness of her kiss.

The justice of the peace cleared his throat several times before finally throwing his hands up in surrender. "I suppose you can give each other the rings later…by the power vested in me by the state of Nevada, I now pronounce you husband and wife. Go ahead and keep doing what you're doing."

Cheers erupted and the family rushed to congratulate Mona and Reno. She pulled the wedding band from a small white pocket, quickly slipping it onto his finger to make it official. In turn, he did the same. They turned to accept the family's love and congratulations. Martha hugged Mona tightly; the older woman was blubbering away and all the words were unintelligible, but Mona knew exactly what she was saying. She, too, was so happy to be a part of this family. For the first time in fifteen years, Mona didn't feel like an orphan anymore.

Reno found himself in a circle of his brothers. They were slapping him on the back and hugging him. Ray seemed the happiest of all, his smile never fading as he hugged and congratulated Reno on being a married man. Lizzie was glued to Mona's side the entire time and made fast friends with Liberty and Cadence. Elina, Lisa, and Meghan found the bar and were eagerly chatting and drinking wine. It didn't surprise Reno that Karen and Rob were uncomfortable being in a strip club. After wishing the bride and groom well, they called a cab and hurried their four children out of the Watering Hole.

Now that the ceremony had concluded, dinner was being served. Tito and Otis were playing waiter, complete with matching red silk vests. Reno was damn impressed with the menu Mona picked out; the simple garden salad, several kinds of pasta, meatballs, sausage, and eggplant patties were to die for. While the family was eating, Mitch and Willow arrived, apologizing profusely for missing the ceremony. Their flight to Reno had been cancelled in Dallas and they ended up having to fly into LAX before catching the right connector. Mona was so happy to see them, she couldn't say a single word for a full ten minutes as she held them and cried. Once she regained her bearings, she threw her arms around Reno. "I can't believe you got them here. This means so much to me..."

"I wanted everyone who matters to be here today," Reno soothed and slung his arm around her back. "I invited Dr. Harris too, but she wasn't able to make it. She sends her best." Curling his finger around a lock of her hair, he pulled her toward the dance floor. "Come on, it's time for dancing." He wrapped his arms around her as Nat King Cole crooned over the sound system. "Let's show everyone how it's done."

Mona laughed, holding him tighter as they swayed to the beat. "I'm a little too pregnant to be tearing it up on the dance floor but I do enjoy being in your arms," she murmured against his shoulder. Reno kissed her again and they lost themselves in the music.

Pretty soon, everyone else joined in. Lana was leading the group in one of the routines she learned in her hip-hop class; it was evident she was going to sleep extremely well tonight. Martha and Richard cuddled against one another. He crooned along with Elvis as the DJ played through the classics.

Instead of the traditional wedding cake, Mona had opted for an assortment of cupcakes. It was clearly the right choice, since everyone helped themselves. People mingled, laughed, and celebrated the love Reno and Mona shared. Before the night was set to end, Reno stepped up on the platform where the girls usually danced. "Don't worry," he grabbed a microphone from the DJ, putting up one hand to stop the chatter, "I am not going to be stripping this evening. I'm going to leave that to the professionals from now on…"

Mona laughed appreciatively. "Save it for later!" she jeered.

Reno winked at her before he continued. "I just want to thank you all for coming. It means so much to Mona and me that you were here on our special day. We love you guys." A chorus of 'awwws' filled the room and he grinned. "Since we started planning the wedding, I got to thinking about how it's really not fair we don't have a place for visitors to stay. My apartment is a dump—"

"You can say that again," Mona snorted. She couldn't help herself, she was giddy with joy.

Shooting her a look, Reno laughed and shook his head. "And the condo is going to be too small very shortly." He cleared his throat and hopped off the stage. He reached into his tuxedo jacket and pulled a piece of paper from his pocket. "Mona, you lost your home when you were a kid. I can't take that pain away but I can promise you this: there is one place you will always be able to call your own."

Shock coursed through Mona as her mouth fell open. "You bought me a house?" Staring down at the gorgeous pictures on the page, she honestly couldn't believe it. "This…" A shaky breath rattled her chest. "This is ours?" Mona was too stunned to cry.

Reno knelt beside her. "I searched high and low for the perfect one. This home has all the things you like. The big picture windows, the fireplace, an open kitchen…it even has a white picket fence. I didn't think I'd find one of those in this area, but I managed it." He chewed his bottom lip. "Foreclosures have always worked out well for me. I put in an offer to the bank a couple weeks ago and I got the keys yesterday morning. It's ours, pumpkin."

"I love it, Reno." Mona threw her arms around him, holding him as tightly as her body would allow. "And I love you!" She buried her face in his shoulder, whispering so softly no one else could hear. "Thank you…" The family was clapping and cheering again, but Mona couldn't even hear it. The only sound she focused on was that of Reno's beating heart.

Holding her tightly, Reno smiled as the baby kicked against his hands. It was almost impossible to pull off this surprise, since Mona was always around but he was glad he managed it. The look on her face was priceless. Her reaction was everything he'd hoped it'd be. The two of them remained glued together, joined at the hip until the very end of the night.

It was nearly midnight when Martha and Richard decided to call it a day. Hugs and kisses were doled out with promises to meet up tomorrow. Reno had called ahead to make a brunch reservation for the entire family. Mona was also preparing a gigantic Thanksgiving feast later in the week. It would take a little doing but they were fairly sure with everybody pitching in, Mona and Reno could be moved into the new house and there would be plenty of space for everyone at the table.

Mona and Reno said their goodbyes to everyone until finally they were alone in the club. He slumped down in a chair, yawning. She slid into his lap and leaned her chin atop his head. "I'd say that was a success. Everyone had a great time. I still can't believe you did all this in such a short time. It's so much more than I ever dreamed I could have."

"You deserve all of it." Reno nuzzled her neck, sighing as exhaustion started to take hold. Mona seemed to get the message. She stood to head for the car and he held his arm out to her. "Well, Ms. Gallo, are you ready to go home?"

"Haven't you heard?" she asked as she linked her arm with his. "It's Mrs. O'Keefe now. And you better be careful where you put those hands, I'm a married woman…" Reno laughed and Mona joined in. "I think it's high time we started our lives, wouldn't you say?"

Reno didn't have a single argument.

The moon was full and bright, illuminating Mona and Reno as they stepped into the night. The pavement shimmering beneath their feet, a soft cool breeze, and owls hooting in the trees set a peaceful tone. As they embraced, the world seemed to still in deference to the awesome power of their love. It had been a difficult road with many obstacles in their path, but truly, entirely, and without a doubt, Mona and Reno were finally bound for life.

Epilogue

Mona's first holiday season with an obscenely large extended family was wonderful and terrifying in so many ways. Between shopping, baking, and prepping the new house, she went to bed exhausted every night. She swore over the last month she'd wrapped no less than fifty gifts, signing each of them 'Love, Mona, Reno, & Baby'. Reno focused on finding the perfect Christmas tree, following all of Mona's orders for decorating inside and outside the house, and finishing all the little projects he'd wanted to accomplish before the baby came.

They'd decided not to exchange gifts this year. Instead, Mona and Reno bought a living room set for the family room. The overstuffed brown leather couch reminded him of the one he'd loved growing up and Mona had claimed the matching armchair and ottoman for herself.

Only a small fight occurred when Reno broke the rules and bought her a locket to open on Christmas morning. Mona supposed purchasing him a spiffy antique-style shaving kit was also cheating. They decided to write off the argument and enjoy their first Christmas as a married couple and their last one without a baby.

Suddenly, it was a brand new year. Mona was heavily pregnant and incredibly uncomfortable. Reno made the decision Mona was officially on maternity leave as of January 2nd. She hadn't agreed and spent two nights sitting in the bar as a form of protest. Eventually, she came to realize she'd much rather be in her warm living room in front of the fire with her feet up and a book in her lap. Reno allowed her to believe she'd come to the conclusion on her own and not another word was spoken on the subject.

Mona filled her days with reading every baby preparation book she could get her hands on, trying (and failing) to learn how to knit, and cooking up a storm. On his days off, Reno worked in the nursery. They'd painted it a soft cream color that was warm and inviting. Mona hung family portraits all around the room for the baby to see. Most of them were of Reno's family but she'd also framed some of her father's artwork and slipped in the picture of her mother as a girl. Mona loved sitting in the rocker, glancing at the smiling faces around her; already she felt right at home.

With her due date still two weeks away, Mona and Reno had lulled each other into a false sense of security. The last thing that needed to be done was to put together the crib and changing table. Reno planned to do it over the weekend with help from Tito and Otis. Mona was also planning on using that time to pack up her hospital bag with all the items the mommy bloggers recommended. That way, there would not be a mad dash for the door when she finally went into labor…

Mona hummed softly as she bustled around the kitchen. She had a freezer full of meals ready to be thawed and cooked for when the baby came, but this lasagna was special. Martha gifted her with a book of family recipes for Christmas and this was the first time she was going to try it out. She fully intended to surprise Reno, since she knew he loved this recipe. Unfortunately, Mona's back kept aching fiercely and she was forced to sit and rest several times. Instead of taking an hour to put together, the lasagna had taken almost all day.

She flicked on the television, the weather was flashing across the screen warning of snow and freezing rain in Carson City. Mona wrapped her sweater tighter around herself, shivering despite the warmth of the room. Gently, she rubbed her belly and smiled as the baby shifted; some of the pressure alleviated and she took a big, deep breath.

Reno was supposed to be back soon and if she wanted to serve the lasagna, she needed to put it in the oven. Mona pushed herself upright, waddling over to the large bay window to peek outside. It was pitch black out but she swore she saw snowflakes beginning to fall. Carrying the lasagna over to the oven, she slipped the glass dish inside and turned the oven on. When Mona stood straight, she suddenly realized she was wet. A curse tumbled from her lips. Had she lost control of her bladder and not realized it? When she took another step, more fluid gushed from within. Mona took a shaky breath…and *panicked*.

Hurrying to her phone, Mona's heart was pounding and her hands were shaking. She called Reno once, twice…but he wasn't picking up. The crunch of tires and lights in the window snapped her out of a fear spiral. He must've been driving and had forgotten to put on his Bluetooth. The new SUV they purchased after trading in his clunky old jalopy was fully tricked out and had all the newest safety features. Once he learned to use them, Mona would feel a lot better. "Reno!" she hollered as he stepped in the back door. "Reno!"

He came dashing into the room with one boot off. "What's wrong?"

"My water broke," Mona gasped. "I'm in labor!"

"You can't be in labor. You're not due for another two weeks!" Reno argued.

"Try telling that to the baby!" Mona huffed at him. "Look, we can discuss this more in the car but I'm pretty sure the pain I've been having in my back all day has actually being contractions. I am *not* going to make the evening news as the former stripper who gave birth in the back of a car!"

Reno was a mess. They didn't have the baby bag packed, he didn't have the birthing music mix completed yet, not to mention the crib and changing table weren't even put together. The only thing he had going for him was that the car was still warm, but even that was fading quickly. In the midst of very gingerly helping Mona into the garage and settling her into the passenger seat, Richard's words came flooding back to him. Reno needed to conquer his fear...but that was easier said than done.

Mona gritted her teeth. She was equal parts scared out of her mind and in pain...it was a horrible combination. "Make sure the oven is off!" She commanded. "And put the lasagna into the fridge!" Barking orders was taking the edge off a little bit, but tears were already burning down her cheeks.

Reno ran back into the house to grab her purse with the insurance cards and a couple essential items. He also called and alerted Dr. Harris they were on their way into the hospital. By the time he got back to the car, Mona was nearly hysterical. He leaned over, gripping her hand tightly. "You're going to be just fine, pumpkin. Just keep doing the breathing exercises we learned. I love you." Just like that, he backed out of the driveway as quickly as he could in the midst of a snowstorm.

For some reason, cranking up the music in the car helped Mona feel a lot calmer. By the time they got to the hospital, she was almost back to herself. Mona was terrified, since the pain in her back kept getting worse, but every time she looked over at Reno he seemed to have everything under control. They walked to the elevators reserved for maternity patients and headed to the check in desk. A kind nurse helped Mona change into a gown and hooked her up to a machine that took her vital signs. They also placed a band around her belly to monitor the child's heartbeat. Everyone fussed over her, offering words of encouragement and empathy for her pain.

Reno had to stay out of the way while they got Mona settled in. He hated it. He wanted to be at her side, holding her hand. Instead, he paced the room: back and forth and back and forth…

"Reno!" Mona finally growled, after everyone had left the room. "Just sit down!" She covered her face with her hands and sighed. He looked stricken after she yelled at him and she felt terrible. "I'm sorry. I thought we'd have another couple weeks to prepare for this moment. I don't feel ready…"

"I feel the exact same way," Reno offered. It wasn't the same for him, of course, *he* wasn't the one giving birth. Mona had to go through all of the pain and difficulty to bring their child into the world. He kept waiting for her to tell him what to do but Mona didn't seem to know what she needed. It was very unnerving. So, he sat down beside her and stared at the clock.

Dr. Harris arrived at the hospital an hour later. She hurried into the room in a pair of powder pink scrubs and grabbed a pair of gloves. "I apologize for my tardiness, I got here as soon as I could. The storm is getting worse by the minute!"

Mona heaved a sigh of relief when her doctor stepped into the room. "I'm just glad you're here now." At Dr. Harris's instruction, she laid back and took a deep breath. She kept staring at the fetal heart rate monitor, taking comfort in the knowledge that her child was doing well.

"You're a hundred percent effaced and approximately three centimeters dilated. And you've definitely ruptured your membranes." Dr. Harris grinned. "In normal people talk, that means I'm admitting you. You're having a baby tonight."

Pulling her gloves off, the doctor settled down in front of the computer. "When was the last time you had something to eat or drink? I need to know in case we have to do a C-section."

Just the word 'C-section' made Mona shiver with fear. "I had a burrito at lunch, around one?" She cleared her throat. "I had a cup of tea this morning and I've been drinking water all day." Reno moved to her side and gripped her hand tightly. She was grateful for his comforting presence. "Do you think I'm going to need that? Is the baby going to be okay? I'm not due for another two weeks."

Dr. Harris shook her head. "You're thirty-eight weeks pregnant, Mona. You have nothing to worry about. Due dates are an educated guess. I've been examining you in the office frequently and I have no reason to believe there will be any trouble. We're monitoring you and the baby very carefully." Leaning back on her chair, she licked her lips. "Now is the time for you to request an epidural, if you want one. It can take a while for our anesthesiologist to get here."

Mona chewed her bottom lip. She'd read everything she could get her hands on about natural birth. The drugs scared her more than pain and suffering. Despite the churning in her gut, she shook her head. "I don't want it."

Smiling gently, Dr. Harris leaned over and patted Mona's hand. "I'm going to finish your admission. If you need anything, just ring in." She stood up. "Feel free to get up and walk around if you so desire. You can have ice chips and sips of water or sports drink. Whatever makes you comfortable, Mona."

Reno watched the exchange between Mona and the

doctor with a horrified expression on his face. When the door swung shut, he turned to face her. "I watched that birth video three times. I'm pretty sure I wouldn't want to feel anything below my neck if something like that was happening to me!" he gulped.

Despite the gnawing ache in her back causing significant discomfort, Mona chuckled. She swung her legs over the side of the bed. "I'm tough, Reno. I'm going to be okay." Leaning her head against his, she closed her eyes for a moment.

A nurse came in with hospital bracelets for Reno and Mona. She also started an IV for fluids so Mona wouldn't become dehydrated during delivery. Pulling the gown closed behind her, she stood up and found Reno standing directly in front of her. Kissing him gingerly, she turned around. "You want to close me up so I don't walk down the hall with my butt flapping in the breeze?" He made sure she was properly covered before they headed to check out the place.

The maternity unit looked a lot different at night than it had during the tour they took with their Lamaze class. During the day there was hustle and bustle, people talking, the sounds of televisions and radios…right now, it was quiet. Despite her nerves, Mona felt almost calm. She held tightly to the IV pole as they walked and Reno dogged her every step. His arm was wrapped around her waist.

To his surprise, most of her pain seemed to be low in her back and he paused to gently massage it. "Oh that feels so good," Mona whimpered. "Keep doing that…"

And she let him do it for another five minutes before another contraction ebbed through her and she didn't want to be touched anymore. Her pain came in waves. Sometimes it helped to be walking but she took frequent breaks, sitting in sturdy plastic chairs strategically placed in the hall.

Minutes ticked away into hours. Dr. Harris found them still walking and ushered Mona back into the room for a quick exam. Mona was still at three centimeters at the next check, which really pissed her off. She chewed ice far more aggressively than was necessary and stared outside. The lights of the city illuminated the darkness, giving her a wonderful view of lazy snowflakes drifting down over the town. "You're awfully quiet." Mona broke the silence finally, glancing over at Reno as he scrunched in a chair.

It was cool in the room but Mona's cheeks were red and her eyes bright with exertion. He could see she was tired. "I'm just thinking…" He licked his lips. "By this time tomorrow, we're going to have a baby."

"At this rate, we'll be lucky to have a baby by the end of the week!" Mona snorted and prodded her belly. "This is your official eviction notice. Do you hear me, kid? Don't make me come in there!" When she glanced up again, she found Reno grinning at her. Mona rolled onto her side and propped a pillow behind her back. "You know, we haven't really talked about names."

"Yes, we have." Reno narrowed his eyes. "You just don't like anything I came up with."

"Barbara? Agatha? Ruth? Our baby isn't a ninety year old woman," Mona scoffed. "I liked the idea of naming her Sophie but I get it, you can't name the baby after one of your aunts and not the other." She picked at a string on her gown. "None of that matters. The baby is a boy. All that mumbo jumbo about carrying high and old wives' tale crap doesn't impress me. Mother's intuition is a real thing."

Reno laced his fingers behind his head. "Too bad all the good names were taken by my mom." He sighed. "Mark, Stephen, Luke, Rob…those are solid boys' names. I don't want our son being called Zander or Xavier or something uppity like that. He should have a strong name that means something."

Mona thought about it long and hard before she exhaled sharply. "We're just going to have to see what he looks like when he comes out. This is too hard!" It was the same conclusion they'd come to every time this conversation arose. "I feel like a bad mother not having something picked out in advance. We're so unprepared…"

"I'm sure we're not the only parents who want to see their baby before saddling him with a name for the rest of his or her life." Reno shifted in his chair. "Speaking of parents…I should probably call my family and let them know we're here." Glancing up at the clock on the wall, he licked his lips. "It's four in the morning in Boston. There's only one person who I know is awake…" Pulling the phone out of his pocket, he opened up the camera. "Smile for the family, pumpkin." Mona gave him the finger. When she finally put it down, he snapped a quick photo and then sent it to Lizzy with the words 'Waiting for Baby'. Not even thirty seconds later, his phone rang and he held it away from him in anticipation of his sister's reaction.

It wasn't on speakerphone but Mona could hear Lizzy screeching in excitement. Ray ran from downstairs with a baseball bat in an effort to protect her and Reno was fairly certain he could hear several neighborhood dogs barking in the background. When she finally took a breath, he brought the phone back to his ear. "Lizzy, I can't talk long. We're hanging in there. Mona says hello. If you can call mom and dad in an hour or two and let them know, that'd be great. I promise, I'll let you know when there's a baby." Lizzy seemed to understand he didn't want to be on the phone a long time and quickly agreed to let everyone know.

Mona closed her eyes for a while. Much to her surprise, she was able to nap on and off until sometime around four in the morning, she wasn't able to ignore the contractions any longer. They were getting stronger and closer together. Dr. Harris informed her that the baby was at zero station and she was now six centimeters dilated. Finally, they were making progress.

Reno could tell Mona was hiding her pain from him and it ached. "Are you okay, pumpkin?" He stood in front of her, his arms around her lower back and her arms rested around his shoulders. They swayed together, almost like they were dancing. "I hate seeing you in pain. If there's something I can do, just tell me…"

"Just being here is enough," Mona murmured. She

rested her head against his chest and let him support some of her weight. She breathed deeply as she listened to the cadence of his heart. "Women have been doing this without epidurals for millennia. I can too…"

Two hours later, Mona wondered what the hell she was thinking. The contractions were one on top of each other now. She could hardly catch her breath before another one slammed into her. Her belly tightened painfully and it felt like electricity was burning in her veins. She shivered violently, even though she was drenched with sweat. "I can't do it," she whimpered.

Reno looked terrible. He was ashen and breathing heavily. Nothing in any of the books he'd read or the videos he watched even came close to preparing him for this moment. Mona was hunched over the bed, her forehead resting against a pillow. She gripped the sheets so tightly he was afraid they'd rip. He didn't care if she did rip them, he'd pay for all that and more if she could just feel better. He mopped her brow with a washcloth and whispered soothing words into her ear. Nothing he did felt like enough, but he wasn't sure what else he could do but pray.

Sunlight began to illuminate the clouds in the East, giving the sky a heavy, grey glow. It was still gently snowing, accumulating on the ground and on the tops of the buildings…it might've been a picturesque moment if not for Mona's violent cursing. Dr. Harris was coming in at twenty minute intervals now and at half past six, she smiled. "It's time to go to the delivery room, Mona. Are you ready?"

"To get this baby out of me? Hell yes!" Mona panted. Reno helped her into bed and the team wheeled her into a large room. The hardwood floors shimmered beneath the flow of fluorescent bulbs. The walls were painted a serene forest green and pictures of chubby, happy babies lined the walls. It wasn't cold or clinical, like he was expecting. Knowing the space was warm and inviting meant he could focus solely on Mona and what she needed from him.

Mona gripped Reno's hand tightly, using him to anchor her in the moment; without him standing there, she was sure she was going to be swept away in a haze of pain and fear. Vaguely, she heard Dr. Harris encouraging her to push through her contractions. The world around her seemed to blur as she held her breath and pushed with all her might. Reno wrapped his arms around her shoulders, helping her to sit up and fight through the urge to succumb to crushing fatigue.

Tears burned down Mona's cheeks and her voice cracked with every word that tumbled from her lips. She was past the point of forming coherent thoughts. She groaned and panted, staring into Reno's eyes in a desperate attempt to absorb some of his strength.

"I just need one more," Dr. Harris urged. "Come on, Mona. I can see your baby's head. I just need you to push one more time!"

Reno pressed a kiss to her temple. "You can do it, pumpkin. I know you've been dying to meet our baby for months now. Let's see our little Elvis—"

"Not a chance in hell!" Mona suddenly found her inner strength; there was no way she was going to let Reno name this baby alone. Dragging a breath deep into her lungs, she bore down and brought a beautiful baby boy into the world. Dr. Harris placed her squirmy, red-faced baby onto her belly and all of the pain she suffered was almost instantly forgotten. Tears of joy slid down her cheeks as she took in the sight of her son for the first time.

Mona knew true happiness the moment she heard her baby's angry cry. Dr. Harris let Reno cut the cord and then she cleaned up the newborn a little bit before wrapping him in a blanket. It felt like a thousand years before her son was finally in her arms. "He's perfect," Mona murmured incredulously. Ten fingers, ten toes, a perfect button nose, and rosebud lips. She brought the baby flush against her skin, letting him snuggle against her shoulder.

Reno was enamored of both of them. He snapped a couple pictures to send to the family before he settled at the edge of the bed. "I've never seen anything more beautiful in my whole life. He looks just like you."

"Yeah, well, he has your hair," Mona teased and rubbed her hand over the baby's bald head. The joke earned her a belly laugh from Reno. He leaned down, kissing her gently. "I couldn't have done this without you, you know…"

"I didn't do anything," Reno sighed. "I felt so powerless sitting there, watching you go through it."

"Just being here was enough. When I looked over and saw you were still there and that you still loved me, even though I'm fairly sure I screamed at you more times than I can count, it made me strong. I love you so much, Reno." Mona brushed a wayward strand of stringy dark hair away from her face. She stroked the child's tiny, chubby cheek.

"I love you too, Mona." Reno glanced down at the baby in her arms. "So, what are we going to call him? A boy this handsome has to have a name to match. He's going to be a huge hit with the ladies."

"He's going to be a perfect gentleman," Mona corrected. "There is one name I've been toying with. I didn't want to tell you, in case you hated it…but after giving birth, I'm not scared of *anything* anymore." She licked her lips. "Noah Vernon O'Keefe…what do you think?"

A lump formed in Reno's throat. The tribute to his late father touched him deeply. "It's amazing, and so are you." He kissed her again, tasting the salt from her sweat and tears. These first precious moments with his wife and child were some he'd treasure for the rest of this life.

The staff gave the new family several more minutes to bond, but Mona needed to be assessed by Dr. Harris and the pediatrician was waiting to check out baby Noah. Mona cried when she had to hand her son back and she demanded Reno follow the baby to the nursery. With help from a nurse, Reno gave Noah his first bath, then waited impatiently as the pediatrician checked him out and finally declared him the picture of health.

Mona was moved into another room to recover. When Reno returned with the baby, she was sleeping peacefully. Now that the newborn was clean, Reno snuggled him in the quilt he'd bought in Boston; the very same one Mona couldn't live without. At the time, Reno had no idea why it meant so much to Mona. Now, he was so glad he'd bought the baby his first gift and was the first person to snuggle him in it. It had taken a little maneuvering—and several tries—but Reno swaddled Noah like a pro. He settled down in the rocking chair, staring out into the chilly January morning.

"Happy Birthday, kiddo," Reno whispered. "I'm Reno O'Keefe…well, my real name is Vincent but nobody around here calls me that. And you can just call me dad…" he licked his lips, trying to come up with something to say to Noah. "I like watching romantic comedies and eating pizza." Reno exhaled sharply. "Geez, it sounds like I'm trying to date you or something." He shook his head. "Here's the only thing you need to know, Noah. I love you so very, very much." Leaning down, he pressed a tender kiss to Noah's forehead. "You're really the luckiest little guy in the whole world because your mom? She's the best thing that ever happened to either one of us. She can be tough sometimes but underneath, she's a big softie—"

"I heard that." Mona feigned aggravation. She smiled

blearily, her head still resting against the pillow. She shifted toward the edge of the bed and patted the space next to her. A smile tipped up the corners of her lips as Reno crawled in beside her with the baby in his arms. She rested her chin against Reno's shoulder, staring down at their son. Exhaustion unlike anything she'd ever known clawed at her but she didn't want to miss a single second. "I..." she let out a shaky breath, "I had the dream again..."

It wasn't like Mona to hesitate. Reno felt a little uneasy. "What was it, pumpkin?"

"When I first found out I was pregnant, I started having dreams that I was having your baby. I would wake up and my heart would ache. In a way, I guess Noah was always *unintentionally* yours." She tensed. "You probably think I'm crazy."

"No," Reno cut her off swiftly. "I've felt connected to you and this baby all along, even if I was slow to realize it. We were meant to be together, Mona. You and me and Noah, we're a family." He beamed. Mona was starting to fade again; he could see she was struggling to stay awake. Carefully, he stood up and arranged the blanket over her shoulders. "I think it's time you get some sleep. Don't worry about us. You've been hogging Noah for nine months. It's high time for some male bonding." Pressing another soft kiss to her lips, he smiled.

Mona chuckled and nodded. She rolled onto her side, her eyelids already drooping. She fell asleep to the sight of Reno and Noah curled on the chair.

Once upon a time, she thought only princesses got their fairy tale endings. Mona knew better now. With some hard work, determination, and a little faith, even strippers eventually found their prince charming. And they were going to live ever so happily ever after.

The End

www.ingramcontent.com/pod-product-compliance
Lightning Source LLC
Chambersburg PA
CBHW060520180626
46817CB00002B/426